Brewing Up a Bad Boy

T0275290

Also by Katherine Garbera

The Bookbinder's Guide to Love
How to Charm a Nerd

Visit katherinegarbera.com or the
Author Profile page at Harlequin.com for more titles.

KATHERINE GARBERA

BREWING UP A

BAD BOY

Recycling programs
for this product may
not exist in your area.

ISBN-13: 978-1-335-57491-6

Brewing Up a Bad Boy

Harlequin Enterprises ULC
22 Adelaide St. West, 41st Floor
Toronto, Ontario M5H 4E3, Canada
www.Harlequin.com

Printed in U.S.A.

For Lucas and Georgina.
Wishing you a lifetime of love, laughter
and unforgettable moments.

One

Alistair Miller stood in the archway that led from the book-shop into the tearoom of WiCKed Sisters in Birch Lake, Maine. Leaning casually against it, watching Poppy Kitch-ener. She moved with an effortless grace that he'd noticed the first time he saw her, before they got married, before he'd fucked everything up. Because she'd been insistent they handle everything through their solicitors, it had been nine years, two months and six days since he'd last seen her.

They spoke via email six months ago, when he'd asked to join the Secret Tea Society Discord, Tea Society, for short, which she ran. He'd heard about it via a mutual friend who was into brewing kombucha. He'd joined mostly as a way out of his isolation and to connect with other tea makers… but he'd be lying if a part of him hadn't wanted to recon-nect with Poppy. She was his first love, after all.

The Secret Tea Society had grown in popularity, along with Poppy and WiCKed Sisters. The Discord group was mainly comprised of independent tea makers who were innovative and a far cry from his family's centuries-old traditional company and views.

In the online group, her profile photo was just a teacup with primroses on it. The cup wasn't anything like the woman he had thought he knew. She was strong and pretty, of course, but also bold, quirky and not afraid to speak her mind.

He thought he was prepared to see her again. With her lush curly hair that she still dyed blond because it suited her coloring. A fair English rose with thick brown eyebrows, a heart-shaped face and a mouth that was always ready with a zinger when he got out of line.

The words she'd said to him when she left him for good still echoed in his mind whenever he let them in. There was no guard against being reminded of the worst parts of himself. Losing his wife in the name of a family business he felt trapped by had been a living nightmare. He shoved his hand through his thick hair, trying to shake off the negative thoughts.

He clocked the moment she noticed him. She'd matured into her face, and he couldn't take his eyes off her. Her body stiffened, the smile she'd been wearing disappeared from her face, and she turned to the tall guy behind her to say something. It took him a moment to recognize the gangly man as Merle, her cousin. The same dude who'd texted him back in the autumn, when he'd first joined the online tea society, to tell him not to mess with Poppy.

Like I'd to listen to her nerdy cousin. As soon as the unkind thought entered his mind, he shook his head. Putting others down whenever he felt cornered—that was old Ali be-

havior. New Ali was more understanding and didn't have
to put up defenses every time he was insecure.

There was no doubt he was insecure at this moment.

Poppy Kitchener.

Of all the people who had been a guiding force in his
attempt at transforming from a grade A douchebag into a
semi-decent human, she was the catalyst.

She wiped her hands on a towel and came around the
long counter, walking straight toward him. Her stride was
long limbed. Even though she wasn't tall, she carried herself
like an Amazon when she got her back up. Obviously seeing him wasn't a treat.

He should straighten to his full height and greet her with
that polite smile that he'd learned at his mother's knee and
had been using for his entire life. But that polite, entitled
boy had been burned out of him with rage, loss, and a hard
look at himself. But he didn't want to look desperate either.

His purpose was clear, yet seeing her distracted him.
Poppy had always been a problem. She'd never been the
woman he expected her to be. That was still true today.
There was no way the co-owner of the highly successful
WiCKed Sisters brand was going to agree to pretend to still
be married to him.

"What are you doing here?" she asked.

Taking a deep breath, he focused on his end goal. Surprising her hadn't been his best idea, but time was running
out. "I'm here to see you."

"Why?"

Why indeed? He was pretty sure he could lead with,
*I've been trying to make up for being a total bag of dicks to you
and everyone else in my early twenties.* "Gemma's wedding is

this weekend. You never gave me a definitive answer about going. I thought maybe an in-person invite would convince you to go with me."

"I didn't RSVP, sors."

"I did for both of us."

"Wait…are you really still on about us being married?"

He didn't like her tone. Or the fact that she was totally right about the situation. If he'd just come clean with his parents, then he wouldn't be here. Poppy, more than anyone, understood how impossible it was to have a genuine conversation with his parents.

"Oh my days, you're out of your head," she said, walking away from him. She muttered under her breath as she collected the teacups and plates left on the tables as she went by.

Ali grabbed some dirty dishes as well, intent on following her into the backroom where she'd disappeared—but Merle immediately blocked his path to Poppy.

"Out of the way, mate." The more time she had to think, the more likely she'd get ticked at him and stop talking to him again. All that work in the Tea Society would be for nothing.

"No. She's not your wife and doesn't want to pretend to be. Y'all are divorced. Let that sink in and go back to London."

"I live in Kent now, Merle. This doesn't concern you." The longer that he stood there with Merle, the more tension built in him. The logical part of his brain tried to raise objections, but the spike in his blood pressure drowned that out. Merle somehow became an amalgam of every person who'd blocked him throughout his life. All he knew was Merle better move or he was going to deck the guy—

"Fuck." He couldn't start a fight with Merle. Putting the dishes on the counter, he said, "Tell her I need to talk to her about tea. It's not just the wedding. It's business. I'll sit over there and wait."

He was so tense it was hard for him to get the words out. But he wasn't going to punch Poppy's cousin. The old piece of him, the man who let anger rule him was…straining to get out. It was harder than he wanted to admit to keep that fucking monster under control.

He usually stayed out of situations that aggravated him. But this time, he couldn't retreat to his cottage in the Kent countryside, where he took long walks, brewed his craft beer and chatted online, pretending he was a decent British gentleman instead of drowning in the chaotic isolation that was always right there at the edge.

"You okay?" Merle asked.

"Sorry for being a jerk," Ali said. "But I do need to speak to her."

Merle just nodded. "I'll let her know."

Poppy stood at the sink, her hands braced on the counter. Had she manifested this?

For fuck's sake.

She hadn't been prepared today for Alistair looking like every sex dream she'd ever had. He hadn't lost his shine in the years since she'd seen him. If anything, he looked fitter. When they first met, he'd been leaner, wearing black and leather to go with the bad boy persona that had preceded him to uni. His black hair was just as thick and curled the slightest bit on the top.

God, her fingers were tingling just remembering how it felt to push her hands through it.

He'd deceived her, broken her heart and filled her with regret. Too bad that late at night when she'd had too much pink Moscato, she still wanted him. Even wanted to be his fake wife. To be the ballsy woman that her friend Liberty was and say yes to the wedding, sleep with him, use him and then tell everyone there they were divorced. *Good riddance.*

Time to take karma into her own hands, leave on her terms, taking back the legacy he'd charmed out of her hands when she'd lost her family's tea recipe to Lancaster-Spencer. She should have heeded her ancestor's warning not to trust anyone in the Lancaster-Spencer family—especially the men.

Except she wasn't Liberty. She'd been born a people pleaser. She couldn't hurt him even if she wanted to because of his eyes. Those same soulful eyes that held hidden depths she'd never really discovered, that suggested Alistair held on to a lot of pain.

Truthfully, that same look had been why she'd fallen for him. Sure, she had thought they were moving too fast, but there was always something about Ali that grabbed at her. That outward charming arrogance that looked a little edgy… and secretly sad.

A strong pair of arms wrapped around her, pulling her into a hug. She recognized Merle's warmth and cologne—and the slight scent of cinnamon, which she knew came from Liberty. Hugging him back, she drew strength from her cousin. "You okay?"

With her forehead against his chest, she groaned. *No.* No way, she was the opposite of okay.

He laughed in a kind way. "I tried to get him to leave.

But he said it's business and took a seat at one of the tables," Merle said. "He almost slugged me but stopped himself and calmed down."

That caught her attention, and she straightened. Alistair always had a quick temper and got into fights all the time when they used to go out. That violence was never directed at her but at the shitty men who would hit on her. Alistair always came to her rescue…just not the way she'd have wanted. It had made her uncomfortable and want to go home. For her, he had only his passion. Everything that Alistair felt manifested itself physically.

"That's new."

"Yeah," Merle said. He waited to see what she wanted to do.

Her cousin was six months older than her. They'd always sort of been the oddballs in their families and had bonded. Her mom's biggest gripe about her was that she lived in Poppy's World and Merle had simply said, *What's wrong with that?*

"Options?"

"You sneak out the back, and I act like you're still in here," he suggested. "Then send Liberty in here to 'talk' to you, she goes back in the shop and kicks him out, so I don't have to go up against your buff ex-husband."

Poppy couldn't help smiling at that and playfully punched him in the shoulder. "I know you're not scared of Alistair."

"You're right. I also know he won't get physical with a woman, and it was a near thing when I blocked his path. I don't want to test it again. Seemed like he was holding himself back, and that's not him, from what you've shared."

She had the same feeling when Ali asked to join her on-line group six months ago. He listened, asked thoughtful questions, and there had only been one incident when he contradicted her and got superior about a tea-blending approach. Both of them had been right, and he was valid in stating there were other ways to do things than the way she did them. But it had smacked of their old relationship.

Ali used to frame her blending skills as lesser because she'd only learned them from the old book that had passed down through her maternal family. The same recipe book that his family had tried to romance, buy and steal from hers for centuries. Not without bitterness, she knew that the romance had worked on her in a way it hadn't on Viola Kitchener. That woman had walked away from marriage to the prestigious Earl of Winfield and his fledging tea company, Lancaster-Spencer.

"You got any other ideas?" she asked. Even living in the romanticized version of the world as she did, she still fought her own battles.

"You talk to him," Merle said. "Get some closure with him. Hate to be that guy, but I can tell you're still into him."

No denying that. "I'm not into him… I'm just *not.*"

Giving her a wry grin, Merle said, "It's a good thing I speak Poppy. So what should I do?"

"Watch the shop. I'm going to talk to him. If it looks like I'm about to do something stupid, intervene."

Merle didn't budge. "Define stupid."

"I won't know until it happens."

She tucked her hair behind her ear, took a deep breath and then walked purposefully out of the backroom, aware that Merle was behind her. But straight-up truth, all she saw was Alistair.

Sitting alone at a table near the front of her shop. His posture was perfect, as it was when he was nervous.

Or around his parents. His family had high expectations of everyone.

Including the woman she should be. She'd joined Lancaster-Spencer believing she'd have a chance to try her innovative tea blends, but they had stuck her in a job that frankly felt like Chandler Bing's on *Friends*…sort of nondescript, doing nothing.

The influence they had on their second son was immense. He felt he never measured up, but frankly, why anyone would want their approval was beyond her. His father was arrogant, looking down his nose at everyone else. His mother was vain, working hard to keep her social standing ensuring that everyone she met was aware of it. And his brother…

George actually wasn't that bad. He carried himself with the same bearing as his parents, but you got the sense he actually cared about people.

Alistair had been this fun-loving, sexy bad boy. Always doing what he wanted and taking her along on the ride of her life. Until their marriage, when he'd done a complete personality change.

So who was she getting today? The bad boy who'd romanced a shy girl and made her believe her love could smooth his rough edges? Or the proud, restrained second son of the aristocratic Miller family? Or the playful man who ran down a deserted street with her after they'd been kicked out of a pub for being too drunk and dancing on a table?

Catching her eye, he gestured to the chair opposite himself. He stood, pulling out the chair.

Stiffening her backbone, she told herself all she had to do

was listen to him. But she knew the hardest part would be to remember what she wanted. She wasn't going to even attempt to please Alistair. That Poppy was long gone.

Nothing worth having was easy to get. Despite his privileged upbringing, that was one lesson that Alistair had to keep learning. Right now, walking away from Poppy and WiCKed Sisters would be the sensible thing. But he couldn't do that.

The lies he'd told were all coming together in the perfect shitstorm. And at the center of it was Poppy Kitchener.

She hadn't even changed her name when they were married. Which was cool, a lot of women didn't. But that had been one more mark against him in his mother's eyes.

He was wound up from the exchange with Merle. Therapy had helped him start this journey, but there was still so much work left. Walking away would help. Removing himself from the stressful situation. Except he was pretty damned sure if he walked away from Poppy, the chances of getting her to talk to him again would be shot.

Meanwhile, the owner of the bookshop kept glaring at him between helping customers. *Serafina*. She was the one with the handmade manifesting journals. He'd thought about buying one.

Word around town was that these three were witches. Something that still surprised him; Poppy had never really seemed to have any interest in anything spiritual when they were together. Truthfully, he probably wouldn't have noticed even if she had. Given his history with Poppy, he wouldn't blame her for putting a hex on the journal.

Joke's on her, he thought wryly. He'd already hexed himself. If there was a way to fuck up a good thing, then he inevitably found it.

Poppy walked over to him. She wore a pink satiny shirt dress with red rhinestones on it. The V-neck of the dress was respectable, but he knew the body underneath that demure dress. Had lain awake at night remembering holding her in his lap, the heat of her against his body.

Not now, he reminded himself as he held out a chair for her. He needed every single etiquette and deportment lesson he'd ever received. He had to be the epitome of a gentleman. Not the man from years ago, who'd taken one look at the woman he was meant to persuade to sell his family her tea-blend recipe and almost forgotten his name.

Not this time.

He wasn't going to allow it. He couldn't. They both needed closure, and Poppy deserved some real compensation and acknowledgment from Lancaster-Spencer Tea Makers instead of having her family and her own name erased from the blend that they'd crafted and cultivated over the years.

"Thank you for coming back to talk to me."

Poppy gave him what he thought of as a *Poppy look*. It was polite but told him he was on thin ice and had better not screw up.

"Explain this fake-married proposal. You said it was for business. Weren't we real married for that?" she asked with more than a little bite.

Poppy came to play. For the first time, he realized just how much she had changed from the woman he'd courted and married almost ten years ago. Her new attitude was going to make everything more difficult. But he liked it.

"Lancaster-Spencer is aware of Willingham's offer," he

said, remembering the email his mum had sent last night outlining what they knew about the offer, made by their biggest competitor. His brother George had texted over more details and a generous counteroffer.

"So?"

Yeah, Ali, so? It's not like you convinced her to sign a contract and told her she didn't have to read the fine print beforehand. Of course, he hadn't read the fine print either. Who did, right? "Lancaster-Spencer will sue you if you sign it."

"What the actual fuck?"

"Turns out that one of the clauses from our first contract was a noncompete. That's why I'm here. I have an alternative for you."

Red crept up her chest and neck and cheeks. In a minute, she was going to lose it, and he didn't blame her.

"I'm sorry. I had no idea—"

"Of course you didn't. You just did what your father ordered. Married me, got me to give you the recipe and then sign a contract giving your family company the rights to the one tea blend that was in my family for generations. The one that we were famous for blending and the one the first Earl of Winfield was unsuccessful in seducing from my ancestors when your family made a subpar blend."

Her tirade was completely justified; everything she listed was truth. "Uh…"

But Poppy wasn't done. "You were just doing your himbo duty. Being sexy and distracting, making sure I didn't look anywhere but at you."

Clenching his fists on his legs, Alistair took several deep breaths. She was winding him up, but what she said was true.

He'd been the party boy in university, and his father had wanted him to prove his seriousness or he would cut him off.

So he'd done it. Gotten something no one else in the history of Lancaster-Spencer had. The rights to a small family-owned tea blend that had eluded them for more than a century. The goodwill from that gesture had opened doors for Alistair that he hadn't realized were waiting for him. He was offered an executive job, but it fed a monster inside of him that he hadn't realized was there: craving his father's approval.

He'd wanted more and more. Until Poppy left.

"I'm a Miller, not a himbo. And you were happy enough to do whatever I suggested," he reminded her.

"Not anymore."

"Believe me, I'm very aware of that. And I'm trying to help you."

"Remind me again how me pretending we are still married is going to do that?" she asked.

Slowly, he unclenched his fingers. "I've been working with George to come up with a fair offer for you."

"Are you two in charge now?" she asked.

"No. Mum suggested that I try to bridge our estrangement, and at the wedding, we can talk to Dad. The family will be there as back up," he said.

"Estrangement?"

"Yeah. That's… Listen I know I should have told them the divorce was finalized, but I didn't… You know how they are."

"I do," she said reluctantly.

"It's become a habit now not talking to them about anything. But I will after you get the agreement you deserved when you married me. What do you say? Will you give it a try? George and Mum both want you to get a fair deal," he said.

"Why now?"

He couldn't tell her that he'd made it a condition for selling his own shares to both of them. They wanted him out of Lancaster-Spencer as much as he did. He had big plans for the money he'd earn from the sale. But they all hinged on Poppy saying yes to attending the wedding with him so he could finally right his wrongs.

Two

It was all well and good that Alistair wanted to help her get a fair deal from his family, but it was also a lot sus. He'd literally never cared about her position in the family before this. Part of why her marriage hadn't been the love match she'd believed it to be.

Grimacing while he nervously kneaded his own legs, Alistair took his time answering.

Over his shoulder, she noticed Sera and Liberty coming closer to them. The doubts that she'd been struggling to contain were assuaged by their presence. The warmth of that bond and friendship gave her strength.

"If you can't answer me, then we're done," she said. Merle had been right about her needing closure, but she wasn't getting back on the hamster wheel that had been her life with Alistair.

"For fuck's sake, Poppy. I'm trying."

"Good for you. Try harder. I need to know what I'm walking into. You and I don't speak the same language."

He inhaled deeply, making his chest flex, something she noted and tried to ignore. But Alistair had always been a physical guy, working out, and it was hard to ignore how ripped he was. One of the things that had originally drawn her eye to him was his body. He looked like a sexier version of Harry Styles, mixed with Timothée Chalamet, with a little old-school Chris Pine—*Princess Diaries* era. One look at him, and she'd fallen hard.

"Fine. I am on a leave of absence—"

"You need me to get you back in?" Disappointed in herself for believing for half a second that he might be here for some other reason. Of course it was about pleasing his father and reclaiming his place in the family company.

"No. NO. Let me start over. I don't want to get back in. I am trying to right past wrongs. I should have read that contract before I told you to sign it. I want you to get what you deserve, not continue being screwed over by Lancaster-Spencer Tea Makers as you have been."

If what he was saying was true... But how could she trust Alistair again? What did it say about her that she really wanted to? It had taken her five long years to start repairing that damage, and it was only the bond she had with Sera and Liberty that made the healing easier. "That's nice," she said.

"If you're going to be like that, then don't bother."

"Like what?" she demanded, feeling her own anger building for the first time. Something she hadn't allowed since she'd walked out of their flat in Kensington.

"Treating me like I deserve to be treated. If this isn't the time and you're not ready to let go of the past, well, I respect that. But my father is going to come for you, and he's got good corporate solicitors that rarely lose."

"Tell me something I don't know," she said. But his honesty here was appreciated. "How would us pretending to be married help?"

"As my wife, you have some sway on the board. Mum and George will stand with us when we go up against Dad. We have enough power to sway him, but they want the tea blend for Lancaster-Spencer, and if you don't do this, they'll side with him. They're both looking at the bottom line."

Of course they were. Part of her understood, because she and Sera and Liberty had to do the same thing. Running a business was eye-opening and sometimes challenging. But at WiCKed Sisters, they never screwed anyone.

"If I went, when would we leave and return? I can't just jet off and leave my store," she said.

"I thought we'd leave on Sunday—"

"In two days?"

He had the grace to look sheepish. "I was afraid if I gave you too much time to think, you'd say no."

"I haven't said yes."

He totally ignored that. "The wedding is on Saturday, and I figured we'd fly back on Monday. I'll pay for everything."

"Legend," she said sarcastically.

He pushed his hand through his hair and looked down at the table before locking eyes with her. "I get it. I'm an ass, and I treated you poorly. I am sorry. You know that. I've apologized. I'm trying to at least get something good for you out of the mess that our marriage was."

Her heart tugged. She couldn't resist Ali when he was sincere, which wasn't as often as she would have liked. But now…when the change in him flashed…

Goddess, don't let me be wrong again.

"Sorry for being a bitch about it. I accepted your apology in that email. But I didn't expect... Well I had no idea what it would be like seeing you in person again," she said.

Damn Ali. At this moment, he embodied all the things she liked about him, owning his mistakes in a way that he'd only done when they were dating. She wouldn't deny that hearing him say she deserved better than Lancaster-Spencer made her melt a little.

"Me either," he admitted.

"I need some time to think." But she already was leaning toward going with him. Did that make her the most pitiful woman on the planet? Luckily, she had "Bad Idea Right?" by Olivia Rodrigo on replay in her head. At least other women also struggled with exes they still had feelings for.

Cutting herself a break, she was going to send him on his way. Chances were, she was going to the UK on Sunday for a week, which meant she needed to get more staff in. That didn't mean that Alistair shouldn't sweat a little. Things came too easily to him the first time...

"I'll give you my answer tomorrow," she said, standing.

Alistair gave her a tight nod and then turned to walk out of the shop.

Watching him leave, she tried to concentrate on anything but the silver lining of this offer. Alistair was clearly different, but that didn't mean he was better for her than he'd been before. Maybe she could finally get over him after this one final adventure together.

She had to be careful she wasn't all *hello, love* when she should be *goodbye, lover*. It was a delicate balance, and one only she could weigh and decide on.

"So that's your ex." Sera threaded her arm through Poppy's. "What did he want? The wedding again?"

"Yes, and his dad is going to sue me for the rights to put out the Amber Rapp tea blend."

"That bastard. I'll curse him," Liberty shouted, starting toward her part of the shop.

Poppy grabbed her arm to stop her. "Not yet. But would you read my cards? I need some guidance."

"Of course." Liberty looked over at Merle, blew him a kiss. "Watch the shop?"

"Sure. Is Greer still here, Sera?"

"Yes, they are. Do you think the two of you can handle everything?" Sera asked.

"Definitely."

Alistair rented a room above the Bootless Soldier Tavern on Main Street. He'd been corresponding with Owen Krog, one of the brothers who owned the place, and Owen offered Alistair his brother's girlfriend's old flat while he was in town. Both of them were interested in beer and brewing hard kombucha, and meeting and bonding online.

The apartment was basically one large room with a kitchen nestled into the corner. The counters were covered with a utensil jar and a large butcher-block cutting board. Owen had told him where the nearest grocery store was. Alistair wasn't here long enough to think about cooking, but this place would be ideal if he were.

There was a bedroom in the back with an adjoining bathroom and a large king-size bed that was comfortable—not that he anticipated a good night's sleep. It had been years since he'd slept for more than four to six hours at night. Part of him hoped if he did this good thing for Poppy, it would be one less blot on his soul. Perhaps the sleep that had eluded him for so long would come at last.

Probably not. He had so many blots that it would take another lifetime to fill them all in.

Walking across the hardwood floor to the window that looked down over Main Street he could just make out the wrought iron sign that hung in front of WiCKed Sisters. It was hard to reconcile Poppy as an independent business-woman. Of course, it wasn't that he didn't think she was capable. It was simply that when she worked for Lancaster-Spencer Tea Makers, she'd hated it. Being her own boss had never seemed like something she wanted.

As if he needed another reminder of how little he'd actually known about her. Had that woman always been there? He couldn't say.

He'd been so focused on fitting in for the first time in his life and earning his father's respect that Poppy had come a distant second to everything else.

There was no way he was going to do that again. This time, he was making things right. For her. His craving to belong was still there, but it was tempered by his need to make sure that he chose the right place to fit in.

It would be nice if Owen was in town to join him for a pint, but he'd gone to Bangor to meet with a distributor. His brother Lars had been friendly but wasn't interested in brewing, so there was no distraction from that fuckup with Poppy. Instead, when Alistair got to his room, he changed into his gym clothes, checked his running app for places near him to run and went out.

Running usually saved his sanity, but today, as he ran out

of the town of Birch Lake and into the rural countryside, all he could see was Poppy's face. Not just the way she was today but how she'd been when they first met.

He'd spent so much time staring at old pictures of her, they'd started to color the way he thought of their history. Poppy had been in love with him. Something he'd missed because she'd been an objective he needed to achieve his own goals. He'd hoped that maybe some residual feelings remained, but he knew that wasn't reality.

He was one of those guys that took everything as far as it could go, even his fuckups. So he'd really screwed over Poppy in ways he hadn't intended. He'd never meant to fall for her, but he had, then he'd felt so damned conflicted. It was hard to balance his family's ambitions against his feelings for Poppy. There was no way she was going to forgive him. He wouldn't forgive himself.

Getting her out of the Lancaster-Spencer contract was the best he could do. He was determined that, even if she turned him down, he'd convince George and Mum to side with him. Maybe he would have been a better man to have worked behind the scenes to just make it happen for her.

But no matter how much he thought he'd changed, there was still a part of him that wanted the accolades. Wanted Poppy to be all like, *Alistair, you're a legend…* Just not in the way she'd said it today.

Also he'd needed to see her again. Was tired of picturing her as that teacup instead of the vibrant, sexy woman she was. Poppy was more than he'd remembered.

Take the hint. She wasn't going to ever look at him again the way she had on their wedding day. That was his fault.

He headed back to his room drenched in sweat, but his

emotions still roiled inside of him like a storm off the North Atlantic, flooding him with all the feels he knew better than to indulge in. Part of him wished Merle had taken him up on the fight he'd been spoiling for in Poppy's tea shop. Of course, if he had, then Alistair would definitely be on his way to London alone.

He showered, then checked the Secret Tea Society Discord. The group had given him space to develop friendships outside of his family and wealthy connections. He hadn't expected that. But most of his life these days was new territory.

No one was online. The tavern served food, so he decided to go get dinner.

The Bootless Soldier reminded him of pubs in the UK. They even had a dartboard in the back and did trivia nights. A pub night might be what he needed. Getting pissed and talking to strangers had always been his jam.

He needed to just be Ali. Not Alistair Miller, second son of Howard Miller, eighth Earl of Winfield and CEO of Lancaster-Spencer Tea Makers. It was time to get his drink on and forget his mistakes, even if just for a few hours. Pocketing his keys, he made his way downstairs and into the tavern.

It was just after seven, and the tavern wasn't that busy, which was surprising given that it was a Friday.

Lars noticed him coming in and waved. The tavern was counter service, and Alistair made his way over to order food. He wanted to try the IPA that Owen had recently brewed.

"Alright?"

"Yeah, I'm good. What can I get you?" Lars asked.

"Owen's IPA. I'm interested to see how his turned out. Mine had a rounded bitterness that didn't fade."

"It's good. Very popular. We're thinking of expanding the microbrewery," Lars said.

"He mentioned that," Alistair said, leaning against the bar to chat with Lars while he sipped his beer and waited for his food.

A woman's laugh rang out in the tavern above the din of conversations. *Poppy.* Trying to be cool, he canted his head to the side. Their eyes met, and her laughter died.

Fuck him.

This was exactly what he deserved after the way he treated her. "Do you think there's a point where it's too late to try to fix the past?"

"Not if it's important," Lars said. "Some things just take longer. Your food is ready. Where are you going to sit?"

Back in his room would be the smart answer, but he knew for his mental health that when he was in this mood, it was better to be around people. On his own, there was a chance he'd spiral and do something stupid.

He glanced around looking for a table and saw Poppy standing behind him. "Want to join us?"

"Us?"

"Sera, Wes, Liberty and Merle."

"Do they all know I'm your ex?"

"Yup."

There was a steadiness in Poppy's expression. His plan to give her space wasn't working because he'd done nothing but think about her before this. "Sure. I like a challenge."

"What challenge?"

"Getting them to like me and getting you to see the ways I've changed," he said.

"It's one dinner," she pointed out dryly.

He'd missed her more than he'd realized until this moment. "Don't underestimate my charm."

"Oh, I never do."

He followed her back to her table with his tray of food and his beer. It was safe to say that no one looked excited to see him. But that had been true of so many first encounters in his life. So he just shrugged and took a seat next to Poppy.

She formally introduced Alistair to everyone. An awkward silence fell around the table. Wes made an effort to get the conversation started.

"How long are you in town?" he asked.

Alistair took a sip of his beer and started to eat the chunky beef and Guinness meat pie that the tavern had on special today. "Until Sunday. Wish I could stay longer. Birch Lake is charming."

"But you have to get back to your family," Liberty said, a bit of an edge in her voice.

"That's right. My cousin is getting married. I think that, Merle, you got an invite, right?"

"Yeah. I'm not really into weddings or England," he said. "Mom and Dad are going. Dad wants to play St Andrews again, so they'll be heading to Scotland after the wedding."

"How are you related to his cousin?" Sera asked.

"I'm not. They...um, invited us because of Poppy. We had a good time at her wedding reception and sort of became friends." Merle's explanation was the easiest.

No use saying that Gemma had been one of her best friends and had come over to visit Poppy in Maine once a year since Poppy had left the UK. She didn't want to rub salt in the wound for Alistair, but the truth was he'd crushed her, and she'd needed the support of Gemma and Merle, until she'd met Liberty and Sera.

"Did your mom and dad take your invite?" Poppy asked Merle.

"I asked if they could attend in my place, and you know Gemma, she was good with it."

"Classic Gemma. She's very generous," Alistair said.

Gemma had always been one of those people who treated everyone like they were her family. Which was how Poppy had first met Alistair. Freshers week, she hadn't really known anyone—none of them had. It was her first week at uni with a bunch of other new freshmen. The university put on a series of events so that all the kids could get to know each other. Gemma, her roommate then, had thrown a pre-drinks get-together at their dorm, and her cousin Ali had been there.

At the time, he'd just been this hot bad boy, but looking back, it seemed his family had used Gemma to connect her with Ali.

"Yeah, she is," Poppy said, not really wanting to take a trip to the past and the night she'd met him. She'd taken one look at him and fallen hard.

"What are you up to these days?" Alistair asked Merle. "Still doing tech stuff?"

"Yeah. I'm a white hat. I write code and algorithms for an online company that tries to stop cyber fraud."

"Wow, that sounds fascinating."

"You still a corporate dou—"

"Dude," Merle cut Liberty off, which made Liberty punch his shoulder.

"Nah, I'm on a leave of absence. I've been brewing beer.

Really getting into unusual blends. Recently, I decided to try hard kombucha. That's why I joined Poppy's tea group."

"What kind of blends?" Wes asked. "My brother got my dad a kit for Christmas, and he struggled with the first batch. So now he's determined to get it right. He keeps trying variations on recipes."

Alistair relaxed as he started talking about brewing and giving Wes tips for his dad. Apparently, most problems stemmed from not getting the yeast right or not having a completely dry, clean container to brew in.

"Hey, would you mind if I called him, and you could tell him what you told me?" Wes asked.

"Not at all. Want to step outside to do it?" Alistair offered. The two men got up and left.

"Why'd you punch me?" Merle demanded of Liberty.

"Why'd you stop me from calling him a douche?"

"Poppy hasn't decided what she's doing yet. If they reconcile and you alienate him, witch, you'll have to apologize, and you'd hate that."

"You did it for me?" Liberty put her arms around Merle's shoulders and kissed him. "Thanks, nerd."

"No problem." Merle was blushing slightly, but he kept one of Liberty's hands in his.

Poppy had almost stayed home tonight but was glad she hadn't. She wouldn't deprive herself of seeing her closest friends in love. Maybe her reluctance was about potentially seeing Alistair again. It was interesting because he seemed more like the guy she'd first met, but mixed with this interesting guy she'd never seen before. A fun-loving man who could talk about anything.

He was good at putting people at ease, and he'd done it

tonight. And his beer brewing was interesting. Ali had never really had passion around Lancaster-Spencer... Ambition and determination, yes, but nothing like the way he was when he talked about brewing. She knew him well enough to see that he was genuinely passionate about it. There was a cute little wrinkle between his brows when he got earnest.

She'd never asked any details about his brewing process in their Discord group. Maybe she hadn't been ready to see that side of him.

"Wes seems to like him," Sera said.

"Yeah. He's a nice guy. It's okay if you guys like him too," Poppy said. "Lots of people are friends with their ex."

Yeah, but they probably don't go all soft and gooey inside when their ex sits next to them at the table. That was something she was going to have to deal with. Lusting after Alistair was nothing new to her. That was easy. It was the emotional cost she'd pay if she opened that door again that would be difficult.

Because as much as she wanted to say she was over him emotionally, she wasn't. A part of her was still in love with him, still dreamed of the good times and wondered if maybe there had been some way to make things work. That fact was driven home to her as he and Wes walked back in, and Alistair gave her a sheepish smile while Wes told everyone how helpful Alistair had been with his dad. She'd never seen that look on his face before, and it sent a zing through her.

The tension left the group after that. They all moved over to the dartboard, and Ali suggested they play Nine Lives, a game where each player threw three darts on their turn. If they missed all three shots, they were out.

They took turns ordering rounds, and everyone was laughing as the night wore on.

"How did I not know you were rubbish at throwing?" Wes asked Sera, wrapping his arms around her from behind.

"It's never come up. Wait… Did you think I was good at it?"

"Yes, you're good at everything," he said.

Sera turned in his arms, whispering something that made Wes lift her up and turn his back to the rest of them while they made out.

Merle and Liberty were both good, but Merle—having grown up in an athletic family—was slightly better and kept beating Liberty's throw each round.

Soon it was just her and Ali standing awkwardly in front of the dartboard.

"Want to get out of here?" he asked. "I'll walk you home."

Home and Ali…two things that totally shouldn't send an illicit thrill through her.

Three

It was late spring; the weather was surprisingly warm, and the sky tonight was clear. The moon was full and lit the entire sky. Looking down on her without judgment. The moon understood. This gorgeous night was a balm after a very chaotic and surprisingly fun evening with Alistair and her friends.

"You've changed," she said, resisting the urge to hold his hand.

"A wise woman told me that I needed to be honest and stop being so full of myself."

"Sound advice. You took it?"

He barked out a laugh that startled her. "Not at first. You know me. I assholed up, determined to prove that I was always honest. Yeah, that didn't go well."

She stopped. Main Street wasn't that busy for a Friday evening at almost midnight. "What happened?"

"You don't want to know. Suffice it to say eventually, I had an awakening and started to heed your wisdom."

"Glad to hear that. How does that correlate to you brewing beer?"

Being buzzed and standing outside under the stars with Alistair was making it really hard to concentrate on anything but the remembered feel of his arms around her and his hot mouth on hers. The way they'd hooked up the first time at her on-campus student accommodation, barely making it into her room before they were on each other.

It felt like this.

He felt new to her.

Not like the ex who had broken her heart and her dreams, burning down everything in her life that she'd always believed. This guy was different; she didn't know him or what to expect, and he was housed in the body of the sexiest man she'd ever been with. The one that she had never been able to banish from her dreams.

Super bad idea. The worst.

Except it didn't feel that way.

The thought drifted in and out of her head like a ribbon of steam from a steeping cup of tea as she leaned toward him slightly. Testing the waters.

Their eyes met for a long moment as he shifted toward her. They were next to Pollens Jewelers; the windows were dark and the street was empty.

No one would know but the two of them if anything happened. Well, only the moon, which saw everything. But there was no judgment coming from anyone. Not even her hyper-critical internal voice was loud enough to keep her from closing that gap between the two of them.

Putting her hand on his chest, she looked up.

His eyes were heavy-lidded, and his lips parted. "Poppy."

Just her name on a low whisper made her shiver, from her core outward. Every instinct she had was muted as desire took over. It had been too long since she'd felt his mouth on hers. Tasted the one kiss that she'd never been able to forget no matter how many other men and women she'd kissed.

Maybe she was remembering it wrong. Maybe one of his changes would be that he was now a sloppy kisser, all saliva and odd noises. Maybe—

His mouth was on hers; his arms pulled her close, and her mind quieted. Her body relaxed into him as if it had been waiting for this. Images of their greatest hits played in her mind as his hand tangled in her hair. He turned so that his back was to the street, and hers was pressed against the jewelry store window.

The glass was cold through her clothes, a contrast to the heat of Ali's body. His hands were still, but hers weren't; kneading his chest, trying to get to his skin but not able to through his T-shirt. Until her brain kicked in, and she pulled it up, shoving her hand against his bare skin.

He was all taut muscles with a light dusting of hair. Holding his waist, she pulled him closer as she went up on her tip-toes to deepen the kiss, brushing herself against his erection.

That was a wakeup call.

Sleeping with Ali today wasn't in her plans. She was supposed to be moving on, not acting as if nothing had happened.

Kissing him hadn't been in her plans either, but it took her more than a minute to pull back and eventually break the kiss.

Well, darn.

Her blood was racing through her body, her heartbeat

pounding in her ears. She needed to be sensible, but that dreamer deep inside of her urged her to ignore the warnings. The pain of the truth of her past. That fear of making the same mistake with the same guy again.

Ali turned away, putting his hands on his thighs, breathing deeply before he shoved his hands through his hair. "That was…"

"Yeah." She didn't want to dissect it. They'd both stopped, so that told her he wasn't ready either. "If I go with you to the wedding, we need to keep things platonic."

"Platonic? Sure we can try, but with that kiss…I'm not sure either of us is going to be able to stick to that," he said.

"We're divorced, Alistair. That has to mean something. We tried being a couple, and it didn't work at all. Let's not put ourselves through that again," she said, giving him the honesty that she'd wanted from him a long time ago.

He nodded tightly. "All that is true, but I'm a different person. You are too. If we decided to try this again, I think it would be a new start."

"Maybe." The pain of losing her dream of what a romantic relationship was still stung. Still, she wanted to try again… Who wouldn't on a night like this, with Ali being so charming and hot and everything she'd always craved?

"Where's your place?" The quiet longing on his face matched a feeling deep in her soul.

"Two blocks behind WiCKed Sisters. I'm good to go alone," she said.

"I'm not good with that," he said, looking around the deserted street. "So, WiCKed Sisters…"

"What about it?"

"I might not have the right, but I'm proud of what you've

achieved. Your tea blends were always something different—special even—and I'm glad to see you being recognized for them," he said.

He reached for her hand, and she almost withheld it, but it was such a nice moment that she couldn't.

They didn't talk as they finished the walk to her place, and as she stood on the threshold looking at her witch's broom decorated with spring flowers and herbs, she was tempted to invite him in. But she was the one who'd thrown *platonic* out there.

Platonic.

Never in his life had he had a platonic woman friend… Well not one he wanted to fuck. This was going to be a challenge.

"So, good night," Poppy said as she opened the door.

He heard the sound of a dog running to greet her. "Pickle?"

The miniature dachshund was on her back legs, her front ones moving up and down excitedly.

He stooped down to pet her behind her ears and then lifted her up into his arms. She was licking his neck, and he put his face down to cuddle her for a minute. He'd missed this sweet dog.

"I didn't know you still had her," he said as he set Pickle back inside the doorway.

The little dog just kept dancing around their legs. "Why wouldn't I?"

"I thought maybe you left her with your mum."

"No. Pickle goes where I go."

"I remember. She looks good for her age," he said. The

dog had been four when they inherited her from Poppy's gran, who'd died six months before their wedding.

"She does. She's had a few health issues, but she's doing good now. In fact, I should get her to bed so she settles down," Poppy said.

"Yeah, right. My cue to leave." Which he started to do.

"I'll go to the wedding with you."

Glancing over his shoulder, Poppy glowed in the warm light from her hallway, Pickle at her feet. He knew this wasn't an easy decision for her. "Thank you. I'll do everything I can to keep Dad from suing you or forcing you to let Lancaster-Spencer produce your tea."

"I appreciate that," she said almost formally.

God. How did this always happen? He had no mechanism for dealing with her when it wasn't white-hot sex or cold, hard business. He could let his guard down around Pickle, cuddle her and let her kiss him. Admit to himself that he missed that sweet little dog, but he wasn't able to do it with Poppy.

"Good night, then." He walked away, and this time, she didn't try to stop him.

Perhaps it was as it should be. Things had happened too fast the first time. It was only in looking back that he'd realized how little he'd actually known about Poppy. Their chemistry had blinded him to anything but how easy it was going to be to get the tea recipe, to finally earn the job his father didn't think he was good enough for. He'd just assumed that she would still be there afterward.

The walk back to his lodging wasn't long enough for the thinking he had to do, so he turned left once Poppy was safely inside her home. Step one on the long list of things he needed to do, clear the past with Poppy, had been achieved.

Having her at his side was just the beginning. He was changing the man he'd been. Brewing beer, taking advice instead of having to be the smartest man in the room and making sure everyone knew it. He'd been a blowhard. That hadn't actually been a revelation. His father was one as well. Only George, who was more like Mum, seemed not to have inherited that Miller trait.

He had already run once today and wasn't dressed for it in jeans and trainers, but his mind was starting to swirl. Poppy under him when he'd slid into her body the first time was on repeat in his head. Running until total exhaustion was the only thing that was going to keep him from going back to her place.

So he started following the track he'd taken earlier. The pace he set for himself was punishing, and when he got back to the Bootless Soldier Tavern, Wes and Sera were making out against the brick wall near the front.

Ali didn't linger, just went to the door that led to the stairs and his lodging above.

That could have been him. Hell, that *had* been him and Poppy, and in the past, they'd be at her place right now, making love on her bed. He got hard thinking about it.

He showered and took care of his erection, toweling off, he sat down in front of his laptop sending a quick update to George letting him know that their plan was a go.

They both wanted to get Dad out of power at the tea company. He was stuck in the past, and his attitude and practices were going to be the end of Lancaster-Spencer. He was classist and racist and still told jokes about women that weren't acceptable.

He was also a bully, and it had taken years of therapy for Alistair to realize he was on the cusp of becoming one as well.

The Lancaster-Spencer motto was *one cup and you're family*. But the Millers had never felt like a family until this moment, when they were poised to take on Dad.

He and George working together, instead of being pitted against each other, to achieve something they'd both be proud to be associated with. Instead of a colonialist company that was stuck in its heritage and legacy. He wanted more.

He logged on to the Tea Society Discord and saw there were two members online. Poppy and Freddie. He scrolled the chat before he joined. They were very friendly… Almost flirty. Had Poppy friend-zoned him because there was someone else in her life?

What did it say about him that he was only just now considering the possibility that she had moved on? Of course she had. They were divorced. He'd hooked up, why shouldn't she?

Which was all good when he was being rational, but the man he was trying to shed was still inside of him. Jealous.

Identify.

That was the first step. His therapist's voice rang loud and clear in his head. It had to be to be heard over the din of anger and regret. He was jealous.

Next, why?

Because he fucking wanted her back. He took several deep breaths and logged off the group.

Write it down.

Pulling out the Moleskine journal he'd picked up in the airport, he started writing, until he realized that his jealousy stemmed from his regret. He had to continue to change to be a better man and know that Poppy deserved love and happiness wherever she could find it.

Punctuality wasn't a strength of hers. It didn't bother her often, because everyone knew she tended to run ten or so minutes late. So when she walked into the backroom of Sera's part of the shop and found Liberty and Sera both waiting for her, she wasn't surprised. Liberty even had an iced coffee from Lily's bakery waiting for her.

"I actually thought I might beat you two in this morning," Poppy said, taking the drink from Liberty and sinking down on the armchair that was wedged catty-corner from the love seat where both her friends sat. Sera's backroom was full of bookshelves and coziness, much like the way Poppy felt when she was near her friend.

"Ha. Merle had to work last night when we got home, so he was still up and woke me when my alarm went off."

"You don't sound annoyed by that."

"He knows how to wake me up the right way," Liberty said with a wink, taking a sip of her mushroom-mud that she drank every morning.

"Wes is still sleeping," Sera said. "But his shop opens later than ours, and he's heading to an estate auction today."

"I love how couple-y you both are," Poppy said. "I was feeling envious, but last night, seeing us all together fixed that. I can't explain it but I'm sorry for it."

"Don't be sorry. You're human, you're allowed to have

emotions. Just don't act like a jerk when you do," Liberty said with a smile. "Did you decide on the wedding?"

"I'm going. Jenny, who's been handling the shop when it's busy, is going to be in all days. I want to make her an assistant manager. Merle said he'll cover for me too. What do you guys think about us all hiring someone? That way, we can start taking some time off. Sera, you're sharing Greer with Wes and Liberty, so you don't really have anyone."

"I see what you're saying, but I don't like the idea of anyone else running our shop. What if we're all gone at the same time?" Sera asked.

"Yeah, I'd have to find someone I trusted to take my place, and right now it's just you two and Mom," Liberty said.

"Just something to think about. I thought the Amber Rapp phenomenon would cool down by now," Poppy said. Their small business in Birch Lake had gained an international spotlight after pop star Amber Rapp had been inspired to write her latest hit album after a visit. Since then there had been a steady stream of Amber's fans to their shop wanting to have the same experience.

"I think they're coming for us now. The exposure we got from her album turned into genuine interest in our shop and products," Sera said.

Which was great. Their shop had moved from a small business to more of a medium-size business on the cusp of going large, but the truth was, they were still running it as they had their Etsy stores and craft-fair booths.

"Should we bring in a business consultant to help us figure out how to grow without burning ourselves out?" Poppy asked.

"I'm taking a Skillshare course on growing small businesses," Sera said.

"Good. Let me draw a card, I want to think about this. I know you're right, but I'm not ready for change," Liberty said who had grown up with tarot and spells.

"And I'm going away for a week. So we have plenty of time," Poppy said. "Can you draw a card for me, too?"

Liberty smiled at her as she reached into her pocket and pulled out her Rider-Waite deck. "Thought you might want to."

"Want me to leave?" Sera asked.

"No. I need you here with me."

Liberty moved to get the small folding table that Sera kept in the corner, and Poppy pulled out a candle she'd been using to help her embrace and love her true self. She put it on the counter and lit it while Sera got some crystals they'd charged at the last full moon and put them on the table. Sitting in the armchair, Liberty started shuffling the cards.

Poppy sat down next to Sera, who threaded her arm through hers.

"What do you want to know?"

There was so much she needed answered. Poppy had learned from Liberty that the card draws made more sense when she had a clear idea of what she was struggling with. Alistair was too much and she had a million thoughts and questions about him. But maybe…

"Am I making a mistake going back to England?"

"It would be better to ask, 'what do I need to know for this trip to England?'" Liberty suggested.

Poppy knew that she'd been too specific, but a girl could

dream. "Okay, that. It's just I don't want to be stupid again with him. You know?"

"You couldn't be," Sera said. "Because you're not stupid."

"Thanks," Poppy said. But she knew that she could be really dumb where he was concerned.

Last night had been a near mistake until Pickle appeared. Poppy had been on the verge of taking his hand and leading him into her house. She'd missed him in her bed last night. And this morning…she woke up feeling not as great as she thought she would.

"You should draw it yourself," Liberty said as she handed over the deck. "Don't say what you landed on out loud. Just think about what you need an answer to in your head."

Poppy took the deck, shuffling it herself and then spreading the cards out on the table as she'd seen Liberty do. Closing her eyes, she asked what Liberty had suggested: What did she need to be successful in England?

She moved her hands over the cards until she felt pulled to one, and drew it.

The Magician.

She took a deep breath as Liberty rocked back in her chair. "Tap into your full potential. Don't hold anything back. So stop censoring yourself."

But could she trust herself to do that?

Four

Poppy sat down to write a blog for the Tea Society. They'd started a Substack, and members had been taking turns blogging about tea and brewing. Alistair was up after her. Not that he mattered, but after last night, he was on her mind.

Pickle was at her feet as she sat at her laptop trying to figure out where to start. There was a knock on her door, and she hurried to answer it.

Speak of the devil. "Hey, I need your passport number so I can confirm your flight and check you in," Alistair said. His phone in one hand, he looked at her expectantly.

He wore a pair of shorts that she suspected were perfectly respectable but seemed really short, showing off his long runner's legs, and a moisture-wicking T-shirt that clung to his muscles.

What had he said?

Pickle greeted him like a long-lost friend again. The dog was a traitor. She'd had a long talk with Pickle last night, reminding her that Alistair was her ex and he wasn't going to be around long.

Poppy turned around with disgust as Pickle rolled over so Alistair could pet her belly. "I'll grab my passport. If you want water, there's some in the fridge."

"Thanks."

His voice followed her down the hall as she went into her bedroom. She opened the lockbox her mum had insisted she buy to keep all of her important documents in. About every three months, when they video chatted, Mum would insist on seeing that she still had her passport, resident visa and birth certificate secured. As if Poppy wasn't almost thirty. But that was her mum.

Glancing at the photo of her and Mum tucked into the side of her mirror made her smile. Everyone said she was Mum's mini-me, but while that was true as far as looks went, they were such different people. Mum wouldn't have fallen for Alistair. Hell, she hadn't liked him. But she'd been pretty cool when Poppy had left him, even though she'd said he was too slick.

"Poppy?"

"Coming," she said.

He leaned against her breakfast bar, alone; Pickle had presumably gone back to her bed. Alistair still had his phone in one hand and one of the hand-thrown pottery tumblers she'd made last year in the other. It was a reminder of when she'd been trying to find something to work her aggression out on as Alistair stalled on signing the divorce papers.

Funny that he was using her IDGAF tumbler.

"Here it is," she said, handing him her passport. She went back to the table, where she had her laptop open. Glancing down to see she had written half a sentence, and it sounded like she was trying too hard.

"Thanks. I booked a car to take us to the airport in Bangor. You still like to get to the airport early?"

"Yes. You still going to be a bitch about it?" she asked.

"Of course not. We have access to the lounge so we will be able to chill before the flight. Do you have any meal preferences?"

Never in her entire span of knowing Alistair had he intentionally cared about any of her preferences. "I sort of like the veggie options, but sometimes they're spicy. So stick with the regular meal, because there's usually a choice."

"I'll get you the veggie, and if you don't like it, we can swap," he said.

"Alistair, stop."

He was trying too hard. "You don't have to act as if you've had a lobotomy."

Looking offended for about a second before he started laughing. "It's okay for you to have your way, Poppy."

"Oh, I know that. When did you start to?"

"I don't want to sound like a broken record, but after you left…" He shrugged and took a long gulp of water. He wasn't chill even though he was trying to act like it.

"You know this is just a one week thing, right?"

He walked to the sink and put the tumbler in it. "It's more than that. I'm trying to fix things."

"Why?"

"Karma. I can't be the man I was anymore."

Except he'd had years to try to fix things with her and had waited until eighteen months after their divorce to try. "Did something else happen?"

"The leave of absence was a huge wake-up call," he admitted. "Truth is, you were on my mind before things exploded at work."

"Exploded how?"

"Let's just say it wasn't pretty."

Okay then. He didn't have to share everything with her. There were a lot of things she would keep to herself until he asked. But he wasn't asking about the personal stuff. Just her meal preferences for a flight to a wedding she hadn't wanted to attend.

"If that's all, I have to finish this blog before opening WiCKed Sisters today."

"For the Tea Society?"

"Yes. How many blogs do you think I have?"

"Just the tea one, according to Google," he said.

"You Googled me?"

"Yeah. Just wanted to see what you were up to."

"Ali, be honest here, do you see us getting back together?" Maybe she was overstepping, but that kiss last night hadn't felt casual to her. Definitely not on her side. Did he want something more? "My life is here. I'm not getting married ever again, and I like the woman I am now," she said.

"Slow down, Pop, it was just one kiss. The wedding is a chance for me to have your back and get you on even footing with Lancaster-Spencer. Am I still attracted to you? I think I'd have to be dead not to be. But you made it clear I fucked any chance of you looking at me that way again. And despite all evidence to the contrary, I'm really not an idiot."

"Of course you're not, but you do act like one sometimes."

"True. I'll stop by the store later and confirm the time to

pick you up in the morning," he said. Then he let himself out of her house.

She stood there for too long. Watching the closed door, dwelling too much on Ali. There were hints of real difference in him. Still, she got the sense he was hiding something.

The sun was hot, something he wasn't used to, but he enjoyed it. Alistair basked in the sun while sitting out back of the tavern and talking to Owen.

Coming to Birch Lake hadn't just been for Poppy. His friendship with Owen had been a big part of it. But he was also doing this for himself. He needed to stop hiding from the past.

The old barn that he'd had converted into his home back in the UK was on a fair amount of acreage, and he'd started brewing out there. His therapist had pointed out that one of the reasons for his short trigger seemed to be a lack of patience, and brewing was a slow process. So he'd started it as a hobby, never expecting he'd enjoy it as much as he did.

He'd stumbled upon kombucha brewing looking for something new to try, which had led him back into Poppy's life. He wasn't a man to look for signs—in fact, he usually ignored them—but there was no denying that he'd felt something more than coincidence when he stumbled upon her online tea group and found advice and camaraderie in his hard kombucha experiments.

Despite her presence in the group, he treated her like a professional acquaintance. He was all about respecting her and her boundaries.

But the core of who he was couldn't ignore that he still

wanted her. He'd never stopped being attracted to her. Kissing her last night had simply reinforced that.

But this time it had to be more than sex. This was a chance that he'd never expected. One that he would make the most of. But he needed to appear cool, as if whatever she decided was fine. It *was* totally fine. If Poppy closed the door on them for good, he would respect it. The plan was to go with the flow.

Ha.

Right now, the flow had him hanging with his new friend, Owen. There was no reason not to enjoy this moment. Even if Owen's first batch of hard kombucha hadn't turned out at all.

"I'm not sure where I went wrong, but it smelled horrible. Probably bacteria. Lars wouldn't even try it, and he's usually up for anything," Owen said.

"Did you?" Alistair asked.

"Nah. Decided it wasn't worth tearing up my stomach. How'd your batch turn out?"

"I haven't had a chance to check. I'd just brewed the kombucha when I came here. It should be ready to add the champagne yeast when I get back home. Did you use ale?"

"Yeah. I think the seal wasn't tight and bacteria developed. I'm not sure where. Are you adding any flavors?"

He was, which was why he'd joined Poppy's tea society. The people in that group were experts on blending and knowing what flavors worked well together. "I want something that is specific to Kent and also tasty. I've been exploring different blends right now. I figure I have about a week or two to make up my mind."

"Good luck with that," Owen said. "I'm going to stick

with the original flavor for now. I think I need a new air-lock for the kombucha. I didn't want to use my ale ones, but had an odd one lying around."

Owen was a big lumberjack of a man with thick hair and a beard that he kept well trimmed. The kind of guy that Alistair never would have talked to in the past, much less listened to advice from. What a yob he'd been.

"I hadn't thought about that." Pulling out his phone, he ordered some airlocks from his supplier to be delivered in two days.

"You said you had a brewing journal?"

Alistair pulled it out and handed it to Owen, who took his time going over the notes in the columns of each recipe that he'd tried. There were times when he thought that he'd gotten nothing from his years at Lancaster-Spencer, but his father had insisted that he and George work in every depart-ment. He'd picked up a lot of skills as a result.

His six weeks in the tasting department had really served him well with beer brewing. He understood the importance of sampling and making notes at different stages of the pro-cess. Each new batch of ale was stronger and better tasting.

Ali still felt like he had a long way to go. But he liked it. Even his fuckups were just chances to try again and get better.

God, if things with Poppy were like brewing a new ale, then he'd have a better understanding of what he needed to do next.

People weren't beer. But frankly, it had been years since he'd felt like he understood anyone or anything. Beer might not be the answer, but it was pushing him closer to it.

Owen had to take a call from Lars. When he came back,

he looked stressed. "Lars isn't going to be back until tomorrow. I need to go and call around to get someone to staff the bar."

"I can do it." Alistair had an afternoon of trying to stay away from Poppy, which meant hanging by himself. "I've pulled a few pints but never worked behind the bar. So I'm not unskilled."

"Sounds perfect to me. Can you start at noon, when we open?"

Alistair agreed and then went to change into jeans and the Bootless Soldier Tavern T-shirt that Owen gave him. The Earl of Winfield would be aghast to see his second son pulling pints. Ali was tempted to take a photo and send it to his dad just to get a reaction.

Brewing a proper cup of tea could cause arguments. There were so many ways to go about it, and everyone believed the way they made their cuppa was the proper way.

Tea brewing and blending was deeply personal. Take Poppy's best friends and co-owners of WiCKed Sisters; for Liberty, the flavors had to be bold and brash. Poppy ordered a brick of huang pian sheng pu'er from Lao Man'E in China. The tea blend was from an old tree, and it sweetened as it steeped, much like Liberty did once you got to know her.

Serafina, on the other hand... Well, when Poppy made special blends for her, they contained black tea, which had higher caffeine and antioxidant levels to fuel Sera's late-night reading habit, but Poppy also added in something floral and sweet, like rose petals. Though her friend's comfort tea was Earl Grey.

For herself, she was always changing. Trying to find the

brew that suited the woman she was. When she was younger, she was always on trend with her teas, like the fruit-inspired blends from France she was obsessed with at uni. Young, moldable, not really sure enough of herself as a tea drinker or maker to stand on her own.

It was only when Lancaster-Spencer Tea Makers had approached her that she'd cracked open Gran's massive buckle book that housed every tea-blend recipe that the Kitchener family had made since 1790.

In 1790, widow Ann Kitchener took over her husband's tea and coffeehouse on the Strand. She ran it successfully for twenty years before retiring to allow her son to take over. But it was her granddaughter Viola who first came in contact with the Earl of Winfield and his connection to Lancaster-Spencer.

While on a diplomatic mission to China, Viola's father had heroically saved the life of a Chinese government official. He was gifted some tea and a recipe to reproduce it, which proved very popular in the family's tea and coffeehouse. A marriage to the earl would see Viola's family's business merged with his. But on the eve of her wedding, she overheard him telling his investors that the long sought-after recipe was soon to be in his hands, and he'd dissolve the tea and coffeehouse her grandparents had started.

Viola confronted him, and he admitted the only reason he'd courted her was the recipe. She refused his hand, vowing that no Earl of Winfield would ever get his hands on it.

The vow had remained unchallenged until Poppy met Alistair. At the time, that first tea recipe seemed so basic and simple. Hadn't felt flashy enough for her at eighteen. But at twenty-eight, she was starting to see the truth in simplicity when it came to tea blending. If the base was weak, the tea would be too.

Could any words be more true?

It had been almost ten years since that April morning when her dreams came crashing down around her. Confronting Alistair and learning he hadn't been in love with her and that *I love you* was just something men said to get what they wanted… Well, that had been enough for her.

Leaving him was the best damned decision she'd ever made.

Now she was acting as his wife again to undo some of the mistakes she'd made. Would it be enough? Could she keep her emotions out of it this time?

Liberty had given her a crystal, which she'd charged over night for strength, and Sera, a handmade journal that she'd reinforced with the love and strength of their sisterhood. It meant more than Poppy realized when they'd both surprised her with the gifts at the end of the day after the shop closed.

Poppy needed to change her destiny and her attitude. She could go after any dream if she had a business plan, but her personal dreams—the ones that stemmed from wanting the kind of marriage and family she'd grown up around—seemed out of reach.

But it wasn't going to happen until she made peace with her past and figured out how to be friends with Alistair.

She lifted a cup of tea she'd just blended for herself. Her magic courage blend. Using green tea as a base, she'd added hints of rose and calendula—a potted-plant type that included marigolds, but she was using a cutting taken from her mum's greenhouse back in Wye, Kent, where Poppy had grown up. The tea was good, but it was going to take more than a cup to help her move on from the past.

She had to deal with Alistair. Too bad she hadn't figured out a blend that could heal a broken heart or erase the chemistry between them.

That was asking a lot from one cup of tea. She smiled at Merle as he walked over to her where she stood behind the counter in the tearoom.

"Hey, cuz. Did you let your mom know you're coming to the wedding?"

"No. Why?"

"My mom let it slip. She also knows that you're going to be in England with Alistair. Just a heads-up."

Before Merle was done talking, her phone was buzzing in her pocket. "I'm not even sorry that Liberty volunteered to watch Pickle, and you're going to have to double up on your allergy meds."

Merle just laughed as he walked away. Poppy answered the video call. "It's late at night, Mum. Everything okay?"

"No. Aunt Regina Facebook messaged me that you are going to Gemma's wedding with Alistair."

"I was going to tell you. Why are you checking messages in the middle of the night?" she asked, walking through the shop to sit at one of the tables and talk to her mum.

"Dad's in France on one of his walking trips."

Mum couldn't sleep when he was gone. "Okay, so we're flying tomorrow. I sent you an email with the information in it." That had been her way of putting off the inevitable.

"Why are you doing this?"

"Alistair thinks he can help me negotiate a better deal

with Lancaster–Spencer. They are threatening to sue if I let Willingham distribute our tea blend."

"Bastards."

"Agree one hundred percent."

"But Alistair?"

Poppy didn't want to defend him only to be wrong again. How stupid would she look? "He offered. I'm cautious, but this time he seems different. And if I'm wrong, it's just one week. I really don't have the money to hire the kind of solicitor I'll need to fight this."

"Dad and I can help. The business is doing good. We could leverage it—"

"Absolutely not. You've done enough. I mean it, Mum."

Her mum didn't look happy with that but finally nodded. "Okay, but if you change your mind…"

"I will definitely let you know."

"Want me to pick you up from the airport?"

"I'm not sure. Alistair's taken care of all the travel arrangements. That's why I sent the email. Let me check with him and get back to you."

"Am I at least going to see you while you're here?"

"I…I planned to make the trip very short. I didn't plan on going at all. Could we do dinner on Sunday before I fly out?"

"Of course."

Talking to her mum soothed her nerves. Seeing her parents would give her some extra strength to deal with Alistair's family while she was in England. Especially since Sera, Liberty and Merle would all be back in Maine without her.

Five

Poppy hated travel. There was something nerve-racking about the entire process of going through security. Like she knew she wasn't carrying contraband, but her pits were sweating as if she were a drug mule making her first run. It was ridiculous. She knew she'd decanted every liquid into properly sized containers, but as she got closer to the security checkpoint, she still worried she hadn't removed every restricted thing from her handbag.

"You okay? You're breathing heavy."

Glancing at Alistair, who looked calm and cool as he shouldered his Louis Vuitton duffel bag while wearing sweats and a T-shirt, she rolled her eyes. Of course he did. Her hair, which she'd taken the time to straighten, had already started frizzing thanks to the humidity on the way to the airport in Bangor. They were on an early flight that connected in JFK before heading to London.

He hadn't shaved and had stubble on his cheeks and jaw, but his thick hair was nicely styled. She inhaled his citrusy, fresh scent, which carried notes of grapefruit, tangerine, coriander and bergamot. She could dissect the scent because she spent so much time around leaves, oils and essences when she blended tea.

Also it had lingered on her clothes after that impulsive embrace the other night.

"Yeah, it's all Gucci." Except it was about as Gucci as that knockoff belt she'd gotten at Primark with two linking circles where the Gs should be.

"Remember that first time I took you on the company jet?" he asked.

She did. One comment that she'd never been to Milan, and he'd whisked her off. They'd skipped two days of class. The jet had been... Well not like this kind of traveling.

Her heart had skipped a beat or two when they'd gotten on the luxury plane with the long couch on one side. He'd held her hand as they fastened their seat belts and took off. He'd proposed to her on that trip. In the Navigli district near a picturesque canal. That was...perfect. Too perfect, it turned out, but at the time, she'd been swept off her feet.

"So different from this. I'm actually surprised you didn't bring it here. I mean, this was totally a business trip for you."

"I told you, I'm not officially working for the company," he said.

"Uh, I guess I thought leave of absence was something else. What's that about?" she asked, noticing that they were next to place their carry-on items in the security bins.

Tossing her bag of liquids in first and then the rest of her stuff. She moved on to pass through the metal detector. Alistair had distracted her, and she wasn't even nervous now. Though she *was* wearing two toe rings and a belly-button piercing that she'd gotten on a dare when she'd been in sixth form.

Should she have removed them? Too late now.

The security agent assured her that she'd be fine. All that energy for nothing. She collected her stuff and watched as Alistair was pulled over for additional screening. She grabbed his bag when it came through the scanner and stood off to the side to wait for him.

"All of your worrying, and I'm the one who got stopped," he said. "Ready for breakfast?"

"I don't think anything is open yet," she said. "I packed some banana-nut loaf if you want a slice. If we can find a place with hot water, I have coffee sachets too."

"That sounds great. The lounge should have some. Let's go."

She'd forgotten about the lounge. She hadn't bothered looking at her ticket either, but she suspected he hadn't booked them in economy. They found a place in the lounge—where they did have food—but she stubbornly ate the banana loaf, as did Alistair, after bringing them both coffees. She wanted to refuse the coffee on principle but freshly brewed was so much better than the instant she'd packed. Hers had two sugars and a splash of two percent milk in it. Just the way she made it for herself.

It wasn't a big deal that he remembered the way she liked her morning java, but she felt that warmth in her stomach all the same. "Thanks."

"No problem."

Silence settled between them, but her mind was running with so many questions. "Tell me about the job thing."

"It's just me trying to figure out what I want to do," he said around a bite of banana bread.

"You're a Miller. Lancaster-Spencer is what you do," she reminded him.

"George can carry on the legacy. I'm not sure it's for me," he said.

"What would you do?" Genuinely curious about him, she told herself it wasn't just because this was Alistair. She did need to go into the meeting with his family armed with knowledge.

"Beer brewing, like I told you online."

"Oh, I thought that was a hobby. What drew you to it?"

"Remember that six weeks I did in the tasting rooms? During the first few months of my leave, I went back to partying and the like. Then stuff happened. The next thing I know, I'm stuck at home—"

"Were you confined to your house?" she interjected.

"Ha. No. COVID. I was seeing a therapist virtually who made me write a list of things I liked. Anyhow, turns out brewing and tasting were things I enjoyed. I ordered a beer-making kit, which was rudimental, but I made my first batch. I was sort of hooked."

She was curious what else had made his list, but it wasn't really relevant to the meeting that she was going to have on Saturday morning. "And kombucha?"

"That's Owen's idea. He suggested trying it after we became friends on a Reddit thread when he found out my family was in tea. That's when I asked to join the Tea Society... I was surprised you accepted me."

Looking down at the table, she played with the crumbs on her napkin. It seemed churlish to say she hadn't. But she wasn't lying to him or herself this time. "It wasn't me. By the time I saw the request, you were a member."

"Would you have declined?"

Shrugging, she wasn't entirely sure how to answer that. "Maybe. I don't know."

A shuttered look came over his face.

"I'm glad you're a member," she admitted. "You've added a lot to the conversation. There have been a few moments when I think you're mansplaining…but I just roll my eyes and move on."

Alistair looked at the Breitling Superocean watch on his wrist, willing time to speed up so he could make things right with Poppy instead of sitting here torturing himself about things that he couldn't change. Their trip to Milan still lingered in his mind. He wouldn't have brought up the trip where they got engaged, but he remembered how nervous a flyer she'd been.

She'd been almost hyperventilating while they stood in line for the security screening. Distracting her was the only thing he'd been able to think of.

But remembering how she truly believed she loved him when he'd gone down on one knee… There was no mistaking the expression on her face when she'd put the ring on her finger and thrown herself into his arms. He'd caught her and kissed her. Getting the response he anticipated had been just a checkmark in a box.

As soon as she'd called her parents to tell them the news, he'd texted his dad to let him know that she was going to be part of their family. Her parents had been cautious and suggested they have a long engagement, but Poppy hadn't wanted to wait to start her life with him.

Those were the words she'd used: *I don't want to wait to start my life with you.*

Not that he'd paid any attention to them until she left him. On drunken nights, he could forget the fuckups of his life. But when he first went sober for a thirty-day stint—which he did frequently now—they became harder to forget. Those words, her face, they haunted him.

He had said the right words for the wrong reasons. Told a woman he hadn't really taken the time to get to know that he loved her. Then tried to mold her into the wife his family wanted him to have.

To give her credit, she'd tried, and he hadn't helped at all. His anger at her failures hadn't been fair. But he'd been feeling a lot of pressure at his new executive position, and that had mingled with the guilt of not being honest with Poppy.

He'd thought he loved her, but all those doubts he'd had about himself combined with his dishonesty about the tea recipe had been a toxic cocktail for him. Making all of his good intentions disappear, leaving only anger.

No excuse for him being a dick to her.

"When did I mansplain?"

"Never mind. I don't want to argue about it," she said.

"I'm not going to argue. I want to know so I don't do it again," he said.

"When we discussed my technique for steeping new blends to test the strength and make adjustments," she said.

Her way of blending wasn't bad… "I was offering another way to do it. Sorry if it came across as inconsiderate."

"Thanks. It sounded like you were the expert even though

I've been successfully doing this for seven years now. You worked in the tasting room for six weeks," she pointed out.

"I'll watch my tone and words next time."

She shrugged. "It's no biggie."

"It's a biggie. Poppy, don't do that. I was showing off. Felt I could finally contribute something to the group that's given me so much. But I shouldn't have done it at your expense."

The words were ripped from somewhere deep inside of him. That kind of behavior smacked of his father's.

"It wasn't that big of a deal. Everyone really appreciated your comments. I think I might be too sensitive where you're concerned."

Leaning back in the chair, he crossed his arms over his chest. "Given our history, that makes sense."

"Yeah, it does."

"Should we try again? Start over? Would that make this easier?" he asked, gesturing to the both of them.

Chewing her lower lip, she fiddled with the breadcrumbs on the napkin, using the edges to move them around. "To what end?"

"Maybe I can stop apologizing for the past that I can't change, and you could stop looking at me like I'm going to hurt you again."

She put her shoulders back, tipping her head to the side to study him. With her hair straight, the angles of her face were sharper and her eyes more direct. She hadn't put any makeup on to travel, so the dusting of freckles across her nose was visible. There was a freshness to this look that made him want to do whatever he could to protect her.

Except when had he ever done a good job of that?

She put her hand on his where it rested on the table. "It's

not you I'm worried about hurting me. It's me expecting too much… Does that make any sense? Please stop blaming yourself. As you said, you apologized."

Expecting too much.

The words lingered between them in his mind. "You can't expect too much this time. I'm going to deliver what I've promised you. Whatever happens at breakfast on Saturday, I'm not walking away until you have a decent deal in place for your tea."

"Thanks for that."

Their flight came up on the board, and they both left the lounge. She wasn't chatty as they waited to get on the plane, which suited him. There was a long day of travel ahead of him, and sitting next to Poppy would be torture. Her sweet vanilla-and-strawberry scent made him want to take a deep breath and close his eyes so he could relive every moment of their kiss the other night.

Not a good idea when they were flying commercial. Besides, she'd been clear about keeping things platonic. He'd do his best to live up to that, but it had been a long time since he'd struggled to keep his thoughts off of a woman like this.

The second flight, from JFK to London, was smooth. Alistair slept from Bangor to New York, giving her plenty of time to think. He'd drifted off again once they were in the air on this flight. She pulled out the journal that Sera had gifted her and started journaling. His aftershave gave her ideas for a new tea blend she wanted to try.

It was hard to be this close to him and not remember the good times.

As with any relationship, theirs hadn't been all fighting

and resentment. There had been laughter and lots of sex. Being this close to him, it took every ounce of willpower she had not to touch him. She could pretend to fall asleep, let her head fall onto his shoulder.

But she couldn't sleep on a plane or with Alistair—that felt too intimate. Even after three glasses of champagne. Instead, she was under the provided blanket because she was chilly. The cabin crew had dimmed the lights and asked everyone to lower the window shades. The flight attendants had settled, having gone wherever they went during a flight. She was as alone as she could be on a crowded plane seated in premium economy.

Alistair yawned and stretched, turning his head to look at her. She had her headphones in and was listening to her favorite playlist on her phone. She paused it and took out one of the earpieces.

"You missed drinks. They said you could ring if you needed anything," she said.

"I'm good with my water bottle," he said.

There was a sleepiness to his face; he looked relaxed…soft. Ali like this was someone she just wanted to curl up next to. He scrubbed his hand over his face and then put his seat up a bit. "What have you been doing?"

"Videoing you snoring."

"Ha. I don't snore." He pulled his water bottle out and took a long swallow, then ran his hands through his hair again, a curl dropped to his forehead. She reached up to push it back into place without thinking.

He went very still. Pulling her hand back and tucking it under the blanket as quickly as she could. "Sorry."

"Nah, it's good. Anything good on the media for this flight?"

Appreciating the change of subject, she struggled to remember what was on the screen. "Not sure. I've been journaling and trying to figure out some new blends for autumn. I like to have time to play around with different flavors."

"Do you have any recipes you return to?"

"Some. I mean, I lean heavy into ginger, nutmeg and cinnamon. Pumpkin spice tea is huge for me."

"Yeah, the Yanks love that stuff. Owen sent me a recipe for pumpkin spice ale. I'm going to try it this fall."

"What other flavors have you tried?" This part of Alistair was new to her. It was fascinating to see him doing the very thing that he'd thought was a waste of time back when she'd worked for Lancaster-Spencer and quietly started making her own tea blends on the side and selling them on Etsy.

"Not many. I figured I should perfect a good ale before I start trying to get fancy," he said with a laugh. "You know how I can be."

"Yeah, I do. So have you got an award-winning ale yet?"

He blushed, and she started laughing.

"You have! Tell me about it."

He shook his head. "No one likes a braggart."

"I asked, so it's not bragging."

"I got best regional light ale for Kent," he said.

"Nice. So now it's time to experiment with flavors?" she asked.

He shrugged. "I'm doing that with kombucha. It has health benefits and naturally has some alcohol content. I'm going to use some champagne yeast in the second fermentation, and then I want to add some flavors."

"What are you thinking? Kent has apples, plums, cherries... Are you brewing it for summer?"

"I've got a growler with kombucha fermenting now. So, yeah. I was thinking of apricot at first because I've got two trees on my property, and they've been blooming like crazy."

"There's a tea I love. Apricot is the dominant flavor, and they use sunflower petals and blue mallow blossoms to add depth and bring out the apricot flavor. Now, blue mallow is usually a nighttime tea, so it might not mix well with the alcohol, but the essence of it would be nice."

"What is blue mallow blossom?" he asked, pulling out his phone and opening up the notepad app.

"It's part of the daisy family. I think it's pretty common. You can probably order it from a tea supplier in the UK. I can give you my supplier, but they ship from the US."

They spent the next thirty minutes talking about tea blending and recipes. It had been a long time since she'd talked tea with anyone in person. She wrote posts and read other's responses on the Tea Society, but this was nice. Alistair had the legacy of his family's influence over tea drinking, but was looking at it from a beer brewer's perspective. The kombucha experimentation was equally exciting and gave her an idea. "We should put this in the Tea Society as a challenge for the autumn after we finish the kombucha one. See what everyone comes up with."

"Good idea. Um...do you think I could invite Owen to join? I think he'd add a lot. The guy is wicked smart about fermentation. Kombucha really requires some different skills."

Poppy had a second of possessiveness toward the group that she'd started, but she liked Alistair's suggestion. One of the strengths she developed after their divorce was letting go. She'd stopped trying to keep things the same, because the world was always changing. Even this conversation was something she'd never thought she'd have.

"I'll show you my setup when we get to my place."

"What? Won't we stay at the hotel where the wedding is?"

"On Saturday we will, but I figured for the next few days, we'd stay at mine."

Six

Stay at his. She hadn't planned for that. Of course, he wanted to show her how much he'd changed. Maybe it was time for her to start giving him the opportunity.

Maybe that explained how she ended up walking around the converted barn that Alistair called home now. It was nothing like the stately manor house he'd grown up in. Even less like the trendy flat they'd shared in Kensington.

It was homey and comfortable. Practically inviting her to take off her shoes and curl up in the overstuffed chair that looked perfect for reading with a cup of tea while a fire burned in the large tiled fireplace.

"You can take the room at the top of the stairs to the left," Alistair said as he completed giving her the tour of the ground floor. "You didn't sleep on the plane, so if you want a nap, that's cool."

"Perfect. Don't let me sleep more than four hours," she said.

"I won't." He stood there at the bottom of the stairs as she started up them.

Tempted to invite him to join her on that double bed while tingles spread through her. Remembering the way his mouth had felt on hers the other night…

"Do we have plans?" she asked.

"No, why?"

"It's the full moon the night of the wedding, so I was hoping to go someplace on the solstice."

"Great. We can take my bike and have dinner at the lighthouse on the pier."

But his body language wasn't giving *great*. Tense and maybe something else that she wasn't able to detect. "It's okay to say no."

"No, it's not. All I did was turn down everything you suggested when we were together."

"Yeah, but we're not together now. We're trying to be friends. Friends aren't twins and don't have to agree to do things they hate. That's not how real relationships work," she said. It had taken her friendships with Sera and Liberty to force her to see that. In the past, she'd spent so much time making sure she fit the mold of whatever someone else wanted her to be. Never again.

"Yeah, but…"

"Honestly, it's okay. You have a great yard. I can meditate in the garden, and I'll be happy," she said.

"Poppy, stop. I thought we'd take the bike and head over to Glastonbury on Wednesday and spend two days there before heading to the wedding venue. I booked a room at a B and B there. The Tor is perfect for your moon ritual. I know it's not the beach—"

She threw herself at him, and he caught her. She hugged him tightly. He couldn't know how touched she was that he'd planned something for her. Not an activity where he needed a plus-one, but something that suited the woman she'd become. "Thank you."

"For Glasto or catching you?"

"Both," she said, kissing him quick because she couldn't resist him when she was this close.

His arms around her were tight and strong. All the feels she wished she didn't have for this man swirled around them like the gusts that stirred the surrounding open farmland. She was buffeted by the past and the present, trying desperately to find her footing in this storm so that she wouldn't make the same mistakes.

But his hands cupped her butt, and his tongue slid over hers, and thinking became impossible. Who wanted to debate the merits of mistakes when there was a hot man holding her?

Turning so her back was against the wall near the stairs, she wrapped her legs around his waist and pushed her hands into his hair.

His hair was thick and smooth as she kneaded her fingers through it while he deepened the kiss. She sucked his lower lip between her teeth before lifting her head. This close, she could see the flecks of gold and green in his brown eyes. His lashes were long and dense. She'd always been jealous of them whenever she tried unsuccessfully to put on fake lashes.

"Uh…" It was like being around Alistair was short-circuiting her brain. All the things she'd planned to say and be around him were gone.

"Yeah," he stepped back and let her slide down his body.

She almost let a groan slip out when she felt his erection against her thigh. And couldn't help running her hand over the ridge of his cock, straining against his sweats. He thrust against her touch.

"Pop…you said platonic… Has that changed?" he asked, his words thready and breathy. He wrapped a strand of hair that had escaped her braid around his finger.

Shivering as his finger brushed the side of her neck, she sighed. *Enough.* There was no way this was part of any plan. No matter how much she wanted to act as if she could manage her feelings for him the way she steeped a cup of tea, she couldn't.

This was Alistair. The bad boy she'd first glimpsed wearing a leather jacket and winking at her. Her favorite romantic hero come to life. Standing close to him, with his thick dick in her hand, she was getting wet just from his fingers tracing a pattern on her neck.

"Poppy?"

"What?"

"Platonic?"

Platonic.

Hell.

Fuck.

Yes. That was what she'd decided before coming to the UK with him. It took all of her willpower to let his dick go, wrapping her arms around herself. She tipped her head back against the wall and closed her eyes. Doing the deep-breathing techniques that she and Sera had learned at the yoga/meditation class they'd started taking at the community center.

But the smell of Alistair was in her nostrils, her breasts were full, and her center was humming; not ready to walk away.

Too bad—her mind was in charge now.

"Yes. Sorry. That one's on me."

"Wish you had been on me longer," he said.

Opening her eyes, meeting his gaze, she couldn't help the smile that teased her lips. "Same. But I'm trying… I need to be smart."

"We both do. When the time is right, it will happen," he said. "I don't want you to have any regrets this time, Pop. Get your nap."

The sounds of Poppy moving around upstairs as she washed up and settled in the guest room were hitting him harder than he'd expected. The walls in the house were solid, but he could still hear the faint sound of her voice as she called someone. Given that her friends and family must all hate him, he guessed that she was going to have to explain her choices.

Or given the woman Poppy was now, she might not bother. He had no right to be proud of the woman she'd become, but having known her at eighteen when she had just a shimmer of the woman she was today, he couldn't help it.

Chances were, the impetus for that growth probably started as a big *fuck you* to him.

Still, that didn't tinge the way he felt.

His own phone had been vibrating in his pocket since they landed. It took all of his willpower to wait and respond to the messages later. Part of his recovery from his anger issues was detoxing from being available twenty-four-seven for everyone.

When she was quiet upstairs at last, it took all of his control not to go check in on her. Instead, he went out to his brewery. Actually, it had started its life as a summerhouse, but he'd slowly rebuilt it over the past year to suit his brewing needs. First, he wanted to check the kombucha he'd put up before he left.

Walking toward the building, he pulled his phone out. There were three messages from his mum, two from George and one from Owen. He opened the one from Owen first.

I'm thinking of a doing a summer beer fest. Want to come as a guest brewer and make your Summer in Kent IPA? Kind of like a residency. You could stay upstairs again if you need a place.

Let me check a few things. But I like the idea. I'd get my own place. What dates?

Don't have anything formal yet but figured I'd run it from end of June through September.

I'll let you know tomorrow.

Owen gave the message a thumbs-up.

Birch Lake was Poppy's place, not Alistair's. It was a small town. But not that small. If things went wrong he'd at least have his own space. He would consult with her, see if she would be comfortable with it, before he agreed to Owen's invitation. As it was, he was more concerned with the details of the deal he was trying to work with George to terminate his employment with Lancaster-Spencer.

He read the text from George, which just said that Dad had had a three-hour meeting with his solicitors that morning. George would update him when he had more info.

It was odd for his brother to reach out. Since he'd gotten married last year, George had been more...brotherly. Was that even a thing? There were four years between them, and they'd never really been close. But after Alistair's explosion at work, George had been sending him messages once a week or so.

At first, Alistair had ignored them, still pissed at everyone. But at his lowest, that weekly text from George had been a lifeline. He'd never tell his brother that, but there were nights when he was pretty sure George had saved his life.

Thanks for keeping me in the loop.

His mum's messages were all about his flight. She'd seen that his plane had landed but hadn't heard from him. The last one, which came in while he'd been texting George, just said, hope you're not dead.

His mum was so dramatic.

He texted back, Not dead. See you at the wedding. Love you.

She sent back a huge block of text that just told him he wasn't funny, she'd been worried and she loved him too.

The shed where he'd stored the kombucha growler to ferment was dark and cool when he stepped inside. Though it was June, it wasn't hot today. The sky was cloudy, and rain had fallen on their way to his place. He checked his brew and it looked pretty good. Thankfully, he'd brewed kombucha before.

It had seemed like a natural bridge between what he wanted to do and his family's legacy. Kombucha always smelled rank to him right out of the growler, and this batch had that vinegary tang, so he figured it would be pretty good. He used a testing straw to sample it. Not bad.

Once he made some adjustments and added in flavors at the last stage, he thought he might be onto a winner.

For now, he was ready to add in the champagne yeast. He checked his watch and saw he still had a couple of hours before he had to go and wake Poppy.

Going to his workbench, he assembled everything he needed. He'd had proper plumbing installed, so he had hot and cold water, and the building was also climate controlled so that his ales and kombucha had the ideal environment to ferment.

The first thing he needed to do was make a slurry with hot water and sugar. He let the sugar and water cool before adding a teaspoon of the champagne yeast and letting it activate. He set a timer for five minutes and then stood near the door, looking up at his house.

Memories of Poppy from their marriage played in his head.

Poppy deserved to be treated with respect, unlike how she had been when he'd married her and brought her to the first board meeting. This time, he wanted to ensure that she was in charge. That Poppy got what she wanted out of this deal.

Not because of what he needed, but because of what she was owed.

He'd put so much bad karma out in the universe. Righting this one wrong wasn't going to suddenly clear that debt, but it would give him less to worry about. Maybe he'd finally have the proof that he could be more than the playboy heir who took what he wanted.

★ ★ ★

Poppy's room had a hardwood floor and a large Persian-style rug under a four-poster bed. There was a full-size wardrobe, with a smaller one off to one side. It had an en suite, which she appreciated, where she immediately washed her face and brushed her teeth.

She eyed the bed, but a wave of homesickness rolled over her. Was it still too early for a call back to Maine? Sitting cross-legged on the bed, she debated for about thirty seconds before messaging Merle.

He called her right away. "What's up?"

"Nothing. Just missing home."

"You're British," he said dryly.

"Ha. You know what I mean."

"Everything okay with Alistair?"

Is it? "Yeah, he's fine. I just…it's odd being back here. Sorry, I know you're working—"

"I called you. I bet it's odd. I feel that way every time I go to a family dinner leaving my hair shaggy and not getting changed into a polo shirt. It's like I've changed but the world hasn't."

She leaned back against the headboard. Once again, Merle seemed to know the right words to say. "That's sort of it. There are some things that haven't changed… I'm struggling. I made a big deal of keeping things just friends between us, but now I want more."

"Tell him. I doubt that he's not going to be all into it. He was watching you when we played darts, and even I could feel the heat."

"That was because you and Liberty put on a show," she said.

But her cousin was right. The heat between her and Ali had never been in question. It was just if she could take it to the next level and not let her emotions get messy. Sera had always been really good about keeping things physical and not emotional with the men she hooked up with, but Poppy struggled with separating her body and her heart.

If it wasn't so early, she'd call Sera. Except there was no way to ask what she wanted to and not have it come out awkward.

"Want some unsolicited advice?"

"I did text you at, what, 4:00 a.m. your time."

"Indeed. Just do what you need to. Stop censoring yourself and acting like if you do one thing, you'll get better results. That's not how life works."

"Yeah, thanks. I already knew that," she said. "It's putting it into practice that's hard."

"Exactly. Didn't say I'd mastered it. I mean, I still try to sneak a baseball cap on to the monthly family Zoom calls, and Liberty snatches it from my head. I don't know if it's like this for you, but I've been living with this one version of myself for so long. Trying to change that is harder than anyone's reaction to me has been."

When she was with Alistair, she struggled to stay in the present and not be overtaken by past expectations for herself and him. She remembered being that girl who felt as if she got the moon when he asked her out. Swept her off to a ball in Vienna and danced with her until the sun came up.

Ordinary Poppy wouldn't get that man.

Except ordinary Poppy didn't need big gestures; she needed truth and honesty. And a man who saw her.

"Thanks, Merle. Love you."

"Love you too."

She ended the call feeling much better about her choices. After the divorce and realizing how wrong she'd been about Alistair, she'd started to beat herself up about every interaction she had with someone. Was she seeing who they were or what she wanted them to be?

But her instincts had always been good. WiCKed Sisters was proof of that.

She set her alarm and then pulled her face mask on, curling onto her side to go to sleep.

Except she was restless. Filled with images of her and Alistair at the bottom of the stairs, fucking against the wall. His hands roving over her body, finding just the right spots. His mouth hot on her neck and breasts as he teased her until she craved him deep inside of her. She knew exactly how he felt inside of her, and she woke up empty and aching.

Touching herself under the covers, she jumped when there was a soft rap on the door. "I'm awake."

"Need anything?" Alistair's voice was a low rumble through the door.

You. Her dreams had been torrid, nothing but the two of them twisting and turning together. Every way they'd ever done it before and new ways that she'd read about and wanted to try.

"Poppy?"

"I'm getting up," she said. Right now, the Ali in her dreams was what she needed. She hopped out of bed and walked to the door, pulling it open just enough to stick her head through. "I'd kill for a sandwich and some tea."

"Let's skip the murder, and I'll order in something. What do you feel like?"

"Surprise me," she said.

She closed the door and got dressed in a pair of jeans and a light top. Her biggest problem was trying to force her life onto the path she'd plotted. More than once, she'd been knocked off of it and the good stuff had been in the weeds.

Her problem had never been trusting the universe had a plan for her. It was trusting herself to recognize it and follow it. She knew her worth this time, so when she did end up across the table from Alistair's dad again, she wasn't going to just back off.

But that had nothing to do with what she felt for Alistair.

If they did hook up, she knew it would be different because they'd both changed. She liked the way he was now. Not perfect, not arrogant. Sort of more human than he'd ever been before. It could just be for the few days they were both in England.

Hopefully she could finally settle on taking that risk before she was on the plane home all alone, regretting not giving him another shot.

Seven

Feeding Poppy wasn't something that he'd ever had two thoughts about. But spending so much time apart, staring at photos of the two of them as he'd processed through his rage, guilt and failings, had changed his perspective.

She acted as if the sausage rolls and yum yums he'd ordered from Greggs were a gourmet meal.

She caught him staring at her and blushed. "Sorry, it's just that Americans don't do sausage rolls… I totally miss them. Also, after the flight and nap, I'm swimming in that drunk feeling."

"Don't apologize. Glad I could provide them. I was surprised when you texted down to order them."

"Yeah? Remember the first time we had them together?" she asked.

"We were hung over…or at least I was. You said they were a hangover remedy."

"I did. Little did I realize that it was going to take more

than sausage meat wrapped in pastry to cure the effects of pitchers of Aperol spritz and Jäger bombs."

He remembered that night. He'd never really before entertained the thought of going to Greggs, the High Street staple and chain restaurant. His normal morning-after was hair of the dog—downing a pint and then an ice-cold shower. Poppy had been outraged when he made those suggestions. Her hair had been tousled from the night before, and she'd tried to tame it into the messiest bun he'd ever seen.

She'd been so cute when she grabbed her debit card and his hand and pulled him down to High Street to queue up in front of Greggs as the doors opened. She'd even turned to him when she first stepped inside, putting her hand on the middle of his chest to steady herself, and told him to take a deep breath.

"Eventually, we did start feeling better," he said.

"Yeah. Remember, you asked me if I was going to eat the entire roll or just pick at it like a squirrel."

He'd been humoring her, but her hangover cure had gone a long way to making him feel better that morning. Or maybe it had simply been the woman with the too-big-for-her-face dark sunglasses who put her head on his lap as they sat on a park bench to eat their breakfast. She'd kept feeding herself tiny bites of the sausage rolls and telling him that her head was going to explode.

Laughing, he shook his head. "You said that your stomach could only deal with the tiniest bit at a time."

"You thought you were immune to it, and then yacked." Shaking her head, she smiled over at him.

He'd forgotten about that. It was too much food when his body had been expecting alcohol. He'd been ticked, but then Poppy had sat up and patted his back, given him water to rinse out his mouth… It sounded stupid, but she'd just been kind to him. Taken care of him.

And he'd never really experienced that before. He'd been shipped off to boarding school at the age of ten, been drunk with his mates and hungover numerous times, but usually he took care of himself. He had to.

"I know I said that you shouldn't have bought into the whole love-at-first-sight thing, but there was something special between us. I was too focused on doing what Dad wanted to see it."

She stopped eating her sausage roll, putting it down on a napkin. "I guess if I'd been in on the plan, maybe I would have viewed everything differently."

"Yeah? I doubt it. What woman wants to be told she's the means to an end?"

"What man does?" she countered.

What did she mean by that? Was she using him this time? If so, kudos to her. He deserved it, and if that was what she needed, he was here for it. "Are you using me, Pop?"

"What do you think?" she asked, picking up her water bottle and taking a long sip.

Leaning back in the leather armchair after he finished his food, he studied her. There had always been something too nice about Poppy, yet she wasn't a pushover. Even when they'd gone in to face his father and sign the contract, she'd fought and gotten concessions from the old man.

Concessions for the two of them.

She'd viewed them as a couple, whereas he'd still been thinking solely of himself.

"I bet you're thinking about it. Using me the way I used you and making me realize what a big fuckup that was."

"I have," she said.

Would she go through with it? It was hard to imagine the Poppy he'd known doing that. But the way she was watching him at this moment sent a bit of a chill down his spine.

It would suck if he'd made her hardened like him. If she was willing to do and say anything just to get what she wanted. The ends justifying the means.

"I'm not planning on anything evil, Ali. I'm hoping we can become friends, or at least friendly."

Yeah. That had been his hope too. "That's partially why I'm sticking around the Tea Society. It's nice to have something other than Lancaster-Spencer to talk about."

"It definitely is. You mentioned your hard kombucha and beer brewing. Can I see your setup?"

Just like that, she'd moved them away from the past and the issues he still wanted to hash out, but he let her.

The land surrounding Alistair's house was all rolling fields. There was a large outbuilding, and then two smaller ones on either side of it. Someone had painted Ali's Brewing on the doors to the largest building. The two smaller ones reminded her of her shed at home, where she dried tea leaves and stored the different elements she used in her blends.

"Ali's Brewing?"

He stood up a bit straighter as he led her to it. "I make more than I can drink, though George says that's not necessarily true. So I started selling it to local pubs and shops. We're close enough to Folkestone, and I have a connection with a pub on the beach there. They like to stock local ales."

"I like it. It's simple and classy."

"I picked that tip up from a woman I used to know."

She'd thought she could simply keep the past where it belonged and focus on learning what she could from Alistair. That was it. But their lives were too deeply woven together. They'd been kids when they got married, so their influence on each other was written on the souls of the people they were today.

His face showed the signs of that life, and there were moments when she caught him watching her carefully. There were those land mines that she remembered hearing mum's favorite singer, Sting, talk about. They'd both planted them on their way out the door, and now they were navigating a dangerous minefield, hoping not to get hurt again.

"She was always too smart for you," Poppy said with a bit of an edge. She hated remembering how much in love with him she'd been and how she'd kept trying to show him how to reciprocate that love.

"Indeed. Also, I have a hard head—everyone knows that. Just took longer for her wisdom to sink in." A look crossed his face that she didn't recognize…maybe regret. "Want to see the brewing operation? Or the kombucha shed?"

"Both. Since you won the right to set the challenge for the summer, I have to brew my own kombucha. I've never been a fan of it."

"I'll let you try some of the stuff I've brewed. See if I can change your mind."

He led her to one of the smaller buildings, and as soon as she stepped inside, she realized that it was temperature controlled. Pulling out her phone, she opened the notes app.

"Is temperature important in fermenting the kombucha?" she asked.

"Not really. When you're making your SCOBY and doing your second fermenting, room temperature is fine," he said.

"The SCOBY is a starter like they use in sourdough?"

"Yes. It's the base for the kombucha. It usually takes about seven to twelve days, but I've heard of some people who let it go a lot longer," he said.

"Then the first thing I need to do is grow the SCOBY?"

"Yes. The next steps all take about a week and half to two weeks. So you should have enough time to do it before the deadline," he said. Then he showed her the kombucha he'd put into the new bottle with the airlock while she'd been sleeping.

When she worked with Alistair at Lancaster-Spencer for those few disastrous months, he'd been impatient and bossy. Here, he took his time showing her all the steps he took to make his concoctions and how he fermented them.

Her questions—which were probably basic to him—were answered. All of them. He even shared his own experience with the mistakes he made and how he learned from them.

"Thanks. I'll probably be DMing you while I do this at home."

"Feel free. I can send you a list of supplies I use… It's the least I can do after you helped me out with the flavors," he said.

A part of her wanted to say he didn't owe her, but they weren't lovers or even friends. They were friendly acquaintances, which meant that he could owe her. No denying it felt good to ask him for something and not feel guilty. "Sure. I'm ready to see the big operation."

"Ha. Dad calls it my 'lockdown hobby' and is insistent I start working again," he said as he led her out of the shed.

"Don't let him do that. Your beer is something you worked hard to make," she said.

He stopped walking, leaning against the side of the beer barn before opening the door. It seemed like he wanted to say something.

She put her hand on his arm to stop him from moving. "Your dad is a bully. Sera would say he probably didn't get to go after his own dreams, so he crushes everyone else's."

"Maybe. What's that got to do with me?"

"Don't be like him. Do your thing if that's what you want. Is this why you took your leave of absence? It must tick him off to know you don't want to be his little clone," Poppy said.

"It does. But he's still got George," Alistair said, opening the barn door and leading her inside.

There were three big vats, and she knew they were for different stages of the fermenting and brewing process. He took her to a tasting table and went to get some samples for them before she realized he hadn't actually told her the reasons behind his break from the family company.

It had always been important to Alistair that he be the heir to Lancaster-Spencer along with George. He had so much pride in his family's legacy and his place in it. Was this something he was doing to distract himself from what he'd lost?

But then he was back, holding a couple of glasses in his big hands. He set them on the table in front of her and straddled the stool next to her.

"This one is my favorite. I was going for something that tasted like summer," he said.

She took a sip, aware that he waited for her reaction. The

beer was good, and she could taste the notes of the fruit he'd used to flavor it. As they talked more about the beer, she realized this didn't feel like something he was doing simply to bide his time.

Since his main repertoire of meals consisted of omelets and ramen, Poppy had suggested dinner out instead of ordering in, and he'd made a reservation at a nice pub near his place.

"Can we walk?" Poppy called from her bedroom.

The clouds from earlier had cleared away. "If you want to. The restaurant is probably twenty minutes from here," he said.

"Great. I need to move after all the time on the plane and then sleeping," she said. "Am I okay?"

She stepped out of her room, and he glanced over at her. She was trying to kill him. The dress she had on was summer weight, a slim-fitting sheath with thin little straps. Due to the heat, she had her hair up, which drew his eyes to her neck. He wished he'd kissed her there, and his fingertips tingled from remembering the feel of her skin under them.

"Great. Me?" He'd put on a button-down shirt and some shorts.

"You know you look gorgeous. You always do."

"I don't know," he said.

"Yeah, right. You were the hottest dude on campus and posed with your shirt off for the calendar."

"You're right. I do know I look fit, but that doesn't mean you like it." Poppy wasn't into giving those kinds of compliments. She'd tell him his eyes were the color of her favorite tea or that his hand in hers made her feel safe when they were out late. But physically...

It wasn't like he needed her words; the chemistry between them had always been off the charts. So he knew there was something about him that still turned her on.

Coming over to him, she stopped when she was close enough that he could feel the soft exhalation of her breath. The bracelets on her arm jingled when she brushed a curl from his forehead. She traced the line of his jaw before placing her hand on his shoulder and rising up on her toes. Her lips brushed his. Heat burned a path from his mouth straight to his dick.

His hands trembled as he tried to keep them by his side, despite every instinct he had telling him to grab her and pull her closer to him.

He wanted to feel the curves of her body against his hardness. She was a summer sprite tonight, bubbly and light, drawing him closer to her even though he knew he should keep his distance.

He wanted her to crave him enough that she forgot about keeping things platonic.

"You look very good. Everyone in the place is going to be envious of me," she said.

She tipped her head to the side as she winked at him and stepped back. Laughing at him. He had to join in. He'd never been the man who needed that kind of compliment. "Just seems like we should keep it fair. Like, why should only women get told they look good?" Ali asked.

"Is this your bid for feminism?"

"Ah...not what I said. I just meant...never mind. I was just playing around."

She shook her head. "It's okay if you weren't. All your life, people have cultivated friendships with you because of who your father is so they could use your connections."

"Not you," he admitted.

"Yeah. How clueless was I?"

"It was refreshing."

The first time they met, she got his name wrong because she'd heard Gemma call him Ali and thought his name was *Adi*. She'd had no clue that he was connected to Lancaster-Spencer or that his dad was titled and that Ali himself would inherit lessor property and land when his father died.

She'd treated him like any other guy. Both humbling and challenging. That worked in his favor when he courted her, because she hadn't realized that his family had been after her family tea recipe for centuries.

"I liked you as just 'Adi,'" she said.

"Too bad Adi wasn't real."

"Nah, Ali has some good qualities too. I mean, he's real, for one."

He followed her downstairs. He wasn't sure that he had many good qualities back then, but in the intervening years, he'd found some. That kid who thought he was the shit had woken up to realize he wasn't, and there was a lot he still had to learn.

It had been hard to admit that a lot of those lessons had come from Poppy after she left him. "You sure you want to walk?"

"Definitely. I'm used to walking around Birch Lake," she said.

"How'd you end up there?" he asked. "I thought your aunt lived in Bangor?"

"She does. Mum and Dad have a rental property in Birch

Lake. I am the caretaker for it, and they let me live in it rent free for six months," she said.

"You had money. I never cut you off from the accounts," he said.

"It was your money. Not mine. You weren't offering the one thing I wanted, so there was nothing you had that mattered to me." She put her sunglasses on and then started a workout on her watch. "Merle and I have a friendly competition on our watches. He pretty much just sits at his desk all night, so I think competing with me for the most steps is good for him."

Alistair's brows drew together. It was too easy for her to switch topics. Her words echoed from the past, stretching out to wrap around his throat. There was a residual tinge of regret that brought him back to something she'd said—or hadn't said—earlier.

He was pretty damn sure that if the opportunity to use him presented itself, Poppy would take it.

Eight

Going to the pub wasn't the worst idea. After the conversation they'd had, he'd tried to keep things light as they walked, and Poppy seemed to be on the same page. It was one of those hazy almost summer days that felt like it would last forever. Having Poppy next to him made his skin feel too tight. All he could notice was the way her skirt moved around her legs with each step she took.

She got a text and took her phone out to answer it.

This gave him too much time to notice how thin the material of her dress was and how, when he slowed down to walk at her pace, the scent of her vanilla body spray surrounded him. Her fingers tapped quickly on the screen of her phone and then she tucked it back into her crossbody bag.

"Sorry about that."

"Your friends warning you to keep your guard up around me?"

"Sort of. I mean, you know everyone in Birch Lake believes we're witches," she said.

He'd heard that. Maybe there was more than a kernel of truth to it. That would be a nice way to explain the hold she'd always had over him even when he hadn't wanted her to. "Are you going to curse me?"

"Who says I haven't already?" she said.

"That would explain a lot," he said, thinking of the past eighteen months. It would be nice to blame otherworldly forces instead of his own cocked-up stupidity. But taking ownership of his own actions was something his therapist had reinforced many times.

"Kidding. I'm not into cursing people," she said.

A memory tugged, and he canted his head to the side to watch her. "Didn't you make a poppet of our econ lecturer?"

Laughing in that small, tinkling sound that he couldn't help feeling all the way to his toes. She nodded. "That's right. I'd forgotten all about that little kit I picked up in the spiritual store. Since meeting Liberty, I know all the ways that those things can go wrong. No wonder I failed the exam."

"I did suggest using the time reading over the notes instead of perfecting the doll," he said as they approached the Cross Keys.

"Yeah, you did, but I've never been good at taking advice," she said.

"Not sure I gave any good tips." He held open the door for her to enter before him.

The temperature inside the pub was tepid, and it was a little stuffy given how hot it was today. "Want to try the beer garden?" he asked.

His local pub had a pretty decent dinner menu, and after eight, they had different local bands play. It was a Monday, so not a big going-out night normally. The sun was out, the pub was crowded, but they managed to find a seat toward the back of the beer garden.

Poppy looked at the menu and gave one of those smiles that sent a zing straight to his heart.

"Pub food. I mean it's a gastropub, so some really nice dishes, but you know I'm going straight for the fish and chips," she said with a grin. "What do you want? I'll order for us."

"Chicken tikka masala and a pint."

"Do they have your IPA here?" she asked.

"They do. Is that what you want?"

It always seemed a bit braggy to order his own beer at the pub. The barrels he'd sent here were from his spring brew, and he'd tried a different way of activating the yeast that Owen had suggested. So it was different than anything he'd tried before. "I guess."

Poppy sat back down and put her hand on his. "It's good. I mean, I already tried that sample. I bet it would be nice with your tikka. Why are you hesitating?"

He rubbed the back of his neck. Years of conditioning from being around his father made him hesitate. If it wasn't his best, then it wasn't worth anything in Howard Miller's eyes. "You sampled a different batch. The one here...I tried something different with the yeast, and it has a good flavor, but it's not as smooth on the tongue as I want it to be," he admitted. "Not saying it's crap."

Poppy leaned in closer, looking him in the eyes. "I find those types of brews teach me the most. The tea bags I brought with me are my third version of Magic Courage."

"I bet the other two were good."

"They were, but not perfect, so I get it. You can get whatever you want to drink. I'm going to try it. I bet you're being too harsh," she said. "The pub owners bought it and are selling it, so that has to count for something."

"They like it. It's light and perfect for a warm day, according to their customers."

"Stop letting your dad dictate your life," she said.

Uh.

He wanted to say, *I'm not.* But that was a lie. Even on his leave of absence. Even away from Lancaster-Spencer. Even as he was plotting the old man's ouster from the company, he still felt the hold of his father. That ridiculous need to get the approval he'd always withheld and was more than likely never going to offer.

"Fair play. I'll have the Ali's Brew Spring."

Poppy went and placed their order and returned a few minutes later with their pints, and the waitress followed with some tap water for them. "The owner told me this was a local ale and that it was very popular. I mentioned I'd heard it wasn't smooth."

"Ha. Tell me what you think," he said, watching her as she took a delicate sip. She let the liquid stay on her tongue before swallowing it.

Staring at her, tension occupying every fiber of his being, he wondered if she'd like it or not.

Her opinion mattered way more to him than his father's did. He wanted to impress her. Wanted to show her that he was more than what he'd been bred to be.

Drinking with Ali gave her all the feels. Most of them seemed to be centered in the very core of her. Technically, he wasn't the hottest man she'd ever met. Surely, there had been other men who'd been more attractive. But she couldn't think of a single one of them right now.

It was like as soon as she'd told her mind that he was off limits, it had started noticing all the little details. Like the way he fiddled with his signet ring just before he said something that made her feel warm and gooey inside.

And the way he ran his hand through his hair when he was getting serious about brewing.

It was so funny to see how much this meant to him. Her bad, but she'd totally thought he joined the Tea Society as a way to get her to come back to him. Turned out, he was really into brewing.

That single fact turned her on way more than him trying to sneak back to her. She liked that he had a legit reason for joining. Like he was sincere about being a member of the society.

"George suggested that if the kombucha turns out well, they'd stock it in the London store," Alistair said.

"Really? He wouldn't even consider my new blends for that location," she said, which really had been the bucket of cold water she'd needed in her life. Everyone had said she was part of the family, but her opinion was never heard at the boardroom table and no one ever backed her.

"Shocker, right? He said that legacy brands were losing traction because they didn't grow with the market," Ali said. "He has moments where I sort of realize he's not mini-dad."

That was good to hear. Alistair had mentioned that he and George had a plan for when they spoke to his parents. "Is the plan you brought up part of that?"

His hand was in his hair again, then he drained his pint in a long swallow. "Definitely. Want another one?"

Once she nodded he went to order them more drinks.

They'd been at the Cross Keys for almost two hours. The food was nice; the fish and chips were delicious. Her nap earlier meant she wasn't tired, but she was starting to feel slightly buzzed.

Spending time with Ali took the edge off of the anger she still had toward him. He was correct that he'd apologized. She just hadn't been able to let go at the time. If they were strangers, she'd be thinking about taking him to her bed. But they weren't strangers, and some petty part of her didn't want to let go of the way he'd hurt her.

It made her feel small. How many times had she messed up and asked for forgiveness? A lot. Never had Liberty and Sera denied it to her. She'd never denied them forgiveness either. Denying him that kindness was unlike her.

Ali was from before. From a time when she thought she was an adult but totally wasn't. Like any kid at uni was truly an adult. Her life had been full of freedom and some choices but no real responsibilities until she got married.

Then the perfect little life she'd crafted had fallen apart.

"Everything okay? You look very serious."

Maybe it was the three pints or maybe it was just her subconscious finally deciding it was time to put it all out there, but she said, "Just trying to figure out why I can't forgive you."

His eyes went wide, and he took a deep swallow of his pint before plopping down across from her. "Fuck. Really? I thought we were beyond that."

"Me too. But I'm not."

"Want to talk about it?" he asked.

No, but totally, yes. There were things she'd never gotten to say. Unfair things, since he'd already said he'd fucked up. But she still wanted to vocalize the hurt that she'd tucked deep inside.

"I hate that you lied to me."

"Me too. I shouldn't have. If I'd been a different guy, I wouldn't have."

"Would you do it again?" she asked.

"No. Definitely not."

She wanted to believe him. She needed to trust him. But she was so afraid of being stupid with him. "Is there anything you're not telling me?" she asked, then put her hand on his lips to stop him from speaking. "Never mind."

"Why?"

She shrugged. "You shouldn't have to prove that you've changed."

"Agree, but if you need me to, I will," he said. "I need some absolution—not that you have to give it to me."

"Didn't mean to ruin our night," she said.

"You didn't. Listen, we both know what our marriage and courtship were like. The more we talk about it maybe we can finally put it in the past."

"Agreed. My mum never said *told you so*, but she thought we were both too young when we got married."

"My parents did too," he admitted.

"Really? Didn't they tell you to marry me?"

"No, that was all me. I was supposed to befriend you and then offer you an insane amount of money if you sold me the recipe."

She had always suspected his family had sent him to marry her. Something that had underscored how stupidly in love with Alistair she'd been. Like, how could she have missed that? But hearing that he was only meant to make her a business offer… Well, that sort of tracked.

There was no denying the chemistry between her and Ali. He drew her in like no other man ever had. That was why she'd put up with so much from him. Stayed as long as she had in a situation that went from happily-ever-after to a nightmare of family corporate dynamics.

The offer that Howard made when she went to work that first day as Alistair's wife and a junior executive had come out of the blue. Though she'd known that Alistair was part of Lancaster-Spencer, she'd never really thought the company was still after her family's prized tea recipe. They'd offered her compensation, but the fine print—which she hadn't truly understood until it was too late—stated that Lancaster-Spencer would own the recipe and Poppy and her heirs wouldn't be able to claim it any longer.

That moment had been a betrayal that cut so deep she'd needed Ali to help her survive. Instead, he'd told her it was just business and her heirs would be his kids, so no biggie.

But it was a biggie. The first of many that led to the dissolution of their marriage. Why had he married her then? Also, if they'd only wanted the recipe…well, that explained why they were never on board with her suggestions in the boardroom.

"Why didn't you?"

"I liked you," he said plainly.

She'd liked him too. But there was more to it than that. "And?"

"Having you by my side with the Kitchener legacy teas would give me an edge over George. For once, I had delivered something my brother couldn't."

His father's approval. Ali had made no bones of hiding his pursuit of it when he and Poppy were together. He talked about his dad all the time. How much he wanted to prove he should inherit the chairmanship.

She had no response to that.

"If I'd been smarter, I would have realized that every plan I made included having you by my side."

Fuck. Tension and anger stirred at his actions. He'd been shortsighted but also so blinded by ambition and desire that he hadn't seen how his path was going to end in a train wreck.

Poppy's eyes went wide for a moment before she chewed her bottom lip. "I think knowing that you wanted me by your side helps," she said.

"How? That makes it worse for me," he said. "What a bastard I was."

"One hundred percent. But you never would have admitted that when we were married. Let's have a toast to letting go of who we were," she said.

"What are you letting go of?"

"Thinking I needed a man to love me so I had worth." Not a single pause. Her answer was automatic.

"You've never needed that."

She shrugged. "I see that now. You gave me that."

"You gave me freedom from my family," he said. He hoped she never heard about his epic meltdown and the anger he exhibited that day. There were no two ways about it: her forcing the divorce had forced him to change.

"Cheers to us," she said.

He clinked her glass. The regrets that were always near

the surface felt…well, better. Not as close or intense as they normally did. Talking had never been something he wanted to do with anyone. But he'd needed this.

"Thanks, Pop."

"For?"

Showing him once again all the things he'd never acknowledged when he was selfish and focused on getting what he wanted. "Being you."

"You're welcome. Sorry I wasn't more my authentic self earlier. Might have helped us both."

"You don't have to take any of the blame. It was totally me."

"It was mostly you. I was in that relationship, and I didn't have the agency to stand up for myself. I just went along trying to please you. That's on me."

This was exactly what he needed.

She tipped her head to the side as the band started playing their version of "Back to You." That song had been on repeat the summer they got married.

"Our song…" He'd never been into that kind of thing, but Poppy had always called it that.

She started to say something, and he held his hand up in protest. He wasn't ready for the truth bomb she was no doubt going to drop. Instead, he held his hand out. Some people were dancing.

Poppy hesitated and then took it, and he pulled her into his arms.

Now, as he listened to the lyrics, he realized how much he wanted to hold her. Was grateful her body was pressed against his as they swayed to the music. Poppy always seemed to embody music. Her arms were over her head, and her hips moved to the beat. He swayed from foot to foot.

His mind always concentrated on the regrets. Like forgetting how it felt to be in her orbit. She might have thought that she needed to feel worthy of him, but there was so much power in her. Whenever she danced and moved, he was utterly captivated.

Poppy was comfortable in her skin in a way he'd never been.

She grabbed his hand and pulled him into the rhythm, her hands on his hips until he found the beat. She danced around him, her hips brushing against his. The coolness of the material of her skirt against his bare legs made him forget everything but her.

He put his hands on her waist and pulled her into his body, his mouth on hers, her hands in his hair. He'd have a million tough conversations with her if it meant she'd come into his arms like this again.

Not just for a few nights. There was no denying he wanted her to come back to him. He'd tried to dress it up to make him feel better about approaching her when she'd clearly moved on. But he no longer could deny that this was why he'd joined the Tea Society.

Sure, he wanted to help her, but he really wanted to help himself. Wanted to be the man who was worthy of being loved by Poppy.

Alistair wasn't sure that he even knew what love was, but he was going to try to figure it out.

She tasted of the spring brew and something that was just purely Poppy. He deepened the kiss for a split second before it trickled into his mind that they were in the beer garden. In public.

"Want to get out of here?"

"*Yesss.* That song…I'm back here with you," she said.

"Indeed."

"Don't fuck me over again," she said quietly as she grabbed her bag and led the way out of the pub.

How could he tell her that he never intended to before?

Did he need Poppy now because he was on the cusp of severing his connection to his family? They might not be the most ideal family, but they were his. Ever since he'd left for boarding school, he'd felt alone. His name and the need to prove himself as a Miller had always driven him.

He was on his own now.

Maybe he was still that guy. Totally making choices that felt right for him but might not be right for her.

He had to remember that he was filtering this through his awakened self. That he was trying to be more temperate and not act on impulse.

He had to be very sure that he wasn't using Poppy once again.

Nine

She was a bit buzzed, but she wanted to assign the past to the done column in her life's to-do list before making any new mistakes. So she turned to Ali. "We good?"

"What?" he asked.

He looked so cute and confused. His hair was tousled from the repeated times he'd shoved his own hand through it. He had some stubble on his jaw, and those thick eyebrows of his were quizzical. She didn't want to feel bad about getting involved with him again, because he was making her feel so good.

For once, she didn't want to look at the two of them and just see a fucked-up mess.

She wanted to relax into this and let him weave that magic that he wasn't aware he possessed. That power over her that made her feel as if her life was the romantic fairy tale she'd always wanted it to be. The one where she wasn't the middle daughter of a very normal family, the odd one that no one else really understood.

Liberty once bluntly stated it was her family's loss that they didn't get her. She'd tell Poppy to take what she wanted from Alistair, and tomorrow morning, she could kick him out, and they could go back to being enemies.

But they weren't enemies. They hadn't been for the past six months or so since he'd shown up online. He'd been slowly reminding her of all the things that made her fall for him the first time.

She was holding on to her own hurt because it made her feel safe. A little anger blanket that she could wrap herself in and use to justify acting like an asshole to him.

Not anymore. Time to find a new emotion to wrap herself in.

Her body was voting heavily for lust.

The moon shone down on them as they turned onto the quiet lane leading to Ali's house. Stopping, she turned to face him. "Do you feel like we've hashed out everything from our marriage so we can finally put it to bed?"

"If we never talked about it again, I'd be good," he said, his smile tight. "I can't live thinking I'm a monster. It makes it harder for me to actually practice the better behaviors I'm trying to adopt."

She wrapped her arms around him, he pulled her closer. He smelled of cologne and faintly of sweat and beer. Closing her eyes, she breathed it in. This was it. She was done punishing him for not being the man she'd wanted him to be. He wasn't a horrible person; he just hadn't been a good husband.

That was okay. She wasn't getting married again.

She stepped back. "I'm Poppy."

"Alistair, but my mates call me Ali."

"And you brew beer?" she asked. How far would he take

this? The old Alistair would never have done something so…unrealistic.

"I just got started, and sometimes I still fuck it up. That's why I joined the Tea Society. Glad we met in that online forum."

"Me too," she said. Honestly, that was when she'd started feeling mixed emotions toward him.

"What do you do?"

She linked her hand to his as they kept walking toward his house. "My friends and I have a shop in Maine. WiCKed Sisters. You might have heard of us via pop star Amber Rapp. She's a pretty big deal."

"You really part of a half coven of witches who wield magic?" he asked.

"Don't be scared, I'm a good witch," she said. "Mostly, it's just charged crystals, moon rituals. I do have some practices I use when making my tea blends."

"Like what?" he asked.

"I have some blends I use in the shop that I mix with the intention of the season. Each season has a different purpose, so I want the tea to aid whoever drinks it in getting the most out of it."

"And your magic courage blend?"

"That one is for me. When I'm a mess mentally and I need a courage boost. It's new. A guy has come into my life. And it's complicated."

Ali leaned against his front door when they arrived at his house.

"How?"

She leaned in closer, her body resting against his. "I'm not sure about him. He's the sexiest man I've been around, and his kisses leave me hot and bothered and wanting more. Truth is, I don't know why I'm hesitating. I'm a divorced lady, so yeah, I get that relationships end."

He put his hands on her hips lightly, making sure their bodies were flush together. His chest was hard under her palm. "Yeah? I'm divorced too. Married life taught me how much I suck at it. This guy…" His eyes darkened. "Poppy, I want you. I'll take whatever you'll offer me."

She put her fingers on his lips. Loving the feel of his full mouth under her touch. His exhalations were hot against her hand, fanning the flames of the fire that had ignited in her the moment she took his hand to dance. Her heartbeat was thundering in her ears.

She was tired. Tired of fighting her attraction to him and denying herself this time with him. There was no reason to keep up the pretense. "Don't let me use you."

His eyes went wide. "I…"

"Last time, we were uneven. This time…if we do this, then it has to be different. No pretending to be anything you aren't," she said. "I'm going to be unapologetically me."

She had to. Denying herself the joy of being back in England with this new Ali wasn't something she was willing to do. This time, she had her eyes wide open. Knowing who she was helped. Having a life she would happily return to also added to it.

The full moon was just days away. The summer night was hot, the sky clear. The moon watched her, challenging her to take what she wanted and to stop hedging her bets.

The magic of the evening wrapped around him. He was done talking and pulled Poppy more fully into his body, turning his head to move her fingers from his mouth, then kissed her long and deep.

His hands roamed up and down her back. He grunted as the thin fabric of her dress almost allowed him to touch her skin—but not quite. Her full breasts were pressed against his chest, her nipples tight buds that he flicked playfully with his finger. A shudder rocked her as he slowly lowered the strap of her dress.

Stepping back, she shoved her hand in his pocket, her fingers brushing his erection as she rooted around for his key. "Let's go inside."

"Why?"

"We're on your front step."

"There is no one around for miles," he pointed out.

It surprised him that the shyness she'd had the first time they had sex was still there. Poppy had a natural passion and sensuality that she had grown into throughout their relationship. She'd had some kinky fantasies that they'd explored. "You're right. I just…"

She didn't have to explain; there were moments like this when he felt he knew her better than he knew himself. Shifting so his back was to the quiet country road, he put one arm on the wall of the house above her head as he tried again to draw down her dress.

Poppy brushed his hands away and slipped both sides of the top down. The fabric fell, pooling at her waist. He couldn't tear his eyes from her body. There was an ethereal delicateness to Poppy making his breath catch in his chest. Her breasts were small and round, and he covered them with both of his hands.

Her back arched as he squeezed her, her hands on his

shoulders pulling him toward her until her mouth was under his. Then she pushed his shirt up, her fingers moving over his chest and back, scratching him lightly with her nails. Her touch moved lower until she stroked him through his pants.

Pulling her skirt up, he rubbed his erection against her center, and she sighed, sucking on the side of his neck as he flicked one of her nipples with his finger.

"Don't stop," she said, her words breathy.

Her head fell back as she moved against him. She was at once the way he remembered and somehow something more. It had been so long since he'd tasted her and felt her soft, tender body under his hands. A part of him was afraid this was another dream that would leave him hard and aching.

Moaning in his arms, her hips moving against his cock, she was clearly close to coming. Dropping to his knees, he pulled her panties down and draped one thigh over his shoulder. He breathed in the essence of her sex.

"God I've been starved for this…for you." He was hungry for the taste of her. He flicked her bud with his tongue, feeling her hand on his head, holding him to her as her hips moved frantically toward his mouth. He licked her, sucked at her, tasting her as if it sated something deep inside of him that had been empty for too long.

He thrust one finger into her pussy and she screamed his name. "More," she gasped.

He added a second finger, remembering how she liked it. Thrusting his fingers into her as she arched into him, begging for more. Her hands in his hair were driving him mad. He was so hard and desperate to get inside of her, but pleasing Poppy came first.

Her fingers dug into his scalp as she let out a long, low

moan, then pushed her core against his face. She all but col-
lapsed around him as he stood and lifted her into his arms.

"You on the pill?"

"No," she said. "I don't… I usually have condoms at home
but didn't bring them." Her breath sawed in and out. "Do
you?"

He did, but this felt like a sign. God knew he wasn't one
to heed them, but this second chance with Poppy was worth
the caution. No matter how hot he was to be inside her still-
pulsing body. "Yes, but…are sure about not being platonic?"

Her legs were shaky as she pulled the top of her dress back
up. His words lingered in the air around them. He had a
point. She was buzzed, and there was that sort of euphoric
feeling from unleashing all the crap about their marriage.

But the truth was right in front of her: there was the dis-
tinct chance she'd feel different tomorrow.

She didn't do regrets.

"I'm not," she admitted. "I guess you're on the fence too?"

"Fuck no. Mentally, I'm between your legs, but I can't…
I don't want to let this—" he gestured to his hard-on and
her body "—affect us. I want to do it differently this time."

She almost smiled. Poor Ali trying to do the right thing.
But the chemistry between them had been electric from the
moment they'd met.

"You are," she assured him.

"I'm on my best behavior," he said, opening the door and
holding out his hand to her.

"I'm not sure I got your best," she said.

"You can have it," he reassured her. "But I'm not sure

one night is all I want, and I have the feeling that's what you're thinking."

He wasn't wrong. There were so many thoughts spinning through her head. She'd come, so the edge was off, but that need for him was still there. How was she going to leave England without being under him?

Did she have to?"

"You're right. I didn't mean for things to go that far."

"I did."

The night had cleared a lot of the gray clouds that she'd allowed to color her world. Sex with Ali always left her feeling mellow. That hadn't changed. Neither had the intensity, the way it built into an intense storm and then crested and left her feeling everything at once.

"Shower? Bath? Drinks in the garden?"

Ali seemed lighter as well. There was always a hint of darkness in the upper-class boy he'd been. Tonight, though, that boy seemed to be gone.

"Drinks in the garden. That's new." Ali hated bugs and being outside most of the time.

"Trying to change things up," he said, wriggling his eyebrows at her. "You said you wanted to see the moon."

"I do. Let me grab my journal and moon stuff," she said. "Meet you back down here."

Stepping away from him, he caught her by the waist and pulled her close, her back pressed to his front. He rested his forehead against her shoulder. "Thank you."

The words were low, but she heard them. Putting her hands over his and squeezed. This was new, so they were both figuring it out. But she hadn't realized how it had been affecting him that she had withheld part of herself from him.

His arms dropped, and she continued up the stairs. Right now, she was just going with her emotions. Spending time with Ali felt right. Though there was a tiny warning in her mind that she still had to meet with his family and deal with their demands.

The Ali she saw here was more like the Ali she'd met at uni. The man who had swept her away. Still, her heart felt wary. Like going with these feelings was a one-way ticket back to the misery that he'd left her in before.

Not fair at all. She'd said the past was behind them. *Easier said than done.*

She washed up, putting on a pair of shorts and a tank top. He said he'd wait in the garden, so she couldn't take too long, but she really needed to talk to Liberty and Sera.

Doing some quick time zone calculations, she figured it was only 5:00 p.m. in Maine. She hit the group video chat button as she sank down onto the floor next to her bed.

"Hey, girl!" Liberty answered the phone. Poppy noticed she was in the backroom of her shop. "I told Sera you wouldn't be able to go one day without checking in."

"Oh, yeah. The shop. How's it going?"

"Good, but that's not why you called. Hold on. Merle, watch my shop for me?" Liberty asked as she moved through the tea shop into Sera's bookshop.

Sera must have had a customer, because Poppy heard her tell them to have a nice day before she was next to Liberty. "You okay?"

"Yeah…"

"That yeah is giving me…no?"

"Ali and I almost hooked up. It was great, and I totally

wanted it. Right now, I'm trying not to project that he's the same guy he used to be."

Sera nibbled her lip and then nodded. "I get it. That fear is hard to let go of. What are you scared of? Naming it helps."

"That's true. Once I realized why I was obsessed with meeting my biological father, things shifted for me," Liberty said.

"I'm scared that I'll fall for him again and believe the changes in him, and he won't have changed."

The words were sort of rambling but came straight from her soul. Her friends weren't going to be able to magically take away the fear.

"If he hurts you, I will curse him. No joke."

"Thanks, Lib."

"You're not alone this time. Also, you've changed a lot, why wouldn't he have?" Sera asked. "It doesn't mean he's perfect now, just different. I'd focus on the differences."

"Good idea. Love you two."

"Love you," they both said.

She disconnected the call and gathered her things. In the past, after sex, he'd usually roll over and go to sleep. This time, it was like he wanted to draw out that emotional connection.

Or at least that was what *she* felt. What she always wanted. Just to keep that closeness for a bit longer.

When she stepped out into the garden, he'd pushed two loungers together. His head was tipped back looking up at the sky.

"Thought you'd changed your mind," he said.

"Almost did. Didn't realize when I said the past was done that I'd be the one still trying to pull myself out of it," she said.

"You don't have to do this."

"Ali, I want this week in England with you. I want to look back on the UK and you and not feel bad."

Sitting down next to him, she started to cross her legs, but he lifted his arm and pulled her into his side. He stroked her arm with his fingers. "Tell me about the moon, witchy woman."

Witchy woman.

She liked the way he said that. She had been afraid to show him that side of herself when they were married. One fear gone; one change noted.

Talking softly, she told him about the phase they were in and all the things that the moon could bring to them during this time.

He asked her questions, listening in a way that he hadn't before. With that, she felt her resolve crumble.

Ten

The summer solstice was always one of her favorite days of the year. The start of the summer season and the opening of all those gorgeous long days that held endless possibilities. The fact that her friends weren't here with her dimmed her joy the tiniest bit.

Keeping her hands off Alistair was harder than she thought it would be. Especially on the back of his Ducati as they wove through the winding country roads that led from Kent up to Glastonbury. As a teenager, she'd begged her parents for tickets to the annual music festival, but they always said no. One, she'd been too young—whatever—and two, the tickets were too expensive. But the third reason, and probably the real reason, was simple: coed camping.

During her teenage years she'd been sort of out of control...with everything. Nothing had changed during her uni years except meeting this man she was holding on to now as the June sun beat down on her back.

As much as he intimated that she'd changed, Poppy didn't

really feel that different. It wasn't like she'd stopped craving love and acceptance after the divorce. Perhaps she'd gotten slightly better at choosing the people she let into her heart.

"Want to stop at Stonehenge? They've really changed it, and you can't get close to the stones at all now," he said. His voice was deep and husky in her ear from the built-in microphones in their helmets.

"No, thanks for the offer," she said. Her spiritual practice was too personal to share with anyone other than those who mattered to her. Plus, she wasn't up to facing the crowds that showed up at Stonehenge on the solstices without Liberty and Serafina at her side. She was looking forward to a somewhat quiet ritual at the top of the Tor tonight.

"When did you get all witchy?" he asked.

"I always was," she said under her breath, momentarily forgetting about the microphone.

"I never noticed. How did I miss that?"

"I didn't want to scare you off, Alistair. You were pretty big stuff, and the fact that you liked me had me…" She trailed off.

It had her trying to shape herself into a woman he would fall for. A woman who would be worthy of being the wife of the second son of the eighth Earl of Winfield. It wasn't like her family hadn't been solidly middle class. She'd gone to a good school and been on holidays in France and Tenerife. But Alistair had been next-level.

Still was.

Which was why, no matter how hot he made her, she was going to be smart and keep it in her pants. She wasn't following her libido back into another ill-advised hookup. There was nothing down that path but destruction for both of them.

Yet clearly he wanted her.

Which made her want to push and see how long it would take until his control cracked. To finally exercise her power.

Would she be the first to break?

Hell no.

"Hey, I liked you, Poppy. Not someone you were trying to be," he said.

"I don't think I felt comfortable showing you who I was. Like when you jetted us to Vienna for the ball. I wanted to be with you. If that meant straightening my hair and wearing a ball gown, then yes, please, I'd change everything about myself I could to keep that ride going."

"I didn't realize," he said.

How could he know that the life he took for granted would be so tempting to her? He wouldn't have realized that she was still trying to mold herself. Her mum said that that was what your early twenties were for. Also for big fuckups. Poppy had scored on both counts.

Which was why she was so determined to stay firmly in the friends-with-benefits zone with Ali. Only a few more days and she'd be back home, and Ali would be out of her everyday life.

Online, he didn't make her heart race or her blood rush through her veins. Like he did now, making her hot as she felt his hips nestled between her thighs.

Of course, once they were off this damn Ducati that would help too.

"It's cool. So this place you booked us to stay...two rooms?"

"Of course. We agreed sleeping together had stupid written all over it. Personally, I think it had 'explosive' written on it, but who am I to argue with a woman?"

He wasn't wrong. It was taking all of her willpower just to keep her arms lightly around his middle on the turns. To not let her hand snake down between his legs the way she had so many times in the past when he took her out on his bike. Being with Ali had unlocked her sensual side, and he'd always been game to try anything she fantasized about. Their time together had been hot. Nothing had been off-limits.

God, this was why she should have said no to the wedding. She should have just signed the damned Lancaster-Spencer Tea Makers deal and stayed safely in Birch Lake.

But she wanted more from life than hiding. And Lancaster-Spencer had fucked her out of control of her own tea blends once. She wasn't willing to allow that a second time.

If that meant days of cold showers and masturbating, then she'd do it. As she'd just reminded herself, it was only a few more days.

She turned her head sideways, resenting that the helmet kept her from leaning forward and resting it against Alistair's back.

It was odd how he still hadn't accepted that most of his plans backfired. Having Poppy pressed against his back for over three hours had seemed like the perfect way to remind her that the attraction between them wasn't something that should be ignored.

Partially he'd also wanted to test his own self-control, which was now at an all-time low. Each time he moved into a turn, her arms wrapped around him, and her entire being molded to him. The power of the Ducati was addicting and put him more in touch with that rebelliousness he'd been working so hard to shed. On the back of the bike it was easy to pretend he was in control leaving the past behind…except today with Poppy clinging to his back.

When he pulled into the parking lot of the Airbnb he'd booked for the night, he had to take a moment to adjust himself while she was taking off her helmet.

She shook her hair as she did, her long natural curls flying around her head. She smiled as she tried to fluff them up. "I bet I look a sight."

One that he wanted to fill his eyes with. Staring at her wasn't wise, because Poppy was too perceptive not to know that the entire ride had been a slow seduction for him. Her voice so soft and intimate in his ear as they talked. Her hands on his body as she clung to him on the turns and then kneading his thigh when she slipped them down his sides.

"Always a welcome one," he said. *Lame.* Why was it that he had no rizz with her? He used to know just what to say.

"Thanks. You too," she said. "How'd you find this place?"

"George recommended it. Bronte is into crystals and all that woo-woo shit."

"Like me."

"Just like you." Fuck. He shouldn't have called it *woo-woo shit*.

"Yeah, anyway, he brought her here for their anniversary."

"That's nice," she said. "I did think it was odd you didn't want to be fake married at his wedding."

"We were still real married then," he said sardonically. "Also, everyone knew we were still fighting."

"Did they? How?"

"You posted on your private social media account about *the bag of dicks you married.* Bronte noticed it and flagged it up to George, who told Mum and Dad."

"I didn't realize," she said.

"How could you? You are totally entitled to your feel-ings," he said.

"I know, and you totally were being that when I posted. I think you wanted me to negotiate to keep my great-grandmother's tea service."

Yeah, not the man he wanted her to see. "I don't like los-ing."

"Believe me, I know," she said. "So this place is close to town, and then are we taking the bike to the parking lot at the Tor or walking from town?"

"Either one. It's a nice day, so a walk wouldn't be bad," he said.

She smiled as he used a code to unlock the Airbnb. They had sent their luggage on to the wedding's hotel and just packed in two backpacks for this overnight trip. He grabbed them from the storage compartment on the bike as Poppy went inside to explore.

Taking a moment for himself, he leaned against the side of the house, in the shade, and put his head back.

He was so close to getting everything he wanted. Re-ceiving Poppy's understanding... Her suggestion that they put the past to bed had been more than he thought he de-served. But there was still the meeting with his parents, the contract with Lancaster-Spencer and Owen's offer to come and work at the tavern for the summer.

All things that were tied to the woman who was singing "Flowers" off-key while she opened the windows.

It hadn't even occurred to him that she'd actually be back in England with him despite his hope she would.

His therapist had suggested that maybe anger had burned all the charm out of him.

It felt uncomfortable, the prospect of being who his parents and brother expected him to be at this wedding. It felt like sliding into a suit that was too tight. He couldn't move his shoulders, and the shoes pinched.

"You okay?" she asked from the doorway.

"Yeah. Just need to stand and stretch a bit after the ride," he said.

"Me too. I found a recommendation for a couple of restaurants in town. Want me to book one for a late lunch? That will give us time to check out a few *woo-woo* shops in town."

"I'm sorry I said that."

She nodded. "I'm teasing you. One of the shops sells some of our products, so I'm meeting the owner around three. I can meet back up with you after that for dinner."

Solange Trenton felt like a kindred spirit the moment that Poppy walked into her shop. She had a table of WiCKed Sisters' products, which included a selection of handmade journals that Sera had sent over with instructions on how to embed the purchaser's intention into the cover; crystals and a tarot card deck that Liberty had charged and designed; and the Amber Rapp Heartbreak Remedy tea that Poppy had made after listening to "Rhapsody for an Ex."

"I'm so excited you are here!" Solange said. Her long red hair hung down her back, and she wore a flower wreath on top of her head that Poppy immediately loved. Her bracelets jingled as she ran around the counter and hugged Poppy.

"Me too. Thanks for welcoming me on such short notice."

"I'm glad you were able to get here. I'm hoping to get to Birch Lake in the autumn for the real-life experience."

"Let me know when you're coming, and I'll show you around," Poppy said.

"Definitely. I've been using the journal you sent me at the winter solstice, and I think I manifested your visit."

Poppy shook her head at the other woman. They'd sent a small gift set to some of the shops around the US and the UK that stocked their products as a thank-you for their support. "In what way?"

"I was so sure we'd get on, and I have been wanting to talk to you about how you got started. I've written a dozen emails to you, then deleted them before I hit Send."

"You should have sent them, but I'm here now. If you have time for a cup of tea and a chat," Poppy said.

Solange's shop was small and reminded her of the first space WiCKed Sisters had leased before they decided to stop doing things by half measures. It had taken a lot of debates and belief in themselves before she, Sera and Liberty went to the bank and got a loan to buy the building they were in now.

Solange's shop had two bookshelves on one wall crammed with books and journals. The scent was so familiar—books, patchouli and freshly brewed tea—it was like returning home. The table with the WiCKed Sisters products was in the center of the store, and there was another long low table that held more crystals and other magick paraphernalia. Some soft chanting music was playing in the background. It was nice and cozy.

Solange got them both some tea before she sat across from Poppy and peppered her with questions about blending teas.

Poppy shared the techniques she'd been using lately and invited her to join the Tea Society.

"Really? That would be fab. Can I get a picture with you and post it? Also put it up on the wall behind the register?"

"Of course," Poppy said, posing for a few photos for Solange. In the smallest way, she was a bit uneasy about how excited the other woman was to see her. She'd had no idea that there was anyone out there who was this into the WiCKed Sisters and the women behind it.

"My customers are all big fans of the three of you. We've started a small monthly group where we all do some moon rituals... Liberty sent me some guidance so I could lead them. We've all been using the manifesting journals, of course, and making seasonal teas. But that's been the hardest to master. I'm not sure how you do it."

"Which part?"

"Choosing which flavors will work best together."

Poppy couldn't really explain that there was a big part of blending that felt instinctive to her. She had the Kitchener journal, which she used as a reference each time she tried a new blend. Some of her earliest memories were being in the kitchen with her grandmother as she blended different teas, explaining to Poppy what she was doing the way her own grandmother had done, and every generation before her since Viola.

"Mostly it's trial and error. Also, I make blends I like. In summer, I want something light and refreshing, so I'd probably try mint. I recommend going for classic combos that sound good to you," Poppy said.

Solange's fingers were moving rapidly over the keyboard

on her phone as she took notes. "Great. I'm going to try mint and strawberry."

"Nice. Let me know how it turns out."

Poppy's smartwatch vibrated, and she glanced down, then burst out laughing. Merle had sent the barfing emoji at her, winning their weekly competition.

"Sorry about that. Once you're in the Tea Society, there will be a lot of experts who can give you tips. We have a seasonal challenge you can participate in. Honestly, those are really helpful and fun. Plus, you get the benefit of hearing from everyone else what worked and didn't."

"I'm looking forward to it. Thank you."

"No problem. I'm always glad to meet someone else who loves making their own teas as much as I do."

Poppy left a few minutes later. Alistair waited for her at a park near the middle of town. Her breath caught in her chest when she saw him. He'd taken his shirt off and was lying on his back in the sun. *God.* That man had a body that was hard to tear her eyes from.

A slow heat started low in her body and spread outward. Licking her lips, she was hungry for something that she knew she could only get from him.

Trying to be smart and safe wasn't working. There was no way she was going to be able to keep her hands to herself much longer. All of her thoughts were on how his sun-heated body would feel on hers. If she lifted the skirt of her sundress and straddled him as he pulled her into his arms. She might spontaneously combust.

Spotting her, he lifted his hand and waved.

Fuck. Keep it cool.

Like that was going to happen.

Eleven

Glastonbury Tor was a conical hill of clay that rose from the Somerset Levels. Its sloping hills were terraced on either side of the path that led to the top. Archaeological excavations had revealed some aspects of the history there from as early as the Iron Age. The Church of St Michael was built on the site in the fourteenth century, but all that remained was a roofless tower.

It was clear that coming here was the right decision. Poppy kept up a steady stream of information as they climbed to the top of the Tor. "I know a lot of people come here at sunrise, but I'm more centered in moon magick. Watching the sun rise with you today as we drove from Kent to Somerset was magical enough."

There was magic present, but he was pretty sure it was coming from her. The incline on the Glastonbury Tor was intense, but he was good in shape. Poppy was sweating a bit, and he offered her his water bottle as they stopped partway up the hill.

"Other than churches, what else makes this spot special?" he asked her. Anything to keep his mind off the way her butt looked in her leggings as she walked ahead of him.

"The Celtic name for it is Isle of Avalon, so that draws a lot of connection to the Arthurian legends."

"Him, I know about. When I was twelve, I was obsessed with Thomas Malory's stories. I even talked George into taking me to Winchester to see the round table that Henry VIII had made during his reign."

"Really? How did I not know this about you?" she asked.

"I guess were both hiding parts of ourselves," he said with a shrug. By the time he'd met Poppy, that boy who used to love legends and myths had been smothered under the weight of expectations and his own need to prove he wasn't just the spare. Though there wasn't a throne involved in their family hierarchy, taking over Lancaster-Spencer was a close second. He'd craved what was only George's by an accident of birth.

"Maybe. Well, you'll love this next bit… In 1191, two coffins were found that were labeled Arthur and Guinevere."

"Seems a little sus," he said.

"Yeah, but it's fun. Another legend ties the Tor to the Holy Grail because the Nanteos Cup used to be in the monastery here."

"What is that even?"

"It's a cup that was reputedly made from a piece of the True Cross and could heal anyone who drank from it," she said with a tinkling laugh. "Is that too *woo-woo* for you, or is it more palatable because it's based in organized religion?"

"I'm not into organized religion," he said. "I'm sorry I called anything woo-woo. It's just that I didn't have another way of describing it. What do you call it?"

"Spiritual."

He repeated the word softly. There was something almost glowing about Poppy now. Another facet that he'd somehow missed even though he'd known her since she was eighteen.

"Don't backpedal when I tell you the last legend associated with this place. It's from Celtic mythology. But when I first heard about it, I thought of Shakespeare's *A Midsummer Night's Dream*. It's about the King of the Fairies. So many different belief systems see the Tor has an entrance to another world. In this case the land of the fairies. Others say it's the land of the dead. A portal allowing both fairies and spirits to cross between worlds."

Was she teasing him? There was a spark in her eyes as she waited to see how he'd react. Honestly, he didn't know if they were closer to the land of the fairies or the undead. But something was changing in him the closer they got to the top.

His fierce conviction that Poppy was the key to his freedom from the past was fading. She no longer seemed a stepping stone to a life he wanted for himself. Just the woman that he wanted to keep by his side.

Except that wasn't happening. He didn't have to have otherworldly magic to figure that out. She was here because she had a good heart. He wasn't ever going to be a man she'd trust with it again.

"Exciting. So which of those is the reason you wanted to be up here tonight?"

"Neither." She beamed at him. "There is one more thing. This entire area is important to the modern-day Goddess movement. There's a festival here where the Goddess leads a procession."

He could see that. A very feminine energy wrapped around him. In the past, he would have felt threatened by it, responding with his own version of masculine energy, which always manifested itself in the worst way. He'd never been comfortable owning his interest in things that weren't necessarily defined as masculine.

"Thanks for sharing this with me," he said, catching up to Poppy and slipping his hand into hers. Their fingers twined together, and a tingle went up his arm and then straight to his core. His entire being embraced this energy.

As the warmth and sensuality wrapped around him, he slowly started to realize that the feminine essence wasn't just for women. Glancing over at Poppy, it was hard to separate these new feelings from her.

Was she The One?

Of course she was. Everything always came back to Poppy.

Touching Alistair should always be approached with caution, but she found right now, in this place, there was no need for caution. The Goddess wrapped her in a comforting embrace that encouraged her to claim her full power.

She always pulled back, afraid of shining too bright or drawing too much attention to herself. Even with Liberty and Serafina. But her friends seemed to know this and saw past those moments.

That was the beauty of finding women who were kindred spirits. They got her, and she didn't have to explain everything to them. They gave her space to make her own way into her strength.

Honestly, she still wasn't sure what her strength was. Tea making was her legacy, something her family had always done and something she had a natural ability to do. But the thing that was Poppy? That was still half formed and nebulous.

She'd been thrilled when Alistair offered to bring them here, because she wanted to be as close to the Goddess and the sun as she could today. She needed to be near the fairy kingdom now, when the veil between worlds was so thin. She'd even made a wreath of flowers after seeing Solange's at the shop. Afraid that Alistair might not get it, she'd been carrying it in her backpack instead of wearing it.

But the energy between them had changed on the walk up. They were more than halfway to the top when they stopped again. She felt the pull of magick the way she did when she was with Liberty and Sera at the top of Hanging Hill in Birch Lake.

She took her long sarong scarf from her backpack, wrapping it around her waist into a skirt before shimmying out of her leggings and putting the flower wreath on her head.

"Titania," Alistair said almost reverently.

That was all it took. It felt like she was being lit from the inside of her soul. There was no need to keep any part of herself locked away. Not here. Not with Alistair.

Maybe for tonight?

Once doubt seeped into her thoughts, she couldn't shake it, remembering how Titania and Oberon fought bitterly over a child in *A Midsummer Night's Dream*, and how Oberon used poison to make Titania fall in love with the first person she saw.

Was there a warning in this realization? Or was she so used to seeing deception and lies when she was around Alistair that even now, at this magical moment where the sun was still full on this longest day of the year, it plagued her? Couldn't she let herself enjoy this time with him?

"What is it? You're frowning. Are you okay?"

Trust yourself, a voice whispered in her mind.

Lingering doubt was drawn away at the same moment, Alistair put his hand on the side of her neck, his long fingers rubbing her nape as he lowered his head. "Is it me? Do you want me to leave?"

"Don't go," she said, turning her head into his shoulder and letting the energy that had been swirling around them before come back.

Alistair wasn't the only reason for the fear deep in her heart. Yes he'd hurt her. But now the truth seemed blindingly obvious. She'd expected him to betray her from the moment he asked her to marry him. By never believing she was enough for him, by twisting herself into what she thought he wanted. Their marriage hadn't stood a chance.

Leaning against Alistair, feeling his strong body holding hers, he supported her. Gave her the space to sort out the mental chaos that swept in from the magic of this night, this day.

The power of the solstices and the equinoxes always affected her and brought clarity, helping her to move forward. Normally, she had her soul sisters at her side to ground her and keep her focused. Tonight there was just Ali and the moon.

"Let's go up. Sorry for that. The energy here is so intense."

"I feel it too. I read that the Tor is built on a ley line. They have powerful energy," he said.

Alistair seemed to be affected by the energy here as well.

She pulled away from him and picked up her pack. "When did you read up on it?"

"As soon as you agreed to come to England with me. I knew this time had to be different than when we were here together before," he said.

"Are you trying to win me over for any reason other than myself?" she asked.

There was a part of her that felt the censure of the Goddess as she asked the question. She had to stop looking for signs and then ignoring them.

But that was a hard habit to break.

Alistair was figuring out what to say, so she shook her head. "Don't answer that. Either I believe you've changed from the man who hurt me or I don't. I can't keep asking you to prove it to me."

"Poppy—"

"No, it's okay. Let's make a last push and get to the top. I brought some fairy cakes and tea for us to have up there."

When they got to the top, they could see for miles and miles. Poppy led him to a spot near the crest of the hill, took another scarf from her backpack and spread it on the ground. She'd told him she wanted to watch the sunset at 9:16 p.m., and then she wanted to watch the moon rise.

"What's special about the moon at the solstice?" he asked her as he filled two picnic champagne flutes from the small twist-top bottles of prosecco he'd carried in his bag.

Poppy tucked a long curly strand of hair behind her ear as she pulled out the fairy cakes she'd mentioned, as well as two salads they'd picked up in town. She handed one to him. "June is a time of heady power, and its moon is the moon of horses. Tomorrow night is the full moon, so that's when the power will be highest, but we'll be at Gemma's wedding... I might try to step out to see it."

He'd be at her side. This feeling stirring inside of him was the answer to the emptiness that had been eating a hole in his soul for so long. He liked the feeling. He liked sharing it with her.

There were still so many unspoken things between them, and he wasn't sure he'd ever have the courage to speak them out loud. "What does the moon of horses mean?"

That tinkling sound of her laughter rang out and wrapped around him like the warm breeze that blew strongly up there. It stirred him, body and soul. Being this close to her was beating at the walls of his resolution to keep his distance. To respect her desire for this phase of the relationship to stay platonic.

Right now, as she talked to him quietly on the highest point in Glastonbury, he was struggling. He wanted to sit behind her and pull her back against his chest. Let his hands caress her body while she wove her fairy magic all around him.

It took all his willpower to resist. That breeze carried the scent of her perfume, and he closed his eyes in a bid to win control over the lust that was rising in him as she softly told him about the moon. Maybe this was how they were meant to be. This pain, a wedge between them that their bodies didn't seem to want to acknowledge.

"This moon is about breaking free from whatever holds you down," she said. "I think it's a portent before meeting with your family tomorrow. I wanted to come up here to step fully into my strength and my power."

Breaking free.

There hadn't been a day in the past eighteen months that he hadn't tried to undo the bands of anger and doubt and fear—and more anger—that had been wrapped around him. Trapping him in a bent-and-bound position that he could never untangle himself from.

"You always have power over me," he said.

"Always?"

"Even now."

"Sexually, right?"

Was there a good way to answer?

"I want the power to stand up for myself. Not allow fear to make me take an offer that I know is less than I deserve. But I'm so afraid if I don't take what I'm offered, everything I've built for myself will fall apart."

How could he help her through this? "Do you want to break away from me?"

She chewed her lower lip and turned her head into the breeze, tipping her head back and not saying a word until she finally glanced over at him. "I think I have to."

Well, that was the answer he'd expected. "Of course. How can I help?"

"You are," she said, putting her hand on his. "Being here with me, talking about the past and letting me work through that girl I was…it's giving me a sense of clarity I never would have found on my own."

"I'm glad," he said. But that tightness in his stomach was back. The power he'd felt on the walk up was so far away from him at this moment. He'd never felt more like the second son. The spare that no one needed once George married and took over the vice-chairmanship of Lancaster-Spencer.

Maybe Poppy wasn't the only one who needed to break

free. Hell, he was brokering a deal between her and his family so he could have his freedom. His chance to step out of the shadow that Lancaster-Spencer cast and become his own man.

Until he broke free of those chains that kept him in this holding pattern, he couldn't be the man she needed or deserved.

"Oh, Ali," she said.

"Oh, what?"

She just shook her head, tugging his arm, and he allowed her to pull him to her. She wrapped her arms around him, and that scent of summer flowers and vanilla filled his senses again.

He put his head on her shoulder as she ran her hands down his back, soothing him in a way he wasn't sure he deserved.

Twelve

The almost-full moon was high above them. Poppy held his hand as they walked back to their Airbnb. Singing and dancing around him when they got back, she led him out into the back garden. She was charged with the energy of the moon in a way that was contagious. This woman. This Poppy. Nothing existed but this moment as she wrapped herself around him.

Her hands looped together at the small of his back as she swayed back and forth, singing under her breath, swaying in the moonlight.

Holding her always made him feel like things were going to work out.

Sure, they were divorced, but he still had a hard time thinking of her as anything but his. Even with the years they'd been apart, he hadn't forgotten how she felt when she was this close. She smelled of the summer night and sun and magic. A heady scent that was foreign to him.

The warmth of her mouth on the side of his neck sent a

shiver straight to his groin. His hands tightened on her hips as he gazed down into her eyes. Her lips were parted. He groaned.

How was he supposed to resist the temptation of Poppy?

"Pop, we said platonic," he reminded her as he drew his finger along the top edge of her sarong. It was knotted on her left side, and the tiniest bit of bare skin peeked out where her T-shirt didn't quite meet the top of it.

Her skin was so soft and smooth, addictive, like everything else about this woman. One kiss wouldn't be enough, one touch, one fuck. She was fire. In his bloodstream, in his body, in his brain.

"We did…" she said as his hands settled on her waist, and hers around his neck. She leaned back so that they could really look at each other. "Would it be so bad if we changed our minds?"

His dick jumped and hardened as his mind raced to plan for all eventualities. He was still keeping things from her. She probably was doing the same. They were both trying so hard to make things right this time, fighting against anything that could mess up these new feelings and the connection that was slowly taking root and growing between them.

God, he didn't want to let her go.

He wanted this for himself. Poppy, just for him, with no external pressures. Whatever happened with the company and his dad and George had no bearing on this moment.

"I can't think of a single reason why we shouldn't," he said against her lips.

She rubbed his lower lip with her tongue and then sucked it into her mouth.

Any chance of a rational argument disappeared. There was

just Poppy, him and the moon. Tonight, these were the only things that mattered, and he wasn't going to let her slip away.

"Me either," she whispered against him. "You're not going to stop us like you did the other night, are you?"

"Even if I wanted to, I don't think I could. I need you."

"You do?" she asked playfully, drawing him farther into the yard.

The spill of amber light from the house and the silvery shine from the moon kept the darkness at bay. The summer air was rife with brambleberries and a rich, earthy scent, which stirred that primitive part of him.

He lifted her off her feet, and she undid the knot at her side as she wrapped her legs around his hips. Cupping her butt with his hands, he stroked her through her thin cotton panties. She deepened the kiss, her breasts pressing against his chest.

Tearing his mouth from hers, he glanced around the yard. There was a picnic table. Bending over, he scooped up her scarf as he continued to hold her.

"I love your strength," she said.

"You do?"

"Yes. All these muscles and the power… You always were so strong physically."

"Is that a compliment?" he asked.

"Of course," she said. "Will you get naked for me?"

"I was planning to."

"I don't mean just the sex parts," she said as he set her on her feet next to the table.

She whipped her shirt over her head and tossed it on one of the chairs, standing next to him in a plain cotton bra and knickers.

"Ladies first," he said, but only because he knew that the moment he was naked, he'd be on her, and he wasn't going to come up for air until he was buried hilt deep in her.

She shook her head, her curls bouncing around her shoulders as she reached behind her back. A moment later, the cups fell away, and she shrugged out of the bra, drawing it slowly down her body. "Now you."

He almost ripped his T-shirt in his hurry to get it off, tossing it behind him, his eyes on her body as her hands roamed over him. Her fingers moving along his chest, his pecs. She took her time exploring him, as if it was the first she'd seen of him.

He'd gotten a new tattoo since the last time they were naked together. He noticed that she still had her belly-button ring and that freckle cluster under her left rib. Had anyone else discovered these beautiful secrets since then?

She traced the tattoo over and looked up at him. "Why this?"

A broken teacup hidden in the Celtic symbol for rebirth. To him, it was his break from the family. The start of his own path, and a reminder that he wasn't whole. That there was an emptiness that he was always trying to fill. That anger and arrogance wouldn't fill it.

"To remind myself that I'm not Lancaster-Spencer," he said.

"Good. I'm glad," she said, then she traced the tattoo that was over his heart with her tongue. Her hair brushed against his skin, and he groaned, realizing that he might not need to have his pants off to lose control.

A broken bad boy. Almost like Alistair knew that was the one thing she couldn't resist. He'd probably never thought of himself that way, at least not until whatever had happened at

Lancaster-Spencer, but she'd always secretly seen him as such. That rich man-boy that everyone tried cultivating a friendship with. The one who wanted for nothing, who seemed to have a path to success just because of his pedigree. But she'd always seen past that.

Which was why it had been so much easier to get over him when they were in separate countries.

Tonight, on the walk up the Tor, the wariness she'd kept between them as a shield had floated away on the breeze. There was no going back. Right now, there wasn't a situation she could conceive of in which she'd need it. Not any longer.

His skin was warm and tasted of salt and sweat. That sandalwood scent that he'd put on earlier was stronger here. She rubbed her nose in it as she closed her eyes, creating this memory for herself. It had been so long since they'd actually slept together. The other night had whetted her appetite for him. *Ha.* As if there had been a time when she hadn't wanted him.

His hand was on the back of her neck, fingers kneading and massaging. Stepping back, he slid both hands down her neck to her shoulders, then paused to cup her breasts.

"You're so beautiful. Even more so in the moonlight. It's like… Never mind, I'll sound an idiot," he cut himself off.

"Say it, I'm not going to judge you."

It was as if he wanted to speak but couldn't make himself.

Wrapping her hand around his bicep. "I love how strong your arms are, and when you held me in front of your house, it made me wet just thinking about them."

He canted his head to the side, lifted both eyebrows and then flexed both arms.

She made a purring sound. Physically, Alistair ticked all

of her boxes. She didn't care if it was clichéd that the quiet, quirky girl was attracted to the bad boy. That was just the way she'd always been.

Well, maybe just with him.

"So?"

"Ah, in the moonlight, you shine, Poppy. There is something ethereal about you, and it's almost like if I touch you, you'll disappear."

"I won't," she promised him, taking his hand in hers and putting it on her waist. "See?"

He flushed. It was easy to read that confessing that wasn't something he was comfortable with, but she liked hearing it. Liked knowing that there was something about her that he couldn't resist. He'd always had some kind of sway over her.

That was something she wasn't ready to delve into tonight. She wanted this moonlit hookup. The moon had listened to her fears from the moment he'd sent that message asking her to pretend they were still married. Stirring all the desires and emotions she'd been happily ignoring since their divorce became final.

But here she was, and tonight, on the eve of the moon of horses, when she should be letting go…she wanted to hold tight. One night to see if he was going to be relegated to the past or if he was going to be part of her future.

She held all the cards this time.

She undid his shorts. They dropped to the ground, and he shoved his underwear down after them.

Her breath caught in her chest. He was turned on, thick and hard from watching her. His big, muscled body made her fingers tingle to touch him all over. Taking his shaft in her hand, she stroked him up and down, swirling her finger over the tip.

She was vaguely aware of his fingers in her underwear before she felt the coolness of the night air against her nakedness. His mouth was on her neck, biting and sucking, making her realize that she had been transfixed by him.

He was the one with the magic power where she was concerned.

But the moon was giving her strength, feminine and uniquely hers. So she took what she wanted, gliding her hands up his chest, then back down. Caressing and teasing his nipples, she drew him toward her, then she gently but firmly gripped his dick until the table was at her back.

He lifted her up onto the surface. She felt the softness of her sarong against her ass; he'd laid it across the table. Her knees fell open, and he stepped between them, his fingers moving over her nipples as she rubbed her clit with his erection.

His other hand tightened on her waist, then he leaned down until their foreheads were pressed together. The words that he spoke were low, harsh, dark and sexual, sending heat through her until she was wet and ready for him.

"I'm going to fuck you until we are both too exhausted to move," he said against her exposed skin. He had one hand braced next to her on the table as he leaned over. His mouth was everywhere, starting at the center of her chest and moving down, his tongue twirling around her belly-button ring and then lower.

The heat of his breath covered her, and then his mouth was on her. She screamed and came as soon as he flicked his tongue against her clit.

But he didn't stop. Alistair kept eating her out until she felt everything building again. Her thighs tightened around his head as he shoved two fingers inside of her, pushing on just right spot. The moon sparkled over her head, and the stars seemed to be shooting from the sky as she rocketed to an orgasm that almost made her pass out.

He shifted around, his mouth on her belly, as she reached for his cock, needing him inside of her now.

"Take me," she said breathlessly.

Take her. There was nothing that would stop him. Not tonight. Last night had tested his limits. Today things had changed.

His emotions, which were always right on the edge of exploding, felt...tamer. The ride to the Tor had helped mellow him out, and the entire day had been one long slow burn of desire. She'd been wrapped around him since sunrise, and now she'd somehow coiled herself around his soul.

The first time they'd been together, she hadn't really been Poppy to him. She'd been that Kitchener girl who was the only way to the tea recipe that had been out of his family's reach for generations.

With the taste of her in his mouth, he felt her nails digging into his shoulders. Then she drew his dick to her center with her hands, rubbing him against her.

There was no way to avoid the fact that this was Poppy. *His* Poppy. His mind was trying to make sense of the implications of it, but every hormone in his body didn't give a damn. He needed to fuck her deep and hard. To take her, and for a few moments, maybe allow himself to believe that this might work out. That he'd be able to mend his past mistakes and that the man he was becoming would be enough for her.

She'd said she wasn't on the pill, so he'd put a condom in his pocket before they'd left for the Tor. He pulled it out and put it on.

"Thanks for wearing one," she said.

He wrapped his arms around her back and lifted her off the table, turning until he was leaning against it. She locked her legs around his hips as he penetrated her, throwing her head back as he drove himself into her.

The moonlight fell around them as, once again, he got an otherworldly vibe from her. His own soul seemed to catch the same fire from her as she rode him. He braced one hand behind him so he could lean back and give her more room to move the way she wanted to. Her breasts bounced with each thrust, her hands on his shoulders for balance.

He pulled her forward until he could reach one of her breasts with his tongue, then he twirled it over her nipple as she started to move more frantically against him.

"I can't get you deep enough," she said.

He held her to him and spun around until she was underneath him on the table. Bracing his feet, he drove into her as deep as he could, pushing her knee back toward her chest. He pounded into her as a red haze came over him, demanding he take everything she had to give.

His lips were on hers, his tongue driving deep into her mouth. Her hand tightened on his shoulder, and the little noises she made got quicker and deeper, until she tore her mouth from his.

"Now."

He came as soon as the word left her mouth. His orgasm

ripped from deep inside him, and he emptied himself, thrusting a few more times to draw out his pleasure. Her pussy kept tightening around him as he fell forward, his head resting in the crook of her shoulder while his breathing slowed.

Her hands moved languidly up and down his back. He glanced down at her noticing that Poppy's mouth was moving, but her words were silent.

"What are you doing?"

"Thanking the moon for this night," she said, her hands still playing with his hair. "And for you."

His breath caught, and hope bloomed in his chest. Fear like he'd never experienced before erupted as well, but he quickly squashed it. "I'm grateful for you, moon fairy."

"Moon fairy?"

"Yes. Just came to me, but it suits you," he said.

"Thanks. But you know I live in this world."

"Something I'm grateful for. Want to go inside and clean up or hang out here?" he asked.

He noticed that she liked to be outside as often as she could. She seemed calmer when she was in nature. It was odd that he'd never absorbed that before.

"I'd love to stay out here, but the table isn't super comfortable."

"Right," he said. "Let's wash up and—"

She put her fingers over his mouth. "Let's just go with it. We don't have to have a plan for every second, do we?"

No. Of course not. He tended to do better when there was a schedule, but he could go with the flow. "Yeah."

She started laughing as he shifted to get up. "Your face is giving you away. You so want to plan."

Using his position over her, he started tickling her as her

laughter filled the night sky. The coldness he hadn't been able to shake from the moment she told him she was leaving him began to thaw.

This time, he wasn't going to try to control the outcome. She had a point when she said they didn't need a plan. He'd roll with things as much as he could.

There was always going to be a part of him that needed focus, but with Poppy, he wanted to try something new. She tickled him back, but he wasn't ticklish, so he captured her hands and held them above her head in one of his. "Gotcha."

Her lips parted as she used her legs to pull him closer to her. "Got you too."

He knew she was playing. That this was just more of the moonlight magic that had wrapped around them at the Tor. But those words felt right.

As in soul-deep right.

He was already back to making a list of all the things he still had to change and do, but right now, they had each other. If only he could let himself just enjoy this moment. Not worry about what would happen tomorrow with his family.

Tonight, it was just him and Poppy. The two of them together.

Thirteen

Poppy looked hot in a midriff-baring bright pink top she'd paired with some high-waisted, wide-legged trousers. She had a fascinator tucked into her bag for the wedding later. This was just brunch with his parents.

He'd be lying if he said he wasn't sweating. He'd worn a suit in green, coordinated with a patterned shirt and bow tie. The dress code for Gemma's reception was "funky formal." He'd taken that remit to his tailor and was pleased with the results. But at the same time, he was slightly uncomfortable. George and his wife, Bronte, waited in the lobby for them.

George's suit was similar to his, and Alistair hated that he relaxed when he saw his older brother in the same awkward garb. Bronte wore a sheath dress in bright orange satin with a large broach comprised of three sequined flowers that pretty much dominated her entire left side.

George was on his phone, and Bronte spotted them first, hurrying over and hugging Ali. "Nice to see you." She turned to Poppy. "I'm Bronte. I've been really looking forward to meeting you."

Poppy smiled. "Poppy. Nice to meet you."

"Sorry, I'm going to fangirl for a minute, and then I promised George I wouldn't do it again. But I'm obsessed— *obsessed*—with everything WiCKed Sisters. We've been too busy to make a trip to Maine, but we are planning one at the end of the summer."

Poppy's smile deepened, something that happened when she talked about the shop she shared with her friends. It was clear to Ali that the business truly fulfilled her in a way that he never had. He had to remember that as he was trying to figure out if he could find a way back into her orbit permanently.

The women were soon deep in conversation. Feeling like a third wheel, Alistair glanced at the bar, which should be serving alcohol even this early. It was a wedding day, after all, and he could already hear some people in there celebrating.

George clapped his hand on Alistair's shoulder before he could bolt for a whiskey to dull the edge of his nerves. This was the kind of situation where being numb would have been his MO not that long ago. Tension was all around him.

So he breathed in. Out. Holding himself in that happy zen garden that his therapist had taught him to create in his head.

Today, there was no running or escaping the situation. He promised himself he'd be here for Poppy and George. They were both counting on him.

"How was the Tor?"

"Nice. Thanks for the house rec. We really enjoyed it," Alistair said.

"Bronte got changed three times because she wanted to

vibe with Poppy," George said. "But to be honest, Poppy seems different than the last time I saw her."

"Yeah. She is. WiCKed Sisters' success, I think, is part of it, but she's…just sort of stepped into herself." Alistair had to admit that he was more drawn to Poppy now than he had been the first time he'd seen her. The years had been good to her. He couldn't get enough of this new Poppy—in every sense of the word.

"Good. I'm here for it. That's the kind of energy Dad needs to see," George said. "You good for this?"

"Yeah," Ali said. Not really wanting to think too far ahead to seeing his father. The old man had mellowed toward him after the breakdown. Everyone had. No one wanted to put too much pressure on him.

"I mean it, if you need to step out—"

Alistair was not going to let his brother cover for him. Suspecting that George was coming from a good place didn't change his mind. He wasn't walking out on Poppy or away from his dad. "No. I'm not going down that road. I need to get out of my head when people who matter to me need me."

"Poppy's not the only one whose energy has changed," George said quietly. "I like this version of you."

The women joined them before Ali could respond, so for a moment, he sat in George's compliment. All that work to shed the old behaviors had started to pay off. The biggest test would be when he was with his dad. The earl was his Everest. Every obstacle that would keep him from reaching the top was going to be present. There would be disappointment, probably—

His thoughts broke off as Poppy slipped her hand into his. Her fingers were long and cool, and when she squeezed his hand, heat moved up his arm, melting the lump of icy panic that had taken hold of him.

"You okay?" she asked under her breath as she reached up with her free hand to straighten his tie.

"Yeah. I'm not going to let you down again." Reassuring her was easy. It was all he thought about. The past was littered with mistakes that he was determined not to repeat.

A sad sort of half smile teased her mouth, and then she forced a full one. "Great. I'm not going to let myself down either."

Ali understood that he and Poppy had the same agenda. They both had allowed themselves to be pushed, manipulated and bullied by his father the last time they met with him like this. As a couple, they hadn't been united because Alistair had only wanted to see pride on the old man's face.

This time, he was here just for Poppy. Praise wasn't something he craved from Howard Miller any longer. And it wasn't something the eighth Earl of Winfield was ever going to give willingly. It had taken a lot of miles in his running shoes to finally process that Ali didn't need that man to be proud of him.

"They're here." George waved his parents over.

Ali felt Poppy tense next to him. Dropping her hand, he put his on the small of her back instead so he could touch her skin. He stroked her gently until she stood taller, shoulders back, and nodded to him.

They were as prepared as they could be.

His mum spotted them first and rushed over to hug him. "Ali. I'm glad you both could be here." She turned to Poppy and gave her a stiffer, more formal sort of hug, kissing both cheeks before stepping back. "Nice to see you again."

"Thanks, Helena."

"Alistair," his father said, holding out his hand.

"Sir," Ali said, giving it a firm shake.

"Glad your wife is with you."

"Poppy and Gemma are friends, so it was easy to convince her to come with me. But she's still not pleased with how our family treated her," he said.

His father's eyebrows rose, but his mum stepped between them. "George is signaling that our table is ready. I think this is a conversation better had when we are all together."

His mum tucked her hand into the crook of his dad's arm. Poppy was taking deep breaths, and Alistair eyed the door. For a minute, he was tempted to just walk away. To escape to his Ducati and get as far away from this situation as he could.

But then he glanced down into Poppy's brown eyes. He wasn't going anywhere. If he exploded the way he had at the Lancaster-Spencer offices, well, he'd deal with it. But first, he planned to set the tone he wanted for the meeting.

Poppy could tell Alistair was all but vibrating with tension as they followed the family to the table. Her thoughts flashed between the man she'd known for the past few days and the man he'd been during their marriage. This kind of tension usually precipitated an outburst. His anger would be hard to control and could take all the attention from the points she wanted to make.

But he'd told his father this meeting would be different from the last. Plus, she could always walk away from this table. She wasn't the scared young bride afraid to stand up for herself anymore.

Bronte looked nervous as well. Was there more than one plot in play?

Poppy almost strutted past the table and out of the restaurant. Of course there was something more going on. When had anything with the Millers been simple and straightforward?

Alistair pulled out her chair and leaned low to whisper in her ear as she sat down. "This is your show."

As he went around to take his seat, she allowed the sentiment to wash over her. She wasn't alone. Liberty had pulled a card for her that morning. It had still been midnight when she called her friend. Sera had video-chatted in too. They'd both agreed that she shouldn't take a shit deal to keep Lancaster-Spencer from suing her. If they did, then WiCKed Sisters was prepared to deal with it.

Don't settle for less than you deserve. Sera's words circled in Poppy's mind, adding to the strength she always drew from her friends. They weren't going to be disappointed if she walked away from whatever Howard Miller offered her.

Their party was seated in the back of the restaurant, with no other tables close to them. Helena signaled to the servers, who took their orders. After coffee and tea had been delivered for everyone, Alistair's dad cleared his throat.

"Poppy, I'm sorry that you feel you weren't treated fairly by us. But the deal you were offered for your family's tea-blend recipe was fair, and you still receive profits through Alistair from the sales of that blend," his dad started.

The earl's age really showed on his face. His thinning gray hair was still perfectly styled, but some of the toughness in Alistair's father was gone.

"I should receive them myself. Alistair and I are di—

estranged, as you know," Poppy said, quickly catching herself. Her hands were clenched together in her lap as she braced herself to make her point.

"We could amend that deal," George said. "We should never have hidden the fact that you were signing away the rights to the tea blend in perpetuity. That should have been spelled out from the beginning."

"Perhaps, but you're getting ahead of yourself, George. We already have a contract that we haven't been enforcing due to you and Alistair working through your marital problems," Howard said. "But given the success you've had in the last year, we can no longer ignore it. I think you are aware that the contract you signed when you joined Lancaster-Spencer has a noncompete clause in it."

"I'm very aware of that. But I haven't been an employee of Lancaster-Spencer for seven years. My noncompete clause only covered a period of three years after leaving Lancaster-Spencer," she pointed out. She'd taken the time to go over the contract as soon as she'd gotten the offer from the Willingham of Hampshire tea company.

Howard took a sip of the Darjeeling tea that he favored, looking a little too smug for Poppy's comfort. What had she missed? She wasn't still employed by them; she hadn't received any money from the company since she'd left London.

"That's not necessarily true. You do receive dividends paid into your joint account with Alistair as an absentee board member."

Alistair put his hand on her leg as she looked over at him. "Poppy wasn't aware of that account, Father. I have held it until our marriage is settled. She hasn't received anything from the company. I think you should consider, as well, that paying me for her work isn't—"

"We weren't paying you. We were paying into the account she had when she started at the company," Howard pointed out. "Whether she used the money or not, we have been paying her."

"Which isn't the point," George said. "We'd like to move past this and talk about what we really are here to discuss—the Amber Rapp tea blend and your plan to license it to Willingham of Hampshire. Instead, we'd ask that you license it to us under a very generous offer that would see you paid into your own account and the contract not linked in any way to Alistair."

Howard's glare should have melted George to his chair. But George ignored his father and kept his gaze on her.

"The terms I've been offered by Willingham include me keeping control of the recipe, and I would have full control over the factory that would package the tea mix."

"Unacceptable. We already have rights to everything you develop," Howard said.

"But we don't," George countered. "She terminated her employment contract in 2019, when she moved to Maine."

"That's right, I did. So I was free to create blends and sell them under my own name. The Kitchener name," she added, because Howard had co-opted her family's recipe as his own when he'd taken their blend and made it into the premier blend for Lancaster-Spencer. "Unlike what you did with Ann Kitchener's famed tea recipe. Taking her name off of it and making it the Lancaster-Spencer Reserve wasn't right."

"To that end, we'd also like for you to change your current offering of Earl Winfield to Kitchener's Earl Winfield," Alistair added.

"Now we're renegotiating that too?" Howard said.

"Everything is on the table because I can't allow you to license another tea blend while this is still unresolved," Poppy said.

"It was resolved when you married my son."

"Would it be undone if we divorced?" she asked.

His father had no answer for that.

"That's not happening. Alistair is making strides, and you are together," Helena said. "Let's focus on doing the right thing for our daughter-in-law, Howie. She deserves to be treated like family. Just like our motto. What are we if not family?"

"I agree with mother," George said.

Poppy wasn't sure what was happening, but there were undercurrents of discord and conspiracy. In fact, it seemed as if each member of the Miller family was using the licensing of her tea blend for their own agenda.

Normally, he'd be incensed by his father, but right now, he also wasn't feeling great toward his mum and George. "This meeting is for Poppy to talk to us and get some sort of fair offer. I understand that the past contract needs to be amended. But she's not going to sign something you offer her at breakfast."

"No, I'm not. What exactly is your offer?" Poppy asked. Her hand found his under the table, and he squeezed it. George had an agenda that Alistair was behind when it came to the future of Lancaster-Spencer, but to his mind, this wasn't the time to make a play for the chairmanship.

"We'll top what Willingham of Hampshire offered, and you'll retain rights to the Amber Rapp blend," Howard said.

"Willingham will be marketing the tea as WiCKed Sisters x Willingham of Hampshire. Since our brand is what is driving sales, I'd expect that in the offer as well," Poppy said.

"Very well."

"It's also a limited run, for six months, coinciding with Amber Rapp's European tour," Poppy said.

"Given the excitement around that blend, we'd want to make it more of a permanent offering than limited," Howard said.

"How about six months limited, and we reevaluate at the end of the term?" Poppy countered.

"That sounds fair," George said.

"I'll have to think that over," Howard said. "I'll also consider the points brought up by Alistair regarding the Kitchener name. You'll have an offer from us in a few weeks."

"Thank you," Poppy said. "I'll make my decision by the end of August."

"I'm still prepared to sue," Howard warned.

"I'd be disappointed if you weren't," Poppy said cheekily.

His father almost laughed.

Alistair noticed his father observing Poppy with something that was close to respect. As it turned out, maybe she hadn't needed him and George and their plan. Poppy had done more for herself than all the back and forth before.

"Good. Where's our breakfast?" Howard asked.

His mum lifted her hand to signal the waitstaff, and a few minutes later, the food was brought to their table. The meal wasn't exactly enjoyable, but it wasn't as tense as it could have been. For the first time, Alistair didn't feel uncomfortable with his family.

It was because he was with Poppy. Their time chatting online over the past six months, and their moments together the past few days, had shown him a glimpse of another life. One that had nothing to do with tea or being the second son of the Earl of Winfield.

Instead, he felt like Poppy's boyfriend again.

How did she feel?

The way she kept giving him little smiles when she thought no one was watching them told him she was happy with the meeting at least.

He couldn't blame her. She'd come to the table and owned it.

God, this woman. How had he never seen her strength? He'd taken for granted that she once bent to his will. It was a miracle she'd lasted the entire six months of their marriage before she left him.

When they left the restaurant, she grabbed his hand, pulling him out to the garden where the wedding would take place later that day. She threw herself into his arms and squeezed him tight.

"That went way better than I expected. George had me worried with all that stuff he kept bringing up."

Alistair held her loosely, so afraid of fucking this up. Of somehow saying the wrong thing and being pushed back out of her life. "He was trying to help."

"I got that. You were awesome. Just laying down the law. Aren't you afraid that he might fire you or cut you off?" she asked, stepping back from him.

"No." That was one fear he didn't have, because he no

longer worked for Lancaster-Spencer or depended on his in-
heritance to survive. He'd made some good investments, and
his life was simpler now. No more jet-set partying.

"Good. I like that for you."

"Yeah?"

"Yeah. God, it's a gorgeous day. I never expected… I
mean, I hoped for this outcome, and I had Sera and Liberty's
energy with me."

He wasn't sure that she needed anyone else's strength. She
was pure steel wrapped in bright pink, curves and soft curls.
He lowered his head and took the kiss he could no longer
deny himself.

Her arms wrapped around his shoulders, she held him
to her as she deepened the kiss. Her thigh slid between his
legs, and he cupped her butt, turning them away from the
windows of the hotel and steering them under the shade of
a large blooming tree.

"Sorry. That was… Where do we stand on us?" he asked.

"Us?"

He didn't clarify. There was still Owen's offer to come
and curate his beer for the summer festival at the tavern. Ali
wanted to do it. Wanted to keep seeing Poppy and trying to
figure out this new dynamic between them.

Still, respecting her boundaries was important to him;
he'd regret it if he pushed his way back into her life if it
wasn't what she wanted. But this…felt like something new
and worth pursuing, as did the opportunity to work in Birch
Lake with Owen.

He had to make it clear to both himself and Poppy that
he was doing it for the right reasons. Not simply to worm
his way back into her life.

"I guess we could call it a holiday fling," she said at last. "I mean, I'm going home on Monday."

He swallowed, taking a deep breath. "Owen offered me a summer job in Birch Lake. I'd like to take it and see you while I'm there. Maybe see if this could be more than a fling."

Chewing her lower lip, she wrapped one arm around her waist. Her gaze moved over him, and he knew she was sizing him up. Trying to cut the truth from the lies. He let her. He deserved her distrust, her uncertainty. But he was working to change that. After he'd seen her show of strength today, he knew that he had to continue the work to be the man he wanted to be.

"If you did that, it would have to be for you. I can't guarantee that we'll ever be more than this," she said.

"Okay."

"Hey, I get that's not what you were hoping to hear. But take it from someone who changed and moved and tried to be a person they weren't. Relationships like ours will only work if we're both true to who we are."

He couldn't argue with that.

Fourteen

They danced all night at the wedding. The Earl of Winfield and his wife left early. George and Bronte were with a group of their friends, but Alistair hadn't wanted to join them, though George had motioned for them to come over several times.

The wedding itself had made her misty-eyed. She hadn't thought she would cry but she had and Ali had handed her a monogrammed handkerchief to dry her eyes.

Gemma glowed as she'd walked down the aisle to Patrick. The man of her dreams. Seeing the two of them so in love, standing next to the man who'd shattered her own romantic dreams and not hating him...that was something else.

But he was different. Which brought her back to the moment.

"Why aren't we joining your brother?" Poppy asked.

"Those blokes are so old me," he said.

"Do you think you'll fall back into old habits around them?" she asked as she danced around him.

"No. But they might expect me to be someone I'm not."

"How?"

This was awkward. There was no way he was having this discussion with Poppy. Telling her that he'd earned a reputation for getting high and taking a different woman home every night after she'd left. It had been a coping method, and he wasn't exactly proud of how he'd behaved. Not that she'd be surprised to learn any of that. He just didn't want to remind her of the man he'd been.

"Different," he said. "That's all past. Why do you want to go over there?"

She shrugged.

"Do you want to?"

"It's just that they all weren't great to me when we were married, and I'd like to go over there and be all 'I've met Amber Rapp, and she loved my tea...' Oh, God. Do you hear me? Could I be any shallower?"

Laughing, he tugged her out of the reception into the quiet hallway. "You aren't shallow. You're allowed to be happy you're successful."

"Yeah, but I wanted to rub their noses in it." She laughed too, that perfect, tinkling sound he loved to hear. "Liberty is totally rubbing off on me."

"I don't think that's it," he said.

She arched her eyebrows at him. "What is it then?"

"Moon of horses power. You've thrown off the shackles and stepped into your full power. There's no stopping you."

Her eyes sparkled. "That's right," she said.

"Poppy."

They turned as her aunt and uncle walked out of the ballroom. "Just wanted to catch you before we left. We're heading up to St Andrews in the morning."

"It was good to see you, Aunt Regina," Poppy said, going over to hug her aunt. Her aunt and uncle fit right in with Ali's family. Alistair could see why Gemma liked them. They were an outgoing, athletic couple who'd socialized throughout the ballroom all night.

Poppy had mentioned that Merle and his dad didn't really have a close relationship, and honestly, Alistair understood why. Seeing Coach, as everyone called him, and knowing Merle as he was coming to, Ali could see that the two men had nothing in common. Not unlike him and his father.

Alistair walked over and shook the other man's hand. "Nice to have met you."

"Same. Looking forward to trying some of your beer the next time we are in the UK."

"You'll be able to try it at the Bootless Soldier Tavern in a few weeks," Poppy said. "You are sending some to Owen, right?"

"I have."

"Good. The next time we visit Merle and Liberty, I'll try some. We'd better leave, Reg. I want to hit the road at four so we beat the traffic tomorrow morning," Coach said.

"Tell your mum I said hi when you see her." Regina hugged Poppy, and the two left.

"It's so odd that your family is nicer than mine."

"They just are better behaved. And they aren't my parents," she pointed out.

"Speaking of which, are you sure I'm invited to dinner tomorrow?"

"Uh-huh," she said. But it didn't really sound definitive.

"That's not a yes."

"Well, Mum is still not happy with you, and my dad apparently cut his walking trip short to get back for dinner," she said. "I have a feeling it's going to be tense. But I'd like for you to come with me. I think they will be open to seeing you this time."

He hoped so. He didn't blame her parents for not liking him. He'd been everything he'd been taught to be around them. He'd sucked up to her dad and talked about hiking the Camino Real in Spain, which he'd done with some school chums one summer. He'd asked about her mum's garden, which was one of the best he'd ever seen. They were nice, honest people. But he'd always been superficial with them, asking questions because he'd been raised to be polite and not because he was actually interested in getting to know them better.

Which, given how perceptive Poppy was…he had to guess her parents had seen through him as well. It was probably why they didn't like him—well, that and the fact that he hadn't made their daughter as happy as she deserved to be.

"Will your siblings be there?" he asked. Poppy had an older brother, Barnaby, and a younger sister, Mae.

"Mae's at uni, so no. I doubt that Barn will drive down from Oxford, so probably not."

"Good. I don't think I could handle the full Kitchener family grilling me," he said. "Maybe you can show me a moon ritual that will give me strength to get through it."

She laughed and took his hand, leading him out into the garden of the hotel. The sky was clear, and the full moon was big and bright above them.

"Tip your head back and look up at the moon," Poppy said.

He watched her instead of looking up at the moon.

"Songs of the wood, words of the fae, guide me and show me the way," she said. Then she opened her eyes to find him staring at her. "Ali."

"I've found my magic in you. I'm letting you show me the way."

"I can show you, but you have to walk it yourself," she said softly.

Words that he'd heard from this therapist more than once. Walking the walk was something that should be second nature to him, but he still struggled with it. "How?"

"Look up at the moon with intention. What do you want?"

He started to talk, and she put her fingers over his lips. "Don't tell me, tell the moon."

Tipping his head back, he closed his eyes, breathing in the heady scent of summer and the woman standing next to him. What *did* he want?

The answer to that had somehow always eluded him until this moment, with this woman. He wanted to figure out a way to find his way back to her. Back to the girl who'd loved him and made him feel like anything was possible.

That girl was gone, trampled beneath the feet of his ambition. But a part of his soul hoped to find new love with the wiser woman she'd become.

Sunday dinner with her parents was really happening. When she'd invited Alistair to join them, honestly, she hadn't really considered what it would be like. Her flight back to Maine was in the morning, and she was staying the night at her parents' house. Ali arranged for her luggage to be sent to the airport and checked in early. So all she had with her was her trusty backpack as they pulled up to the house on his Ducati.

It was a semi-detached home in a nice neighborhood. Poppy had grown up in the house and had gone to the school that Alistair had driven them by once they left the motorway. Driving through the town stirred memories of her girlhood, when all she wanted was to be something more than a regular girl from this medium-size town.

Marrying Alistair had done that. Her wedding had been covered in the papers and had even gotten a small mention on ITV news. But that had had nothing to do with Poppy. That had all been Alistair and the spotlight that followed him around.

WiCKed Sisters fulfilled that desire to be more. To find the thing she was good at. Most people wouldn't recognize her on the street, but that wasn't why she wanted to be more. She'd wanted it for herself.

After all they'd experienced together—the Tor, their lovemaking under the moon, the meeting with his family—she'd been too much in her feels to know what to say to Ali. Today, after dinner, he'd be gone.

It was bittersweet. To finally again see the man she'd had fun with before they were married. She'd liked it. Too much? The jury was still out on that.

Her mom was at the door as Alistair turned off the bike. Poppy hopped off, then took off her helmet before hugging her mum.

"Dad's not happy he's here," Mum whispered in her ear.

"I hope he'll give him a chance," Poppy whispered back.

Maybe this hadn't been a good idea, but she wanted her

parents to see this side of Ali. To understand that the man he'd become during their marriage wasn't the man he was today. Maybe they'd stop blaming him for what happened. Maybe they'd see it all as Poppy did now: that they had both simply been too young.

"Hello, Alistair," her mum said, leading them into the kitchen and out into the garden where her dad was manning the grill. She was surprised to see her brother and sister both sitting in chairs, talking to him.

"Poppy's home!" Mae exclaimed, running over to her and hugging her tight. She completely ignored Alistair.

"Hey, Pop," Barn said. "Drinks?"

"I've got that pink gin we like," mum said.

"That for me. Alistair?" Poppy turned to him.

"Beer, please," he said to Barn.

She'd rarely seen Alistair look as uncomfortable as he did now. Taking his hand in hers, she wasn't sure what to do next. What could she say? *He's not a dick anymore?* That wasn't going to help.

"Aunt Regina called to say she had a great time with you two at the reception," her mum said.

"We enjoyed seeing them too. I had a good meeting with Lancaster-Spencer, and they are going to make an offer to distribute the Amber Rapp tea blend," Poppy said.

"Are they going to be fair this time, Alistair?" said her dad, finally breaking his silence.

"I believe so. Your daughter really left them few options other than that. We also asked for them to return the Kitchener name to the Earl Winfield tea blend," Alistair said.

"Glad to hear that. About time Lancaster-Spencer stepped

up. What are you doing these days? Still a junior executive?" her dad asked.

"Nope. I left the company about a year and a half ago and started brewing my own beer. I really like it," Ali said.

When he started talking beer and brewing, Ali relaxed, and soon the men were all huddled around the grill while Poppy, Mae and her mum talked in the kitchen.

"He seems different," Mum said as they finished making a salad to go with the chicken on the grill.

"Still hot," Mae added.

"Yes, to both. He is different. He's serious about not being a part of Lancaster-Spencer. I like him this way."

"I do too," Mum said.

Walking Ali to his bike to say goodbye, she was totally aware that her family were probably watching from inside the house.

"That was…"

"Nice," he said. "They treated me way better than they should have."

It hurt her heart a little to hear him say that. Putting her hand on the side of his face, she wanted to find the words to thank him for these last few days.

Her perspective and her emotions around Ali and their marriage had changed. The angry girl/woman she'd been when she'd left wasn't someone that Poppy identified with anymore.

"You've changed. You wouldn't have been aware of that before."

"I'm glad that you noticed. It's not easy but the rewards are worth it. I wouldn't have had this time with you. Wouldn't have gotten to see your special magic, moon fairy."

Her heart melted a little more, making her very glad she was heading back to Maine where she would have some time away from Ali to process this all.

He turned his head, brushing his mouth against the center of her palm. "Goodbye."

He got on his bike and she watched him drive away before going back inside. After Ali had left and everyone was in bed, her mum sat on the couch with her arm around Poppy. "Don't feel like you owe him anything. Just because he's changed doesn't mean he'd be a better husband for you."

"Believe me, Mum, I know that. I'm not getting married again," Poppy reminded her.

Her mum didn't say anything else, but on the plane ride home the next morning, Poppy couldn't help but wonder what her mum had seen to give that warning.

Had she fallen under Ali's false spell again?

Fifteen

Poppy was glad to be home. Pickle danced on her back legs and peed all over the floor when she came in the door. Liberty laughed as she hugged Poppy tight. Sera got a towel to clean up the mess and then hugged Poppy as well.

Exhausted from the flight, Poppy immediately slept a solid ten hours, only to wake up at 4:00 a.m. and go sit outside on her patio.

Ali had been on her mind all night. Dreams that were a blend of hot sex and complicated emotions. Life would be so much easier if she could say she didn't really care for him. If he'd simply been a lover from her past that she hooked up with at a wedding.

Simple, right?

Except it was Ali, so that went straight out the door.

He hadn't mentioned Birch Lake or working for Owen again. Perhaps it was for the best. It would be too much pressure for her if he moved here with expectations of anything other than late-night, lonely calls and hookups…which would make her feel like a loser.

Despite the time she'd spent with him and the resolution she'd found with her own part in their marriage, she still didn't trust him. Or, to be fair, anyone else.

That was part of why she'd wanted closure. There were two—okay, three—people on the planet she trusted not to let her down. Merle, Liberty and Sera. That was it. That was enough.

Wasn't it?

Except the wedding had made her misty-eyed and nostalgic. Watching Gemma say *I do* and knowing her friend had found a guy who was going to love and cherish her for the rest of her life had caused a pang in Poppy's gut. She'd had the fancy wedding and all of the trimmings; she knew the rest of someone's life could be six months—hell, not even—just because your spouse turned into a dick.

But the butterflies she felt in her stomach when Ali drifted into her thoughts told a different story. There was a part of her that still believed the right person could come along. Ali? That's what had her worried. Could she trust herself enough to believe in him and them again?

Someone knocked on her door. Poppy walked through her house with Pickle barking and running around her ankles. When she opened the door, Liberty and Sera stood there. Liberty held a bag of pastries, and Sera had three coffees.

"We knew you'd be up, and we couldn't wait to see you. You seemed a little out of it when you got home last night, so we didn't want to press you for details," Sera said.

"I missed you guys so much," Poppy said.

"We missed you too," Sera said. "We want to hear all the details. I loved your outfit for the wedding. Did it slay?"

"Yes. Thanks for the help picking it out," Poppy said. She missed her tea shop. Her regulars, the smell of tea brewing and just glancing around and seeing her friends. "How was the shop without me?"

"Okay. Merle knows your operation so well, but having him there distracts me. I almost gave Mrs. Parson a virility blend instead of the one for her arthritis," Liberty said in mock horror.

Sera chuckled. "She didn't do that, but I did catch her and Merle in the backroom twice."

"Like we haven't all caught you and Wes back there," Liberty said. "She's not wrong. The energy isn't the same without you. I'm so glad you're back."

Liberty hugged Poppy tight from behind. "How was England? Did the meeting with Alistair's family go okay?"

Poppy hugged her friends back, drinking in the love and friendship that they gave her. She knew she was tired from all the travel, but the tears that stung her eyes came from a deeper place. Being at the table with Howard Miller had made her realize how far she'd come from the eighteen-year-old girl she'd been.

A lot of the woman she was today was down to these two. There was something so special about knowing that they always had her back and if she made the wrong decision, they'd still be there to support her.

"You okay?" Liberty asked, leaning forward to take her hand.

"Yes and no. I'm just feeling so much love for you two and realizing how glad I am to be home."

"We're glad too. How was Alistair?" Sera asked as she arranged the pastries on paper towels she'd grabbed in the kitchen.

"Ali was..."

"What?"

"Different. I mean really different. I think I might have finally found some closure with our marriage," Poppy said.

"Good. I hoped you would," Sera said, leading her into the kitchen. "It's not good carrying around the resentment you had toward him."

Was it resentment? Poppy hadn't realized until she'd talked to him that she'd been angrier at herself for not seeing the truth. She'd let herself change to please him. That behavior was hard to swallow because she always prided herself on her strength and sense of self. To accept how easily she'd thrown it over to make a man happy was a lot to take. Though she wouldn't do it again.

Liberty and Sera would both give her a dousing of reality to bring her back to herself if that were ever the case.

"It was that. But also coming to terms that, at eighteen, I had no idea what I wanted for the rest of my life. Ali brought his A game, and I was all starry-eyed there for the romance, never really remembering that Prince Charming pretty much does nothing to save Cinderella. She does it all herself."

"Are you Cinderella? I always pictured you as more Mulan, with the tea and the sword," Sera said.

"I'm Meera," Liberty said.

"No arguments. Sera's definitely a Belle."

Sera laughed. "I am. But back to Poppy. Why did you think you were Cinderella? Did your mom make you do all the cleaning?" she asked. "One of my foster moms was like that."

"No. It was more a class difference. Like I was middle class, but I had a part-time job at uni and struggled to pay for everything, and meanwhile, he'd say, 'Let's take the jet to Vienna,' like it was the most mundane thing in the world."

"That would be fun and exciting," Sera said. "I mean, I get the Cinderella thing because I've felt it a lot as well. Like I didn't fit in until I moved here. At eighteen, I couldn't have done this."

"Me either. That's what I meant. That girl was still figuring out every single thing. She had no business seeing a hot guy and thinking it would last forever."

Which really didn't help her at this moment. Ali was more likeable now that she'd gotten to know him. He was humble, funny and still so hot that all she had to do was think of him to get turned on.

Nope, not really helping.

George showed up the day after Poppy left, just as Alistair was packing to leave for the US. Poppy's reminder not to move for her had changed him. It was one thing to believe strongly that they were meant to be together, but another to accept that this time, he might be the only one who was vibing with it.

"Why are you here?"

"Super friendly, I see. Where's Poppy?"

"Back in the US. You knew she wasn't staying," Alistair reminded his brother. George didn't know about the divorce. Like everyone else, he believed it was just an estrangement.

Oddly fitting word since Ali felt hella strange with her

gone. His house seemed imbued with her magic. He found himself standing on the front porch the past few nights, right where they'd made out, just to feel closer to her.

"I did. Is that why you're back to being an ass?" George asked, walking to the fridge and taking out two beers. He opened them both before handing one to Alistair.

"Did I ever stop?"

"Yeah, mate, you did," George said. "I wanted to apologize for how I was at breakfast."

"You did like seven times when you were drunk at the wedding." Alistair couldn't help his smile. His older brother had started to relax since marrying free-spirited Bronte, but seeing George drunk wasn't something he'd been prepared for. Once his friends had left and George was in his cups he'd come over to himself and Poppy.

George turned into a dreamer when he drank. He'd regaled them with all of his plans for the company, told Bronte she was the most beautiful woman in the world and apologized to Poppy for not allowing her to own the meeting. Then when the girls went to dance to a Steps song, George slung his arm over Alistair's shoulder and told him that he should do everything in the world to get Poppy back.

George's words were still rattling around in his head. *No man should live alone once he's been in love.*

"Yeah...glad Mum wasn't there," George said. "So we need you back in the office if I'm going to make my move on dad."

"I'm not going back. You know that. I will back you at the next board meeting. Mum will too, but that's it. Then I become the silent shareholder, and you continue to vote my shares."

"Won't Poppy object? She gets a say too," George pointed out, taking a long swallow of his beer.

Well, fuuuck. "Yeah. I mean, I haven't discussed it with her. But since she's not moving back here, I think she'll want to let things ride."

"Is everything okay with you two?" George asked.

It felt like this was the first time his brother had noticed something was going on with Ali. Other than that time he hulked out at the office, of course, and verbally eviscerated a coworker before punching the wall next to the poor guy's head.

Things with Poppy had been a really bad bag of dicks. George and Bronte were about to walk down the aisle, and Stephen had pointed out that if his last name weren't Miller he'd be fired for his poor performance at work. It had been the final straw, and Ali had lost it on Stephen. Not his finest hour, and one that should have served as a red flag, but being who he was, it had taken Alistair a few more months of drinking and drugging before he finally figured that out.

George had been the one to escort him out of the building and tell him to get help.

This was different. His brother sat across from him expectantly. "I'm…" He wasn't sure he could do this. Open up and tell someone who wasn't being paid to keep things confidential about his relationship with Poppy. "We're… Fuck."

"So that's a no," George said. "Bronte left me before Christmas for two weeks. I came home from India, and she was gone. The cat was gone, her clothes were out of the closet, and her mug wasn't on the counter. I stood in the flat fucking confused for twenty minutes. She wouldn't return my texts, and I knew better than to call. I had to track her down and wait outside her house like a creeper until she came out to go to work."

"Why did she leave you?"

George shoved his hand through his hair, walking to the French doors that looked out on the back garden. He shook his head. "I was dictating our marriage and life. She felt strangled by the plan I put in place. When she left...I had to do whatever it took to get her back."

"What did you do?" Ali asked. George wasn't like him. His brother was always the smarter one, but they'd been raised by the same parents, who had their own fucked-up relationship, so this made a kind of sense.

"I thought about you and how hard you were working to figure things out to get Poppy back, and I realized it was time I did the same. The thing with how we were raised is that I felt..."

"Superior," Alistair supplied. "Like we had manners, lifestyle and all that shit nailed."

"Took Bronte for me to see I didn't. I have the surface-level stuff, but after that, jack all."

"I'm still working on me, George. But I had further to go than you. I'm glad you and Bronte are back together, and you two seem good for each other."

"We are. But it's a struggle some days. I keep backsliding and spending long hours at the office. I missed her exhibit at the British Library. I can't do that. But it's hard to balance being a Miller of Lancaster-Spencer with being her husband."

"Why are you telling me all of this?"

"Probably should have a long time ago. I don't express myself like you do, but we both bottle everything up. Product of our upbringing, no doubt. Bronte is slowly making me realize that there is a lot more to being a Miller than just running the company. So if you don't want to come back, I'm not going to make it a condition for getting Poppy the deal she deserves."

"Great. I'm sure she'll appreciate that, especially since we're divorced."

"What?"

The shocked look on George's face was oddly satisfying. Ali felt freer than he had in months, if not years. "Yeah. For eighteen months now. You figured out things a lot quicker than I did. I think there's a chance with Poppy, but not if I slide back into the man I used to be."

"Okay. So what can I do?"

"Nothing. This is something I have to do for myself. Actually not keeping that a secret is something my therapist has been bugging me about. I don't have to feel like a failure."

"You don't," George said. "You're not. So what's next?"

"I'm going to Birch Lake to curate a summer ale for a festival run by a beer-brewing mate, and I'm going to try to see if I can convince Poppy to give me a real second chance."

Summer in Birch Lake was all big blue skies and verdant trees. Poppy loved all the seasons, but being British, there was something about a sunny day that drew her outside. She'd slathered on sunscreen before she'd left her house. Leaving her staff to handle the shop for a few moments, she brewed a peach and ginger tea and poured it over ice. It was the perfect thing to cool her down on this warm day.

Most days, she took her break in the shop's backroom. Sometimes she sat at the picnic table behind the shop that Liberty's mom had given them, but today she needed to walk. And think. Thinking was paramount to whatever was going to come next.

Lily at the bakery had let her know that Alistair was back in Birch Lake—her boyfriend was one of the owners of the tavern. Lily had made a joke about how surely Poppy didn't know everyone in England, but a potentially familiar British guy was helping curate the ales for the summer beer festival they were running.

Oh, she knew that British guy. She'd thought he would let her know if he was coming, but they'd left things so open… she didn't blame him for not saying a word.

Returning to England with Alastair had been eye-opening in so many ways. The man she'd demonized after their separation had turned out to be a shadowy image of Alistair and not who he really was. The other big bad in her life, Howard Miller, had seemed to respect her when she stood up and drew a line that she wouldn't cross.

She'd grown in that short week in England, learning lessons she thought she already had. Her mum had quipped, *Welcome to adulthood*, when Poppy told her. Which was a joke they shared. Poppy often told her mum the same thing when her mum went on about the rise in council tax.

Sitting on the bench that overlooked the park, she closed her eyes, tipping her head back toward the sun.

"Want some company?"

Alistair.

She didn't open her eyes. Maybe it was the sun-induced haze that was making her think he was here. But the breeze brought with it the scent of sandalwood and citrus: his aftershave. She put her hand over her eyes as she opened them.

"So you decided to come back." She gestured to the spot next to her.

"I did. It wasn't as easy a decision as I expected," he admitted. "But in the end, the chance to grow as a brewer and to see you again swayed me."

Obvs all she heard was that he wanted to see her again. It had taken all of her willpower to not text him as soon as she landed at JFK for her connecting flight.

"I'm glad you're here. Want to tell me about the ales and walk me back to WiCKed Sisters?" she asked.

She'd made up her mind that if he showed back up, she'd be open to getting to know him better. This time, if they fell back into bed, they had to know each other first. Not just their messed-up past. This man who wore a collared shirt buttoned to the neck, shorts and loafers without socks was vaguely familiar to her. But the wedding week had shown her how little honesty either of them had brought to their marriage. This time, with him, she wanted more.

"Sure. I'm meeting a realtor later to try to find a place. Any recs?"

"Liberty used to live in an apartment complex on the outskirts of town that was pretty nice. Merle lives in a subdivision that has some nice houses."

"I don't want to live near your cousin."

"Where do you want to live?"

"With you."

"With me? You didn't come here for me, right? You know we're not—"

"Stop. Yes, I know that. But I can't pretend that I don't want you back."

Want you back. Of course, her mind immediately went to Take That's "Back For Good."

Her heart raced, and she was already picturing him living with her in the little house she'd bought for herself. Except that was her place. And this time, she was going to be smart.

"I want to be friends," she said, blurting it out as if she had no emotional literacy and couldn't navigate a conversation with her hot ex.

"I want that too. I'm not pushing you, moon fairy, but I'm also not going to pretend I'd be happy in the friend zone forever."

Moon fairy.

God, this man, when he saw her, made her feel like she was one in a million. If this was going to work, she needed to feel that way all the time. To not feel lacking.

Now if only she could believe that this was real.

Why wouldn't it be? What could he possibly need from her now that he would use her for?

Nothing.

That was what her mind said, but her wary soul and bruised heart weren't sure. Not yet.

Sixteen

Poppy had a large greenhouse in the back of her home where she grew Camellia sinensis and other plants for blending in her teas. Alistair had been surprised to see how large it was and how much she was growing.

It was Sunday evening and he'd already worked his shift at the tavern. WiCKed Sisters closed early on Sundays, so Poppy invited him over to use her shed to brew his kombucha for the Tea Society. It would need to be bottled and sent to the participants by August 30 for judging.

"Thanks for bringing the yeast and for your knowledge. I've never tried fermenting alcohol before," she admitted. "Kombucha's not really my thing."

"I'd never have guessed based on how hard you argued against it." Each season they set a challenge in the Tea Society. Ali had suggested one for brewing hard kombucha while Poppy had wanted to do different iced tea blends. His kombucha had gotten the votes but she'd still argued to try to persuade the group. It seemed obvious now that she'd simply wanted to win so Ali would lose.

She punched his shoulder lightly. "That was only part of the reason. You were the other."

She wore a pair of denim shorts that brushed the tops of her thighs and a blousy top with fluttery sleeves. It had a V-neck, and he tried very hard not to notice the swell of her breasts as she bent over to pull a weed or a leaf from one of her plants. She was barefoot, her hair hung around her shoulders, and the heat of the day reminded him of the two of them on top of the Glastonbury Tor.

The same magic that she'd woven around him that night was back, seducing him with the vibrant scents of summer and woman. He closed his eyes, reaching for his self-control, thinking if he couldn't see her body, he'd cool down, but it just heightened his other senses. Unable to breathe without inhaling vanilla, rose and bergamot—everything that was Poppy.

"Well, you won, so um…I ordered the supplies we need to make the kombucha. I got enough for both of us," she said, walking out of the greenhouse.

It was slightly cooler outside but still hot. Or maybe the heat was coming from inside him just from being around her.

To clear his mind, he'd taken a run this morning before the sun came up, and he would run again later tonight. But even if he wore through his shoes, he was pretty sure nothing could cool him down or distract him from wanting her back in his bed.

All those pictures he had in his head of the life he wanted with Poppy felt within his grasp. He just had to keep being her friend and keep it in his pants. He could never reveal that he ached to touch her again.

Even a brief brush of their fingers as she handed him some leaves to smell as a potential flavoring for the kombucha sent a tingle straight to the tip of his dick.

"Thanks for that," he said, realizing he'd never responded to her last statement. It felt as if he were wading through a pool of lust and need. His head was muffled, and he was trying to keep it together, but damn.

Just damn.

"No problem. Least I could do since you offered to bring the champagne yeast," she said. "I also ordered two growlers and airlocks. You said we'd start with sweet tea, which is so generic. Black, white, green, oolong?"

"Any," he said, laughing at the frustration in her tone. "It's really down to what you like. The base is going to influence the direction of the kombucha. I used black tea because I had a bunch from Lancaster-Spencer."

"Okay. Well, I brewed all four bases, and I wasn't sure on the sugar. I mean, sweet tea in the American South is very sugary—"

He laughed, and she stopped talking. She was so cute like this. The tea blender in her element, wanting to make sure everything was perfect.

"What?"

"You're cute," he said, tempting fate and Poppy's resolve by leaning over and kissing her gently on the lips. He pulled back before he lost all sense. "I'll use the black again. You should try that magic courage blend for yours."

"You think?" she asked. She rubbed her finger against her

lower lip and then shook her head. "I will. Okay, so we put the tea and SCOBY into a large jar and seal it up?"

"Yeah," he said, moving to the bench where she'd set out jars in different sizes, all with lids. He noticed that there were two of each size. She'd spent a lot of time setting this up, and here he was, being all horny. He shoved his lust into a large chest in his mind and locked it. Poppy wanted them to be friends. God, he craved that too. So he needed to be that guy.

"I think this size will work for what we're doing," he said, indicating one of the jars.

They both assembled their ingredients and then sealed their jars. He took a photo of Poppy holding her jar, and she did the same for him. Then they posed together.

"That's it," he said. "Now we wait."

"Six to ten days, right?" she asked.

"We can check on them and see how they're doing in a few days," he said.

"I will." She turned to a pad of paper and made a few notes. "Do you keep track of your recipes?"

"I do. I keep them on my phone. Want to see the recipe I used last time?"

"Did it come out good?"

"I gave the growler to George because I was coming here," he said. "It should be ready any day now."

"Let me know what he says. I'd love to see your recipe from the first time," she said. "Want to show me over dinner?"

"Yes."

"Good. I invited Liberty and Sera and their guys for a cookout."

So not just the two of them, which was fine. Really it was,

because if he couldn't learn to get along with these people she considered family, then there was no place for him in her life. "I can run back to the tavern and get a pony keg of my summer ale."

"That sounds great. I'm grilling, and Liberty is bringing sides. Sera's on dessert."

Alistair had his shirt off, which was distracting her from the book discussion she was meant to be having with Sera and Liberty. They'd all picked up the latest release from their favorite author. She really had stuff to add to the discussion, but her eyes kept straying back to where Ali was talking to Wes and Merle about sweet fuck all for all she cared.

It was that chest and those abs that kept her gaze locked on him. That super-hot alpha-hero body on a guy who looked relaxed and humble as he was sweating and talking… It was a potent cocktail.

Sera nudged her. "If you don't want to talk about books, let me know. I'm fine with staring at men."

"Yeah, but we are strong independent women," Liberty said. "Let's discuss, or next week, we'll have to not invite the guys."

Poppy turned so that her back was toward Ali. It wasn't like she couldn't have him in her bed if she asked. He wasn't hiding the fact that he wanted to be there. It was her waiting for some sign from the universe that she wouldn't get hurt if she let him in. Really let him in.

England had felt different. That hadn't been real, because her life was here. Holiday flings weren't real, everyone knew that.

But Ali in Birch Lake? That felt like solid reality.

"For fuck's sake, Poppy."

"Ugh. I'm sorry. He's been here all afternoon. We were brewing tea together, we kissed—well, he kissed me and then ended it just when I wanted it to never end," she said. "I sound like an idiot."

"Never. You sound confused. That's completely okay," Sera said. Sera was the kindest of all of them. She had the most reason to not see the best parts of humanity, but somehow she always did.

"I am, and I'm not. I sound like that guy from *The Traitors UK* who freaked, don't I?"

"A little bit, but I get it. He's your ex for a reason, and you are right to take things slow, but make sure you're doing that for the right reasons."

The right reasons. What were they? Saying out loud she didn't want her heart broken by him again wasn't something she needed to do. The girls knew that. They didn't want her heart broken again either.

Liberty watched her with that wise-goddess gaze Poppy had noticed more and more often in her friend since last fall, when everything had happened with her ailing nan and her newly discovered biological father. Since starting a serious relationship with Merle, Liberty had unlocked some hidden feminine power.

"What do you see?" Poppy asked her.

"I'm not sure. I've been pulling cards for you all week, and they aren't clear. What do *you* see?" Liberty asked.

"That even though I told him the past was resolved, I still am plagued by it all the time." There. It was out there.

It ate her up inside how she melted every time he smiled at her. Staying present was never harder than when sweet, charming, irresistible Ali was around. Still niggling at the back of her mind were the times when he'd been charming and then lied to her. How he'd seduced her with that same charm…and she'd fallen for it.

How?

If she could figure that out, then maybe she could really move forward. Somehow, the more time she spent with him was both helping her get closer to getting over that fear and making her more aware of the fact that she'd never really been able to know him. Never been able to trust him.

How was she going to figure this out?

There just wasn't some magical card that Liberty could pull out of her tarot deck or a journal that Sera could bind for her that would manifest peace of mind. There wasn't anything but her own soul-searching and answers that she was no closer to finding than she had been the day he'd walked into WiCKed Sisters.

"Honey, you take as much time as you need," Sera said. "If he's the man for you, he'll understand and realize what's going on."

Poppy glanced over her shoulder, realizing the men had gotten quiet. They turned to the grill as soon as she did.

Sera laughed. "They were watching us."

"Of course they were. Probably realizing how lucky they are we are nice witches and didn't curse them," Liberty added, raising her voice.

"Witch, you know I'm not afraid of you," Merle said, grabbing Liberty's glass and refilling it as he came to perch on the arm of the chair she was sitting in.

Wes and Ali came over as well, but Ali scooped Poppy up and sat down, holding her on his lap. He smelled of the smoky grill and man. She looped one arm around his shoulder and leaned back against him. His thighs were hard and solid underneath her as she and her friends and their men all sat in a circle. It wasn't that hard to let the fear that had been taking hold melt away.

Talking about summer and tourists and really nothing, they drank the ale that Ali brewed and ate the sausages and burgers he'd grilled. Poppy started to feel like this was what she needed. Not white-hot sex alone, though she was ready to take this more physically with Ali now. But this quiet intimacy that came from being part of a tight friend group.

Laughing and talking and living.

That had been missing from their lives in London. He'd been busy, she'd been scared, and they'd had no real friends. Just acquaintances that had really only cared about their own status and Ali's position in society. She had been looking for a sign from the universe, some big neon arrow that would say that Ali was reformed for good and that she could trust him with her heart, but…

Her heartbeat always sped up when he walked into a room. Her eyes always sought him when she knew he was near.

There was no letting herself fall for him again. It was going to happen. She just had to be careful not to make him into something he wasn't.

He fit in so well with her friend group, but she had to be careful that he also fit in with her.

Somewhere between the greenhouse and grilling, he'd decided to stop letting her set all the terms for this new relationship they were developing. Or rather to stop being passive in what was going on between them. He'd never been a man to keep his passion locked up in a box. For Poppy, he'd been willing to try, but this summer was the first in a lifetime of expectation. He was creating his own destiny.

Not touching or kissing her didn't feel right, and he wasn't going to do it anymore. As soon as her friends left, he intended to talk to her about it. But for now, he was enjoying an impromptu D&D game that Merle and Liberty were leading them in.

"Remember, guys, if you stay within thirty feet of me, I can use my bonus action to heal anyone in my radius," Liberty said.

"How the mighty have fallen, witch. I don't throw the word *nerd* out often, but I think you're becoming one," Merle said.

"Nerd?" she repeated pointedly.

"When did you start talking about radiuses?" Merle shot back.

"I thought we wanted all of our friends to survive this encounter."

"What's the radius?" Alistair asked. "I'll take all the help I can get."

"Six squares. Also, if you get hurt, I'm a very strong healer, and I've been rolling well tonight," Liberty said.

Alistair laughed, enjoying the interplay between all of the couples. Unlike that first night at the tavern, they'd all sort of accepted him tonight, and he felt some genuine bonds developing. Of course, Liberty had specifically cornered him and warned him that if he fucked with Poppy, she'd come for him. But otherwise, they were nice and fun.

Alistair looked down at the page where he was tracking his health. "I'm down to three if you want to heal me."

Liberty looked over at him. "I'll heal Puddgurr."

Everyone else had a character they'd been playing for a while, so Merle had helped him create Puddgurr. He was a barbarian, which suited Alistair, as the character could rage and destroy things in the name of saving the day. It had been a long time since he'd felt the kind of rage that his character used as a strength. Honestly, he'd never felt like rage was an asset, but in this type of fictional fight, it did come in handy.

Liberty healed him and looked very pleased with herself.

Poppy threw her arm around his shoulder, pressing against his side. That haze that he fell into whenever she touched him was back. Everyone else was muted, and the focus of the summer evening was on her as twilight fell and fireflies danced around the yard.

The scent of her was tinged with Pimm's, which she'd declared they needed after the beer ran out. He'd helped her use the gin-based drink to make a cocktail with fruit and herbs picked from her garden before they'd added fizzy lemonade to make a batch big enough for the group. It was funny that she admitted she'd never made it for her friends before this. It was quintessentially British summer.

"Why haven't we had Pimm's before? I love it," Sera said. "Who knew a gin-based liquor, fruit, cucumbers and mint could be so yummy?"

"The British," Poppy said with a laugh. "I just hadn't thought about it in a while."

"I'm glad you did," Liberty said. "I could do without the cucumbers, but it's not bad."

"Liberty doesn't like cucumbers," Poppy said in an exaggerated aside to Ali.

"I figured that out," he said, turning to face her.

She sighed, touching his hair with a soft hand. "Please don't be fake."

Her words drove an ice pick into his heart. He'd hurt her before, and this entreaty that she would never have made if her guard had been up told him just how much. "I'm not."

"You feel real," she said as she rested her head on his shoulder.

He wrapped an arm around her waist and pulled her closer. *Real.* That was what he was trying to get more comfortable with.

They played the rest of the game with his arm around her. It was fun, and though he doubted he'd play other than with this group, he enjoyed it. On the way out of Poppy's house, Wes talked to him about his father's brew, which had gone much better after he'd used Alistair's tips. Soon he and Poppy were alone and cleaning up, and Alistair knew he should leave.

Poppy had switched to lemonade after her entreaty that he not be fake. The slight buzz she had seemed to have left. She was quiet...pensive, really. What was she thinking?

He had no idea, but frankly this wasn't the first time he'd had no clue what was going on in her head. "What's up?" he asked.

"You kissed me earlier."

He waited, but she didn't say anything else, just leaned against the counter, crossing her long legs and watching him.

"I did. I don't want to be just friends. I want to keep getting to know you, but this not touching, kissing... It feels odd."

She tipped her head to the side. The sun had left her cheeks reddish and drawn some freckles on her shoulders. Her hair had loosened from her ponytail due to the heat, strands lying against her neck.

The loose-fitting top she wore pulled taut over her chest as she crossed her arms under breasts. "Yeah, it's not us to be just friends. But I don't want to go back to being just lovers."

"Me either. I want to take this friendship to the next level. I don't know if I'll be any good at it," he admitted. "But not trying feels fake."

A slight smile teased her lips. "Fake isn't what we're going for. I'd rather have something that's real and true that burns quickly like the summer heat than something fake."

Seventeen

Possibility was in the air. She told herself that all she wanted was one kiss. That was all she needed for tonight. But that was a lie that her mind didn't even bother acknowledging.

He'd left his shirt off. That light dusting of hair on his muscled chest was too tempting for her to keep her hands to herself. That she'd resisted even with her Pimm's buzz was saying a lot for her self-control.

The other bit keeping her contained was that her first whirlwind romance with Alistair had been witnessed by everyone. They'd made the society pages, everyone at school had known, and that had added to the pressure for her to be the girl worthy of being with him.

This time, she wanted Alistair for herself. Wanted to see if, behind closed doors, he was the man for her. She'd already admitted to caring for him. But anything else… That was dangerous. Her heart and soul had already gone all in on him, and no matter how hot he made her feel when she was in his arms, it wouldn't be worth that cost again.

"So…" he began.

"You've never been this…tame before. Why are you now?" she asked him.

"I'm trying. Hell…" He shoved his hands through his hair. "I want to be what you want, and I'm struggling because it's not me."

"You think I don't want you?" she asked, carefully coming closer to him so she felt the heat coming off his body.

"You want me in your bed. What about your life?" he asked.

She had no answer for that and didn't want to go there tonight. This had been pretty much the perfect summer day. She wanted him to kiss her. To continue the heat that had been simmering between them all afternoon. Since the moment he'd kissed her and told her she was cute.

"Am I still cute?" she asked.

He muttered "fuck" under his breath, cupped her butt and pulled her into his body. "You're always cute, sexy, frustrating, smart, infuriating and enchanting, moon fairy."

His mouth came down on hers, and she twined her arms around his neck, holding him as his tongue brushed over hers. He slid his hand under her shirt and up her back. His palm was big and hot against her skin, his fingers spreading out as he lifted her off her feet.

She wrapped her legs around his waist, falling into his embrace fully. This wasn't the moon weaving her magic around them. This was something else, something different, something that seemed to come from them.

Was there magic here? Or was she seeing what she wanted to see?

Shut up.

Her subconscious urged her on as she sucked Ali's tongue deeper into her mouth. She felt the edge of her breakfast table under her thighs as he set her down. He undid her bra and shoved her shirt up over her head.

Her bra hung loosely on her arms, and she shrugged out of it. He growled, his hands coming up to cup both of her breasts.

"That blouse has been driving me mad all day. When you leaned forward, I could see these beauties. I tried not to look, but it was too late. The image was in my mind. All I could think of was this moment," he said, leaning over her, his words low and husky against the skin of her neck.

"I had no idea—"

"That you were driving me out of my ever-loving mind?" he asked.

"Yeah. I would have done it more often," she teased.

He flicked his tongue over her nipple. "Until I did this?"

She sank her nails into his shoulder. *"Yeesss."*

He laughed against her skin, sending sweet shivers down her stomach to her center, where heat gathered. Her denim shorts felt too restraining, and she reached between their bodies, going for the button, but his hands were there first. "Not yet. I want to make it last."

She didn't bother answering, just undid the button and zipper of his shorts, shoving her hand into the opening and stroking his erection through his boxer briefs. His hips moved as he rubbed against her touch.

She loved the feel of him—so hard—and couldn't resist pushing her hand inside his underwear and rubbing her finger along the top of his dick. The skin was so soft as she circled her finger around the tip again and again. Until he shoved his pants and underwear down his legs.

Standing back, with his legs spread, he watched her as she touched him. Their eyes met as she wrapped her hand around his shaft, tightening her hold on him. He groaned again, and then she felt his fingers at the waistband of her shorts, undoing them.

"I thought you wanted to wait."

"Fuck that," he said, lifting her up with one arm around her waist and trying to shove her shorts off.

Finally, they got them off together. He leaned over her, plunging his tongue deep into her mouth as she rubbed the tip of his cock against her clit. He felt so good.

A dizzying sensation burned through her, and she arched her back, touching herself with him. His mouth moved down her body, his hips pulling away, and she wanted him back, but his tongue was on her clit. He flicked it over the nub until her thighs spasmed around his head, and she threw her head back, stars exploding behind her closed eyelids.

His hands were on her waist, holding her to him as he continued sucking and tasting her until she came again, another burst of fire spilling out of her center. She needed more. These orgasms were nice, but she wanted him inside of her.

She twisted, reaching for his cock. He felt harder than he had before, and she was on fire to get him inside of her. She tried drawing him closer, but he resisted her.

Then she leaned down and licked the side of his shaft, taking the tip of him into her mouth, and he groaned. She felt his hands on the back of her neck as she took him deeper into her mouth.

★ ★ ★

Her mouth was doing things to him that there was no coming back from. The way she swirled her tongue around the tip of his cock had him close to coming. Not in the plan, he thought, and he imagined the cords on his neck standing out as he tried to keep it together. He thrust his hips, then pulled back and out of her mouth.

Her skin was flushed. Looking down at her naked on the table in front of him made his heart clench. Her smile was seductive and knowing. His moon fairy was channeling her inner feminine power, knowing she owned him. He wanted to be inside her. Wanted to fuck her long and hard until they were so much a part of one another that there was no room for anything fake or pretend.

Her fingers were still rubbing the tip of his cock. He was on edge; another moment and he was going to spill himself into her hand. Not what he wanted. He reached down for his shorts and dug around for a condom, then cursed. "I don't have a condom."

She started laughing. "Your face…"

"Yours isn't disappointed."

"I have a box in the bathroom." Hopping off the table, she beckoned him to follow her down the hall. The sway of her full hips and the glide of her long legs as she moved with languid grace had him hurrying after her.

She opened a drawer in the bathroom cabinet and tossed the box to him. He took one out and stroked his hand over his naked cock as she watched him.

She licked her lips and reached for him.

They needed an entire day in bed. That was the only way he was going to get the time he needed with her over him, under him, around him. He was desperate to make up for the long years he hadn't had the right to touch her and take her.

"Stop teasing me," he begged.

"No," she said, reaching for his cock.

He pulled his hips back, got the condom on and then caught her around the waist, turning her in his arms. He urged her forward until her hips were pressed back against him. Then he rubbed his dick against her ass, sliding into the crease before bending his knees so he could enter her pussy in one long, slow stroke.

He caressed one of her breasts with one hand, reaching around with the other to flick his finger against her clit again. He felt her pussy walls tighten on him, and she turned her head, looking over her shoulder at him.

"Now who's teasing?"

He couldn't help the proud look that he knew was on his face. He'd somehow gotten the upper hand.

Then she tightened around him again, grinding back against him. Taking his hand in hers, she moved his fingers over her clit in a different pattern. The noises she made tore through his control, and this was no longer a game.

It was heat and need and craving.

A craving for something that he could only find when she was in his arms. Her body moving against his. He leaned over her, bracing one hand on the counter next to her. His chest rubbed against her back as he explored her neck with his mouth, sucking strongly.

He was trying to consume as much of Poppy—of this moon fairy and her magic—into his being as he could. But his body demanded more. He moved his hips more frantically as she clamped hard and screamed his name, her pussy throbbing around his cock.

He drove himself deeper into her, riding her orgasm until it drew out his. He thrust into her until he was empty and then rested his head between her shoulder blades. The smell of sweat and sex, Poppy and him, mingled in the air. He closed his eyes.

Don't let this be fake.

That was all he was thinking. These feelings that she stirred in him were intense and scary. If he sat in them for more than a second, he wanted to rage. Not at her, but at the universe for making him feel something so deep and then giving him no assurance that it would work out.

If this was what falling in love felt like… Well, he wasn't ready for it. Wasn't entirely sure he ever would be. These emotions were too fragile.

He lifted his head, and their eyes met in the mirror. Her eyes were sleepy and sated. She smiled at him and his heartbeat sped up.

How could he run from this? From her? He'd done it once, but that time he hadn't allowed her this far into his psyche. This time… Was there a way to push her back out? He was afraid it was too late for that.

"Want a bath or a shower? It's so hot tonight," she said, her voice soft and sweet. So Poppy was talking about ordinary things while he was falling into a maelstrom, searching for something to hold on to. He drew his finger down the line of her spine as he pulled out of her. She was so vulnerable to him. She'd told him that with her booze-fueled entreaty to be real.

Maybe that was partially why he felt this fear. It wasn't just himself he had to protect. It was Poppy's heart. If he couldn't stay, if this wasn't going to last, if the man he thought he was becoming wasn't real…then he had to stop this now.

"Ali?"

"Yeah. Shower would be great." *Get your shit together.* He wasn't going to have a fucking meltdown after having sex with Poppy.

"Good. Together?" she asked. There were clouds in her eyes now as if she sensed the fucking shit going on inside him.

"Yes. I want that," he said. God he wanted that more than she could know. He wanted this to just feel normal and safe. But he wasn't sure that he was going to be able to allow these feelings to stay.

She debated asking him to spend the night.

Pickle jumped up on the couch and curled into his lap. Even the most hard-hearted person wouldn't be able to resist Alistair cuddling the sweet mini dachshund. She felt tears stinging her eyes and got up to go to the kitchen, making an excuse that she needed water.

The past few years had been a lot. Like, more than she'd ever expected. She wished being an adult had been that rosy tale she'd painted for herself as a kid. Where she'd get to eat cookie dough from the bowl, stay up late and just hang out with her friends.

Her reality had been harder, more intense. The divorce, moving here. The months when she wasn't sure she'd ever make enough money to move out of her parents' rental house. Pickle getting sick and having to have her teeth removed. Liberty's nan being put into a nursing home. Sera losing Ford. They had all been through a lot.

They'd helped each other through everything. Even her divorce. But how were her friends going to help her through this?

Ali was on her couch after having just fucked her and left her boneless and then taken a shower with her. She glanced at him sitting on the couch, flipping the channels. He stopped on *Pride and Prejudice*. "You like this one, right?"

"It's my favorite."

She hated to admit that for years, she'd refused to watch it because everyone loved it, and Poppy had never wanted to be like everyone else. Even when she morphed into what she thought Ali wanted as a wife, she'd taken care to not be like any other new wife. She liked being original. But *Pride and Prejudice* was so good. Like, way better than it should be.

Indulging in a comfort film *would* help vanquish her vulnerability. But she couldn't watch *Pride and Prejudice* with him. If she did, he'd *know* that she always wigged out when they got to the scene where Darcy met Elizabeth at the pub and went to save her sister... That scene always made her heart ache. The emotions on Matthew Macfadyen's face would make her squeeze Ali's hand and want him to feel like they had that love...which they didn't right now. They might later, but at this moment, it would be too real.

As much as she was determined to be real and keep this relationship grounded in truth, she wasn't ready for him to know that the sex had been so good tonight, it had been more than sex. It had been falling-in-love-with-him sex. Which she knew was her mind running away in the heat of it all. Like, soul sex wasn't a thing.

But tonight had felt extra.

Like this time, they were really communicating and seeing each other. He wasn't perfect, he wasn't Prince Charming sweeping her off her feet this time. She wasn't fake Cinderella losing her shoe so he'd find her. She was Poppy. She was his moon fairy, but she was totally in his world. There was no fae realm waiting for her.

Her life was here.

With him? She wasn't sure.

"Pop? You okay?" he called.

"Yeah, debating popcorn. But Pickle can't have any. Maybe I'll get her a treat," she said. Like her mind was on the mundane and not this whirlwind of everything that was out of her control.

She took a deep breath.

Make tea.

Her mum's voice was in her head. *Which leaves would you choose?*

It was nighttime, so something herbal. Maybe a nice blend of chamomile and strawberries. In her head, she was already blending the leaves. Then putting them in a mug.

"Poppy?"

She jumped. Ali stood behind her. "You scared me."

"I can tell. You were miles away. It's me, right? Want me to leave?" he asked.

Oh, it was him all right. "No. I like hanging out with you. It's sort of giving me all the vibes I wanted when we were married, which I totally wasn't going to bring up, because we put the past to bed."

"Except it's still there," he said. "For both of us."

"You doing okay?" she asked.

He took a deep breath and then started opening cabinets. "What are you looking for?"

"Whiskey."

"Above the microwave," she said. "Is it going to be that kind of talk?"

He stopped. "Tea would be better. Alcohol is my crutch. It gives me something to do with my hands, and it takes the edge off my emotions…"

It wasn't just her. Tonight's sex made her want to do everything she could to protect both of them. But she wasn't even sure she could keep herself safe. "I don't mind if you drink."

He shook his head, taking another deep breath. "I'm scared."

"Scared? Of what?"

"This." He gestured to the both of them. "Us. What if…"

"It ends again." That was what was keeping her in the kitchen instead of on the couch being present and enjoying this moment with Ali. "I get it. I love seeing you and Pickle cuddling. I wanted to curl up next to you and just be with our…" She trailed off.

Their little family.

That was what she'd called them when her grandmother couldn't take care of Pickle anymore and gifted her to them. A little family. But they hadn't been.

"I'd like that. No pressure. Take your time. Just know that I'd like to be part of it."

She chewed her lip, then realized what she was doing and stopped. "Let's just go with it."

"Except how can two chronic planners and a massive type A ever just follow the flow?"

"True. Maybe we'll both have to just be there for each other. Remind the other to stay present."

"I can do that." He took her hand, tugging her into his arms, and she wrapped her arms around him, squeezing.

She held him tighter. But she couldn't hold on to him this tightly forever. It wasn't good for either of them. He had to want to stay.

They made popcorn, drank iced tea and watched her movie. When it was midnight, he left.

She toyed with asking him to stay, but in the end, she hadn't. Everything had been rushed the first time, she was doing it different with Ali.

Eighteen

The summer days were long and felt like they'd last forever, but as July bled into August, Poppy knew they wouldn't. The hints of fall were in the air, and she and Alistair weren't having discussions of the future.

She wasn't entirely sure if that was her idea or his. But so far, it was working for them. Working in a way that made everything feel as sweet as the sun-warmed strawberries she'd found at a farm stand on her way home from work.

The last of the season. That was what Charlotte, the woman who owned the farm stand told her as she put them in the basket on her bicycle.

Liberty was even talking about the end-of-summer ritual. The plan was to go up to Hanging Hill to celebrate the transition of the seasons. Poppy was looking forward to that. The last transition, from spring into summer, had been powerful for her at the Tor. The start of her and Ali.

He was leaning against her front door when she pulled into the drive of her cottage. She loved her little house set a few blocks off Main Street. She wasn't sure she'd see Ali today, as he'd been working with Owen to get ready for the Beer Fest, which they were hosting this weekend in the park.

"Hey."

"Hiya. Hope you don't mind me just showing up."

"Of course not. I picked up some strawberries on my way home. I was going to try to dehydrate some to put in my end-of-summer tea blend," she mentioned. "I haven't checked our kombucha today."

"I climbed your fence and checked them. I think they might be ready," he said.

"The gate is never locked, so next time you can just walk through it," she pointed out as she unlocked her front door.

"Good to know," he said.

Pickle ran to greet them, dancing around both of their legs until they petted her. She followed them into the kitchen, where Poppy put the strawberries on the counter next to the fresh-cut flowers she'd also picked up.

Alistair pulled a vase from the cabinet under the sink and put water in it while she got them both some herbal peach iced tea from her fridge.

What felt like an attack of vertigo overwhelmed her. There were moments when she wanted to stub her toe really hard so she'd know this was real.

He was everything she'd wanted from him when they were married. All the things she'd asked for that he never had time for, which was nice. But it was the unspoken things that really got to her. The way he seemed to know when she needed him. Making her laugh about nothing or having a serious conversation about how much they'd changed.

It felt like a dream she'd never expected to come true.

She could almost believe it was real, except there was one thing he never talked about. Him.

He talked about her, his brother, Lancaster-Spencer, beer brewing, kombucha, even D&D and WiCKed Sisters. But when she broached how long he was on leave from Lancaster-Spencer, he always changed the subject.

She sighed to herself as she followed him out to the shed where their jars of kombucha were. They'd added the champagne yeast a week ago, so anytime now they'd be able to sample it and transfer it to bottles. But it would have to taste dry and boozy first.

"Poppy?"

"Hmm?" She hadn't been paying attention at all. She wanted to ask him about his future with Lancaster-Spencer. But she also didn't want to ruin these perfect long summer days with him.

Now who was being fake?

Not fake, exactly, just not wanting to lose this unexpected happiness. Was there really anything wrong with that?

"Should we try it tonight or wait a few more days?" he asked.

"The recipe said seven to fourteen days, and it's been seven. Maybe we should try it at ten days?" she suggested. "Will it be ruined if we take the airlocks off too soon?"

"No. Also, it will take three to ten days to add flavors in the sealed bottles. So if we want them for August 15 and the Tea Society tasting, we're going to need to sample and then bottle them which might be pushing it."

"Yeah. What do you think?" she asked. Instead of asking the question she really wanted an answer to. *Why did*

*you leave your family company? Why abandon the one place that
dominated your life?*

"I like the idea of doing it at day ten," he said.

"Good. So are you working tonight?" she asked.

"Yeah, and Owen has a date," Ali said with a teasing tone.

"He does? I'm not sure why I'm shocked, but I am. I mean,
he's always just in the tavern."

"According to Lars, you should be shocked. She's from
Bangor and they met online," Ali said as they walked back
to her house.

"Nice," she said. She was happy for Owen, really she was.
But Ali's past was heavy on her mind. And so was what that
meant for the two of them.

He stood next to her, his head cocked to one side after
he'd whipped his shirt off and tossed it on the back of a chair.
"The heat… I hate to be that British guy, but I'm ready for
some rain."

"It is hot," she admitted. "Speaking of England…"

"Were we?"

No, of course they weren't, but there was no way to ease
into the prying questions she had for him. No way to let
them lie either. She needed to know. It was time for answers,
and she'd about run out of ways to distract herself.

It would be different if she wasn't falling for him. But she
was. There was still so much about him she didn't know.

"I was," she said. "Why did you leave Lancaster-Spencer?"

"That's a long story," he said. "I'm not sure I can do it
justice before I leave for my shift."

He took his shirt off the back of the chair and walked
into the house.

★ ★ ★

Of course she wanted to know why he left. It was surprising she'd waited this long to ask.

"Fine. I just… It feels like you're hiding something from me," she said, following him into the house. "It's okay, we don't have to be each other's confessor or anything like that, but this feels important."

It was. Way more than she'd ever guess.

But he didn't want her to know what had happened. That he'd lost it in such a big way that even his family, with all their connections and influence, had been left with no option but to put him on a permanent leave and in therapy.

It wasn't the way he wanted her to see him. The work he'd done since that moment was what helped him keep it together now.

Anger and guilt and shame were a potent cocktail running through his veins. He'd be unpredictable if he didn't take control.

"You're right." He bit the words out angrily.

Poppy took a step back from him.

He clenched and unclenched his hands, breathing deeply through his nose. *God, don't let me be like this.* He repeated the words until he felt more centered.

"You're right," he repeated, the words calmer and more rational this time. "Trust me when I say it's not something I want to tell you about and then leave. But I said I'd be at the tavern at seven, and it's six thirty now. I will tell you," he promised.

An eternity passed before she nodded and then came over and hugged him. She wrapped her arms around him, putting her head on his chest.

He circled her with one arm, blinking to keep tears back. Her acceptance of this broken version of the man he wanted to be got to him, hard. He cleared his throat. "Want to come to work with me?"

"And hang out while you work? Maybe. Let me see if anyone's free to join me. I think Wes and Sera are both back from an estate sale. Could you save a table for me?"

"I will," he said.

An alarm buzzed on his watch, and he knew he had to leave to get to the tavern, but he didn't want to. Everything felt off. His fault. Again. Was he ever going to do things right with her? Would anything be easy when it came to Poppy? Or was he always going to be on the back foot with her?

"I'll see you later. Probably in about thirty minutes or so. I want a shower," she said.

"I want one with you," he said. All he could see was her naked, water sliding down her body. He knew how she tipped her head back and let the water run down her face before she started washing. That she uttered her thanks for clean, cool water. He'd watched her too many times for his body not to react to imagining showering with her.

"Maybe after work," she said, pushing him toward the door.

After they talked. He was pretty sure she wasn't going to let this get swept under the rug. He didn't want to either. Things had been so good between them for the past few weeks. He kept trying to tell himself that he was ready for this life.

But there were parts of his past that didn't involve her. Things she still didn't know that he felt she deserved to.

Their divorce had stripped away the mask of civility he'd

always hidden behind. It had taken a few months for him to become the monster he'd always felt he was at his core. That man who was nothing but a servant to his hormones and emotions. The ones that he'd never learned to really deal with.

He had to get out of here now, or he was going to confess it all, and then, depending on how she reacted...he had no idea what would happen.

At first, he kissed her hard because of the turmoil inside of him, and then more gently, because this was Poppy. His moon fairy. Her magic had wrapped itself around him and wasn't letting up, making it easier to be the man he wanted to be.

But when she learned how far he'd fallen, would she still want him?

"See ya later." He forced himself to calmly leave her house.

He'd jogged over earlier, but a full run now would do him good. He took the shortest route back to the tavern, even though his mind was desperate for a longer run. There was no time.

Ironic that, in the past, he would have just blown off his shift at the tavern. But he'd given his word to Owen, a man who was probably his first true friend, and Ali wasn't going to break it. That guy was in the past. As was the man who let anger take everything he'd worked his entire life for.

That guy was gone.

He got to the tavern with five minutes to spare. He hurried upstairs to use the shower in Lily's old apartment and changed into the jeans and Bootless Soldier T-shirt that served as the tavern's uniform.

When he entered the bar, it was noisy and busy. Crowded.

Just what he needed. No time to think or dwell on whatever would happen later when he talked to Poppy.

He spotted Lars behind the bar. "Alright?"

"Yeah it's good," Lars said. "I'm going to grab dinner, and then I'll be back, so you won't have to cover the whole night. Thanks again for helping out."

"It's what mates do."

Lars just smiled and left.

Alistair was kept busy with drink orders and keeping an eye on the rest of the seasonal staff, who sometimes had questions about the curated ales in the summer festival range.

He was busy, but not so much so that he missed the moment that Poppy entered the tavern wearing a sundress, her hair in a braid. Their eyes met, his heart raced, and that fear that he'd been trying to control since she asked why he left Lancaster-Spencer snaked its way into his stomach.

As if nothing was wrong and things were the exact same as yesterday, he smiled over at her and gestured to the table he'd saved for her.

Poppy's eyes had drifted to Alistair so many times, she finally just sighed and turned her attention back to her e-reader. She was meant to be reading a book on traditional kombucha brewing.

"I need a large glass of wine," Sera said as she plopped down next to her.

"I'll get you one. What's up?" Poppy said.

"Liberty's parking the car. I promised I wouldn't spill until she was here. She wants a large as well."

"Should I get a bottle of rosé?"

"Definitely," Sera said.

Sera was never like this. Standing, Poppy hugged her friend and then went to order a bottle of wine and three glasses from Von, one of the summer staff that worked at the tavern.

Ali, who was talking to a customer, glanced over at her, one eyebrow raised. Poppy shrugged, tilting her head back toward Sera. He nodded.

As she took the glasses from Von, some of the stress she was feeling about her and Ali disappeared. They just communicated the way couples do. That was reassuring. It wasn't something they did at all when they were married. Mainly because Ali had been so into himself and his goals.

The panic she felt from the moment he told her they wouldn't be talking until later eased a bit. Plus, right now, she wanted to concentrate on Sera. Concern for her friend had her hurrying back to the table.

Liberty came in just as Poppy sat back down. Von delivered the wine in an ice bucket, and a few minutes later, the nachos Poppy ordered arrived too.

"Okay, what's going on?" Liberty asked Sera. "We've needed a girls night, but your text sounded urgent."

"What text?" Poppy realized she hadn't glanced at her phone since she'd gotten to the tavern. "Sorry, I was busy…"

"Watching Ali. We know. That's why we came here," Liberty said.

They all had the friend tracker on their phones, so Poppy would have been easy to find. "What is going on?"

"Wes wants to get married in January," Sera said at last.

Poppy watched her friend carefully. Why wasn't Sera happy? "Okay, I don't get why that's a bad thing… I thought you were both talking about it."

Sera cleared her throat. "We were, but tonight he said once we're married, we'd start thinking about kids."

Ah, kids. Sera had grown up in the foster care system. It wasn't a topic she spent a lot of time talking about, but Poppy knew her friend still had some triggers from that. She was deeply aware of the instability of families and how fragile children were.

"Did you tell him it's a hard no?" Liberty asked. "You can set limits. For what it's worth, I think Wes loves you so much he'd understand."

"I agree. He knows you, Sera," Poppy added.

"What if this is the breaking point for him? I mean, it's taken me forever to agree to marry him, and now that he's brought up kids, I just panicked," she said. "I told him we should take a break. Which he…"

"Um, he's here," Liberty said.

"What?"

"Just walked in the door, and he's spotted us. Uh, he's coming this way," Liberty said.

Poppy hopped out of her chair and moved to the other side of the table as Wes approached. He looked…determined.

"I got your text," he said. His jaw was clenched, and he looked tense as he sat down next to Sera.

She texted him to say she wanted a break?

"I'm sorry. I should have called you, but I wasn't sure what to say, and I needed—"

"Your sisters. I get that. For years, I've shut down and walked away from the people in my life who are important, afraid of letting them see what they mean to me. I'm not doing that with you. I asked the question because I thought you might want to look into fostering to give kids a chance at a real home," he said. "I meant it as a discussion starter, not a relationship ender."

Sera shook her head. "You know how I am."

"I do, which is why I'm here," he said. "Talk to your girls, figure this out for yourself. But know that I love you, and I'm not going anywhere."

Sera threw herself into Wes's arms, muttering something against his neck that Poppy couldn't really hear. She made out "love you" and "scared" and "Robinson Crusoe." The couple started kissing, and Poppy and Liberty looked at each other.

"So how's things with Ali?" Liberty asked, leaving the other two to make up in their way.

"Good."

"Too good?"

"Maybe. I'm not sure. He's on a leave of absence from his job and has been for a while. I've never asked why until today. We're going to talk after he's done working," she said.

"Is that a big deal? I thought rich dudes didn't have to work and that jobs at their families' companies were just for show."

"You watch too much TV. It was a big deal. Think *Succession*, not *Love Island*," Poppy said.

"Ah. And he's the second son, so the pressure was always on him to unseat his older brother," Liberty said.

Poppy laughed. "I'm not sure that's accurate, but he did want to please his father. Our marriage secured a recipe that no one else in the history of the company had come close to getting."

"So him leaving is a big deal?"

She shrugged again. Who knew? He and George had been

friendlier than she had ever seen them at the wedding. His father hadn't acted like there was anything untoward about Alistair. So it was only his reaction to her question that had fear niggling the corners of her brain.

What was he hiding? He had admitted that he hadn't told her everything, but he also promised to reveal it all soon.

Sera turned back to them and asked if Wes could stay. Though Poppy would have liked it to be just the three of them, she smiled her yes.

Liberty squeezed her leg under the table. "You don't have to always be nice."

But she did. That was how she operated.

Nineteen

Poppy walked quietly next to Ali as they headed back to her place. It felt more like a home than the apartment he rented on the outskirts of town. That place was as homey as his first-year room at boarding school. But Birch Lake was starting to feel like home, and he had Poppy and the tavern.

Small talk was needed, but his mind was blank, until he remembered Sera and Liberty showing up, and then Wes.

"What was going on with Sera and Wes?" he asked.

"Just couple stuff. You know how something small can feel huge," she said, tipping her head back to look up at the sky. It was cooler in the evening than it had been during the day, and Poppy rubbed her hand over her arm.

"Yeah," he said.

Right now, he wasn't sure she wasn't trying to give him some hints about talking about the past. Did she think it wasn't a big deal? She'd change her mind in a moment, when she heard what he had to say.

"Want to talk in the park?" he asked.

"Why?"

"Just in case you don't want me at your place after," he said.

Stopping, she pulled him to her. "If you tell me that Lancaster-Spencer is a toxic workplace, and you had to ghost, I'll get it."

"It is toxic. Not for most workers, but for me," he said.

"I get that. With your parents both working there and George in that office down the hall. I felt stifled there too. It was hard to get up and go into work," she said.

"I'm sorry I never saw that," he said.

She linked their fingers together. "We can talk wherever, but truly, unless you've done something that involves me and my family, I think I'll be good with it."

He could almost believe her. Until he remember the fear and revulsion on his own mother's face when she saw the hole he'd punched in the wall.

They got to her house a few minutes later, then fed Pickle, who wouldn't leave Ali alone until he scooped her up and cuddled her. He ended up seated at the end of the couch with the tiny dog sitting on his lap. Poppy curled her legs under her as she sat at the other end.

Watching him and waiting.

"After our divorce was finalized, something inside me sort of snapped," he said. "I think I told you that, right?"

"Yes. Snapped in what way?"

"I just… Ah, Poppy, I was a bigger dick than you can imagine. I was angry and blamed everyone for the fact that our marriage failed."

"Including me?"

"You, the company, George, my parents. The fact that

some of the people who worked under me were underperforming."

"Oh, so everyone but you?"

"Exactly. One day I'm at work, and you posted about
WiCKed Sisters and how good the shop was doing, and I saw
red. I was sitting at my desk looking out over the Thames
reading profitability numbers on our new tea ranges, and
they weren't great."

"Were you jealous?"

Jealousy would have been preferable. Or maybe it was
part of the mixture of things that drove him down the hall
to the manager of product development after the CFO had
sent an email outlining that the departments under Ali were
underperforming.

He'd yanked that man out from behind his desk, put hands
on an employee and let his rage fly. Screamed into the man's
face about how incompetent he was.

George had to pull me off of him.

Poppy's gasp made him realize he'd been talking out loud.

"I was gone. I mean, not even thinking rationally. I apparently yelled at George, punched a massive hole in the
wall and walked out of the office, giving everyone the finger as I left."

"Alistair."

Just his name. He couldn't look at her. Instead, he stared
down at Pickle on his lap, calmly petting the tiny dog, who
snuggled closer to his stomach.

"I know. Obviously, there was no letting me go back to
work. I was put on a permanent leave. I've apologized to
Stephen, and George compensated him. He accepted my

apology and, through his lawyer, suggested I start anger management."

He leaned back, resting his head against the back of the couch, turning to look at her. Trying to see the effect his story had on her.

She watched him, waiting to hear the rest of it.

"I didn't go to therapy until six months after the incident. I got really drunk or stoned every night, partying and getting into fights until I got arrested. Mum came and got me and took me to a rehab center."

Her face fell even further.

He shut down for a moment, going to the place in his mind where he could block his feelings. He didn't blame Poppy for her reaction. He'd already guessed that she would be disgusted by his actions. He was.

"I started seeing a therapist in rehab and have been in therapy ever since. Stephen and I had a dinner right before I reached out to you on the Tea Society. I finally realized how much of my own failings and flaws I was always taking out on everyone else."

"Oh, Ali," Poppy said, scooting over to sit next to him on the couch. She wrapped her arm around his shoulder. "I'm both sad and happy that you went through all of that. I wish you'd found your way to therapy without that incident."

"Me too. But I don't think I could have. It took a total meltdown. Stephen's forgiveness was the first step to pushing me forward in my therapy. At first, I was doing it to get back to work, but the more sessions I went to, the more I realized that going back to Lancaster-Spencer wasn't the answer."

"What was the answer?"

"I still don't know. I'm still trying to figure out who I

am and where I fit in. I'm getting closer to it, but there is a part of me that wonders if I'll ever really figure it out," he admitted.

She put her head on his shoulder. "Thank you for trusting me."

When he was raw and open with her, she couldn't resist him. This was all she'd wanted from Ali from the beginning. To feel like he could be her soulmate. She hadn't wanted to spend her life with a roommate she had sex with.

His honesty just now was almost painful.

She saw the torment on his face when he told her about his anger. The way he'd calmly kept petting Pickle assured her that the anger that had exploded out of him with Stephen was no longer an issue. Even Merle had witnessed Ali's new sense of control at WiCKed Sisters, that first day he came back into her life.

This wasn't like when they first met, when everything felt like a fairy tale. But it felt right.

Pickle hopped off his lap and headed to her bed in the corner next to the fireplace.

"So…?" Ali asked.

She shifted around until she straddled his lap. They were face-to-face, and she could see him more clearly this way. His hands were on her hips to steady her, but there was nothing overtly sexual about him in this moment.

This was the most vulnerable he'd ever been with her. It made her heart beat faster; her entire being was drawn to him. Similar to the almost-solstice at the Tor, when she'd felt the moon's energy wrapping around both of them.

Truth had a power that was stronger than either of them.

"You're brave," she said.

"I think I just proved I'm not."

She put her fingers over his lips. "That took a lot of courage. Showing me your worst moment. That is something you wouldn't have done before." Resting her forehead against his, she stared into his gold-flecked brown eyes, ringed with those sinfully long eyelashes. Her heartbeat sped up as she turned her head to angle her mouth and kiss him.

But he evaded her kiss. "Are you sure you heard it all?"

She shifted back, looking down at him as he slouched on the couch. "Yes. Do you think you're the only one who doesn't know who they are or what they are becoming?"

He flushed. "Ah, when you put it that way..."

She almost laughed and would have if she wasn't caught in this painful longing for Ali to be the man she needed in her life. Not the one she was expecting. Not the one she wanted him to be. But the one she needed. That secret craving that even she couldn't define for herself but that her spirit would know when he was in her arms.

Perhaps that was why she was trying so hard to uncover every change in him since they'd split up. Trying to ascertain that this time, when she took that leap into him, she wouldn't crash to the ground.

Looking for a guarantee in love was honestly the dumbest sort of ask. But there it was.

She wanted to know that if she let her heart go where it was heading that it wasn't going to be shattered. She didn't want to start over again and wasn't sure that she would ever let herself if Ali wasn't what she wanted him to be.

No, *needed*.

Still, want was always a part of it.

"What do you feel broken about?" he asked.

"Telling me about your leave of absence wasn't a trade," she pointed out.

"I'm very aware of that, moon fairy. I'm looking at you, as I have been all night, trying to figure out how you could feel broken. You seem to have this magic that holds everything together."

"I wish," she said.

"But you do, it flows around you, and sometimes, if I'm close to it, I can feel that spell wrapping around me, keeping me safe."

Hearing Ali talking about being safe broke her heart a little bit, but in a different way. She understood how scary it was to be lost inside yourself.

"When I walked out of our flat…I am surprised my legs carried me. I was shattering a little more with every step. Everything I had ever believed about the woman I was had turned into a lie. I had told myself I wouldn't be one of those women who blindly gave up her own agency to be with a man…yet I had."

"I never meant for that to happen."

She shook her head. "It wasn't something you could control. I lost all sense of who I was and had been. Hiding my witchy practices and playing down my tea blending to make something more commercial instead of taking risks. Being safe turned out to be the most detrimental thing to my own health."

"God. How are you even here with me? Don't you hate me?" he asked.

Hate him? Of course, she'd said that a million times or more when he dug his heels in about the divorce or wouldn't answer her emails, but the distance had helped. "No. I mean

I did, but that was more hating myself. I hated that I allowed you that much power over me. Once I realized that—and it took a hella long time—everything started to get better. Where do you think your anger comes from?"

"Dad."

That made sense. "I noticed you weren't as much of a kiss-ass as you used to be."

"Kiss-ass, really?"

"Yeah. I mean, you used to be like, 'Of course, Dad, we'll do whatever you want.'"

"Ha. I mean you're not wrong, but pleasing him…it was such an old behavior. Took me a long time to break that down," Ali said. "I'm sorry I hurt you. You were right to hate me."

She wasn't sure that hate was ever the answer. It was time to make peace with the past. She kissed his nose. "Did you hate me?"

"Oh, fuck yeah," he said. "I told everyone about the bitch I married when I was out drinking, but when I got home, out of my mind, I would reach for my phone and look at your picture, still wanting you back."

"Is this—" she gestured between them "—about you wanting me back because it means you haven't failed? Or was it to make a real change for yourself?"

"It had to be for me, because there was no situation I could foresee that you'd ever be with me again. Until Amber Rapp."

Poppy let out a humorless laugh. "Amber Rapp continues to change my life."

Poppy nestled on his lap wasn't something that his body was going to ignore for long. This conversation that he dreaded having was actually something that he needed.

"Amber Rapp, huh? Her songs are okay, but I never thought she'd have this much influence over me."

"Not your usual listen?"

"You know I'm all death metal."

"Ha. You're a pop man. Amber seems like your kind of listen."

"She would be if her lyrics didn't cut so close to home. Hearing myself in *Rhapsody for an Ex* sort of soured me on her music. Then George calls out of the blue to tell me you're famous."

"You weren't stalking my socials?" she asked with a fake pout that made him lean forward and take the kiss she'd tried to give him earlier.

Poppy shifted up onto her knees, her hands on either side of his face as she sucked his tongue deeper into her mouth. Her sundress was thin enough that he could feel her body heat through it.

He pulled the fabric up, bunching it until his hand was on her back. Lowering his hand to her butt, he massaged her cheeks as he held her.

There wasn't a moment he didn't remind himself how lucky he was to be back in her arms. To be in her house and see her every day. It was a gift he never thought he'd have.

She lifted her head. "We're wearing too many clothes."

"Agreed," he said, flipping her onto her back on the couch.

She shimmied out of her panties as he fumbled for the condom he'd put in his pocket earlier in the day, before he knew they were having this talk.

"Thank you for being here with me after everything," he said. His emotions felt too big to keep inside. He was seconds from spilling it all when she took the condom from him.

The moment her hand wrapped around his dick, he almost forgot about the gratitude and love—there was no denying that he loved her—and his need to express that to her. He would show her instead.

The condom on him, she shifted, pushing his erection down until he was at the entrance to her body. "Fuck me."

"Are you ready?"

"Yes. I have been since the moment you were honest with me. That was the biggest turn-on," she said, pulling his head down to hers. She whispered into his ear, "Nothing is sexier than you when you are unfiltered."

He could deliver that. He leaned over, rubbing his chest over her body. The fabric of her dress in the way, he shoved it up and toward her neck. She hadn't worn a bra, so he felt the press of her hard nipples against his chest. He groaned.

God, she felt so right. There wasn't another woman who had ever been able to erase the memory of how Poppy felt in his arms. There never would be.

He knew that.

Entering her in one long thrust, he held himself there. The emotions he thought he'd caged for the moment were back. It took all of his willpower to keep them bottled inside instead of letting them spill out while he fucked her.

She felt so good and tight around him. She clawed at his hips, urging him deeper and faster until he was caught up in a haze of need and demand, driving himself into her frantically. His orgasm was right there, but he wasn't even sure if she was close.

Reaching between their bodies, he rubbed her clit the way he knew she liked it, and she arched her back, screaming his name as her pussy throbbed around his cock, and he came.

Thrusting until he was empty, he let himself lean forward, resting his head next to hers on the couch.

She turned her head to look at him. "Hi."

"Hi," he said.

He loved her. The words were on the tip of his tongue, but he kept them back. This moment wasn't perfect, but it was as close to it as he imagined it could be.

For years, he'd been searching for his place and his purpose. He'd tried a few different things and finally found true happiness and contentment in brewing, but that was just something to keep him busy while he waited.

He hadn't even realized what he'd been waiting for until now. *Poppy.*

She was what had been missing. Not the Poppy who married him at eighteen, but the woman she was now.

This woman.

He kissed her, then rolled to his side, tucking her against his chest so that he wouldn't be tempted to blurt out the truth of his feelings. There was still so much she had to sort out for herself.

Which was only part of it. The other part was that this felt so new and scary, and what if he was wrong? What did he know of love? Maybe this feeling in his stomach and soul was just him trying to keep something good for himself.

He couldn't manipulate her again for his own means. She needed to figure out how she felt about him before he would ever admit that sometime between the Tor and tonight, she'd become his entire world.

Twenty

August was a heady month. Usually, the end of summer was full of sun and fun. This year was, well, uncommon with Alistair by her side. He'd shown up at her place at 5:00 a.m. with his Ducati—he'd bought one here and taken her for a ride up around the countryside, ending at Hanging Hill.

They were holding hands at the top as they watched the sunrise. Releasing her hand, he bent over to the bag at his feet and pulled out a thermos filled with her magic courage tea and mugs for both of them.

Typically, August was the month of maturity and gratitude for earthly sustenance. For the first time, Poppy felt that she was leaning into her own maturity.

When Ali had come clean about his leave of absence that night one week ago, something within her had been unstoppered. There was a lightness to her bones that wasn't there before. As if she'd released the weight of the past, even though she thought she exorcised all of that when she signed her divorce papers.

"Nice. It's not the Tor, but I hope it will do," Ali said. "One of the books I was reading on the ritual of tea spoke of welcoming the sun each day and taking time to be present in the day."

"This is a great way to start it." She took a leisurely sip from her mug, taking a deep inhale of the fortifying steam. "I've been working on a new tea blend for you."

The more time they spent together, the easier it was for her to figure out which leaves and essences to blend to create one as unique as he was. It would have to have heat, so she started with the huang pian sheng pu'er that she used in the mix for Liberty. It was strong like Alistair.

She added in bergamot because of his heritage and lineage. But she also wanted the new flavors to represent the man he was becoming. That was the tricky part.

She wanted to use something that represented the Kent coast where he brewed his beer. Summer flavors of brambleberries and strawberries. But they were too delicate for the harshness of the sheng pu'er, so she'd had to scrap it and start over.

"I'm intrigued. What will it include?" he asked.

"That's the problem. You're a bit of an enigma. I thought I'd use some Kentish flavors and a strong fiery base. But the sheng pu'er I started with is dominating the tea," she said. This was the first time she'd brought up brewing around him, she realized, other than the kombucha they were working on together.

The one time she'd tried to talk to him about unique blends when they were married, he'd mansplained tea blending to her and told her that her flavors weren't going to work. He'd been wrong. The blend he didn't think was good enough was the first one she'd made and sold at markets and her online shop. It was still popular.

She called it FUAM. A lot of people assumed it was some mashup of a region or her just trying to sound exotic. But it was simply *Fuck You Alistair Miller.* It had been the first step toward WiCKed Sisters.

"You're smiling."

He slid his hand into the back of her hair, his fingers massaging her scalp as he leaned forward and kissed her. He'd been very touchy-feely lately, always reaching for her when they were together. It suited her, because as much as she felt they were good and solid, fear sort of crept around them, reminding her of the last time everything had fallen apart with Alistair.

"Just remembering the last time we talked about tea blending."

He shook his head, pulling back from her. "Fuck me. I was an ass. I'm sure I told you you were doing it wrong."

"You were, and you did," she said, unable to stop the grin from spreading across her face. "But it worked out for me. FUAM is one of my top sellers."

"Does everyone know what it means?"

"Just Liberty and Sera," she said. "So my way back to tea is now for you, not in spite of you."

"Yeah. Well, my favorite is black tea," he said.

"I didn't know that. You always drink oolong."

"Just to annoy Dad because he insisted we have Earl Grey at home," Alistair said.

So black tea. "Black tea is a nice base. What else do you like?"

She'd made a lot of assumptions about Ali. Spent a lot of

time dwelling on all the ways he'd never seen her, mainly because lately, he seemed to really see her. Not realizing that she'd never really tried to see him either.

She'd had an idea of him. Howard Miller's second son, bad boy, player, reckless. The tabloids' favorite fodder. He'd been all of that during their courtship and marriage. And to be fair, he was still those things, but she saw depth to him now.

That one-dimensional image of what she thought he was… One of the hardest things to accept was that she'd been just as culpable in the downfall of their relationship. She wasn't going to take the blame entirely, but there was a lot she was doing differently this time that never occurred to her before.

"Vanilla and strawberries," he said. "Those are two of my favorite flavors."

"Really? Strawberries make you break out if you eat too many of them," she pointed out.

"Thanks for the reminder. But yeah, they remind me of you," he admitted. The alarm on his watch pinged.

"Ah, that's sweet that you're willing to risk skin irritation for me," she said.

He shrugged. "I can be sweet, you know."

"I do know. I like it. It's just unexpected."

"Good. I like keeping you off-balance."

"You do? Why?"

"Because that's how I feel around you, moon fairy. Only fair to try to keep things even."

But they weren't even at all. She was falling for him. Although her mind was going to figure out a way to keep her heart safe from him again, every part of her being wanted to be with him.

★ ★ ★

Alistair dropped Poppy off at her place and headed back to his apartment. The beer festival had gone off without a hitch, and Owen was now talking about brewing some autumn ales and doing an Oktoberfest if Alistair wanted to stay.

He did want to stay, but he had obligations in the UK. His own place and brewing business that he'd started. He also needed to go to the board meeting in September to relinquish his voting rights in the company. Though George had mentioned Poppy's voting rights, she'd already given those all to Ali in the divorce. All she'd asked him for in return was that he made no claim on anything involving WiCKed Sisters.

So was he going to stay? If he did, he needed to find a real house. This apartment was okay, but it wasn't anything special. And he'd like to have Poppy at his place once in a while, so when he was alone…he wouldn't be, not really.

George had sent him an email with the offer that they were sending to Poppy today. Ali had read it, and it looked pretty fair to him. But he saw a few places that he suspected she'd argue and a few that he knew she could get them to back down on.

He'd been toying with offering her his advice, but the truth was, it was *her* deal. He wasn't even sure George should have sent it to him.

Which made him feel edgy and tense. So he ditched the Ducati, changed into running clothes and went for a long run. As his feet pounded the pavement, his mind wandered through scenarios. Each one had a different outcome.

It had been years since he'd felt this calm when it came to making a decision. He knew his therapist would be pleased.

He was going to have to call her when he was back in the
UK. He wanted to have one more session and get her take
on everything with Poppy.

Poppy.

She was really what had him in this scenario mode. He
thought he loved her. Honestly, he had no real stick to mea-
sure love by. He cared for his mum. A lot. He liked George
and Pickle. But these emotions he held for Poppy were
deeper and more consuming. As if there was a part of him
that no longer belonged solely to himself.

Was that love?

Or was he just obsessed with his life in Birch Lake? It was
easy and almost relaxing here. It was nice to show up for his
shifts at the tavern or stop by Poppy's and end up playing
D&D with her and her friends.

This life had no real demands. It suited him. Or it suited
him in this phase of his life. Would he be content to be just
Ali for the rest of his time on earth?

He got back home and changed and headed to the tavern. He walked past WiCKed Sisters and saw Poppy, Liberty
and Sera outside, welcoming their customers in for the day.
Poppy waved at him, and he waved back.

This felt…safe.

That was the problem. Was he taking the safe path? Was
he morphing into someone he wasn't just to keep Poppy?
Was he being true to the man he was?

How was he ever going to know? He'd have to leave.
Go back to the UK and maybe Lancaster-Spencer to figure
things out. It was the only way he'd know for sure.

But what if he got sucked back into his old life and lost
Poppy for good?

What if you don't?

That voice was louder than the noise pulling him into a whirlpool of doubt and fear.

Love was at the heart of it. He'd been afraid to ask for it in any of his relationships. He knew that he'd taken comfort over love so many times. But now he didn't want that. He wanted Poppy to love him. Even if they couldn't be together, he wanted her in this emotional quagmire with him.

"Dude, you're very early," Owen said when Ali let himself into the tavern with his key.

"Yeah. I wanted to talk to you."

"About?"

"Autumn."

"Ah. You're going back to England?"

"I don't know. There is a lot I want here. But I can't just abandon what I had there," he said. "It's not fair to you, but I would like to work with you on brewing some ales for the Oktoberfest and possibly come back."

"That's cool. Your brews are unique, which I really like, and the customers do too, but you've got to do you. I'm still going to host it. Maybe make Lars step up on the brewing front."

"Cool." That was truly the only answer that Owen could give. So why didn't Ali feel better about it? He got what he wanted. Except he didn't.

It would have been easier to make the choice if Owen had said he needed him. *Fuck me.* Was he still looking for external approval? If he was, then he wasn't ready to be the man that Poppy deserved.

"What are your typical autumn brews?" Owen asked.

Alistair grabbed his notebook from his backpack, and as

he looked at it, he saw his future in the pages. His love for Poppy wasn't going to change this. He didn't have to go back to Lancaster-Spencer to know that his future wasn't in tea making. He'd always have an interest in it, but that was all it was.

His heart was here in the beer he started brewing as a way of saving his soul. It had done that and more. Given him a world of his own. A place where he could stand out because of something he'd earned instead of how he'd been born.

This morning, sitting in the moment had rattled him. He wasn't used to just letting himself be. Worry had nipped at his heels on his run and sent him into a spiral. The kind that he would have punched his way out of before his breakdown.

They always closed the shop at seven. It didn't make sense to stay open after that. Foot traffic on Main Street died down; tourists usually had headed back to their rooms, and locals were home or at the tavern. It was sort of a magical time of day for Poppy when the doors were closed and she and Liberty and Sera sat down to just talk.

Lately, with how busy summer could be, they hadn't had time for this. Most days, one or all of them needed to be somewhere else. But tonight it was just the girls, and Poppy needed this. The final offer from Lancaster-Spencer had dropped in her inbox an hour ago. They'd already gone back and forth with different versions a few times until they got to this point. She'd skimmed it while making pots of tea for her customers.

Taking a moment to get the antique coupe glasses that her mum had given her when Poppy moved to Maine, she set three of them on the table and then went to check on the

Moët she'd put in the fridge in the back. Sera and Wes had officially announced their wedding date…the first Wednesday in January, the day they met. It was also the anniversary of Ford's death, and they were going to honor him.

Ford, Wes's grandfather, had been Sera's mentor in bookbinding and restoration. The two of them had met when Ford passed away and left Sera a box of books that Wes wanted. It had been a bit dicey at first but they'd worked together and fallen in love.

Liberty and Merle had officially moved in together. For some reason, Merle had been oddly stubborn about it, until Liberty told him that she liked his nerdiness and to stop being afraid.

Lancaster-Spencer had come in with a very generous offer that more than matched the offer from Willingham of Hampshire. Poppy had also received an amended contract regarding the Earl Winfield blend, which would now be labeled Kitchener's Earl Winfield, and the rights were only licensed to Lancaster-Spencer and would revert back to Poppy's family in fifty years' time.

As much as she had never expected it, she was contemplating a relationship with Alistair as well. Something felt settled deep inside her. But hesitation still seemed to be her vibe around him. At times, she was frustrated with herself for not just trusting him, but she hoped that would come in time.

"All right, celebration time," Liberty said.

"What's the good news?" Sera asked as she joined them.

"All three of us have something to celebrate," Poppy said, sitting down next to her friends after pouring them each a glass of champagne.

"We do? Are you and Alistair serious?"

Her cheeks got so hot, she was pretty sure it looked as if she'd been baked in the sun. "I don't know. I meant your official engagement, Liberty moving in with Merle and the really nice offer I got from Lancaster-Spencer." Really, it would have been better to lead with that. No questions or guessing what the celebration was about.

"Nice! Have you accepted it?"

"Of course not. It's a WiCKed Sisters product, so we all have to decide," Poppy said. Her sense of fairness wouldn't let her cut her friends out of success that had been earned by all three of them. Amber Rapp didn't just love the tea but the entire experience.

"It's tea, so whatever you decide is fine with me," Sera said.

"Yeah, same," Liberty chimed in.

"Really? What if the bagged tea product means people don't come here? What if our business slows?" Poppy asked. "I don't want to be the source of anything like that."

Liberty shook her head. "Business will slow. Amber will release a new album in a few months, and something else is going to engage her fan base. We will still be here doing what we did before she stopped in."

"Yeah, our success isn't tied to Amber. It's all down to the three of us," Sera said. "I think putting our products in shops is a nice next step. That business class I've been taking on Skillshare was talking about that."

"So I should do it?" Poppy asked.

"If it's a good deal. No underhanded clauses like whatever happened when you married Alistair," Liberty said. "I can read it if you want me to."

"I'd love that. Both of you, actually. It looks good to me.

I was clear that there would be no option or first right of refusal on any other blends I produce," Poppy said.

"Perfect. Champagne time," Sera said.

"To magical journals, intuitive tarot readings, tea that warms the heart and soothes the soul," they all said together, clinking their glasses and taking a sip.

As they laughed together, Poppy reflected that this here was the closest she'd found to a home. These two women, this shop, the men and parents and friends they'd drawn to them. Poppy wanted to believe that this was all she needed, but she knew that in her heart, she was including Alistair in the mix.

He wasn't even really here for longer than the summer. Could she have fallen for him again without any thought to the consequences?

That was one hundred percent a yes.

He'd changed. But change alone wasn't going to make them suddenly live in the same country or want the same things.

His dreams… She didn't know what they were. He was determined not to return to Lancaster-Spencer, which she totally approved of. But what was next for him?

Was she going to just wait for him to tell her? Or was it time to ask him and tell him that she wanted more?

"Can we go to Hanging Hill on Monday night? It's the seasonal blue moon," Poppy said.

"Of course, why?" Liberty asked.

"Alistair." No use pretending there was any reason other than that man.

"Definitely. Want to talk?" Sera asked.

"It's nothing bad. I just don't know what to do. He's here

for the summer. I mean, I knew that when he came back. But my heart is starting to count on him. To expect to see him every day... It's so much more than it was before."

She was rambling, but that was how she felt about Ali right now. Just this gush of need, want, craving, all wrapped up in the joy of sharing everything with him.

"I'm scared."

"The moon will help," Liberty said. "I don't know what to say. I wanted to hate him, but he's not really a dick. I mean, I'll totally hate him if he hurts you."

"Thanks, Lib."

"I like him too," Sera said quietly. "But there is something...I can't place my finger on. Like he's uncertain."

Which was what scared Poppy.

Twenty-One

"Ready?"

Kombucha was an acquired taste. The first time Ali had tried it, he wasn't expecting something that smelled so funky to actually be palatable. Poppy looked skeptical and cute as she tried not to breathe in the initial whiff of vinegar.

She had on a pair of incredibly short denim shorts that showcased her long legs. A T-shirt printed with Edward Robert Hughes's *Midsummer Eve*'s moon fairy completed her look. It was all he could do to keep his hands off her. The shirt, the kombucha brewing shed, Poppy... They were drawing him back to that night on the Tor.

He'd truly believed his life had changed when he put hands on Stephen, but the truth was, that had only been an awakening. He'd found his path on that long walk up the Tor on the magical midsummer night with Poppy.

"Did you change your mind?" Poppy asked. "You're staring at me like...you're not sure I'll survive."

"Ha ha. Of course you will. At worst, it will taste bad," he said. "Want me to go first?"

"No. We agreed to do it at the same time." She held her free hand to him, and he took it, lacing their fingers together. "One."

"Two," he said, lifting his own bottle to his mouth.

"Three."

She took a deep swallow, and he did the same. The taste was…not bad. Actually, he got the faint hints of strawberries and mint that Poppy had suggested they use in the last fermentation.

"Not bad," she said. "I think we'll beat Freddie with this one. He was determined to get summer boardwalk in his kombucha. Pretzels and all that."

"I don't know. Is winning important?"

She shook her head, putting down her bottle, and then put her hand against his forehead. "Seriously, did you just ask me that? Alistair Miller, who has to beat every car to the red light? The man who was determined to get the one recipe that had eluded the rest of his family?"

Yeah, that had been him. Intent on being first at the cost of everything else. "Winning doesn't matter if you don't have someone to share it with."

He hadn't meant to let those words out, but that was where he was. Who he was. For the first time in his life, he wasn't hiding behind anger or class. Not acting like he was better than everyone else to prove he was number one. He was just Ali.

Old fears and expectations stirred. As if he wasn't good enough without the trappings of his family, of his name.

But Poppy wrapped her arms around him and hugged him

tight. "This one is for both of us," she pointed out. "You're not alone at the top."

Hugging her wasn't enough, so he pulled her into his body and lifted her up onto the table, moving to stand between her legs, his mouth hot and hard on hers.

His feelings for her were bottled up inside of him, and not unlike his past anger, he felt like they were going to explode out of him. When had that ever been a good thing? He kept his mouth on hers so he didn't blurt out how he loved her.

The past few weeks had been a good run, and now the kombucha had turned out successful. The better things were, the tighter that knot under his heart got. The one that warned him not to fuck this up. To say the right things and be the man that she was digging.

Her arms were wrapped around him, pulling him closer, when he heard the fence gate slam.

"Poppy, you back here?"

Pickle started barking from her spot in the sun on the patio. Merle.

Alistair pulled back and put Poppy back on her feet. "Later."

She walked out of the shed to greet her cousin. Alistair stayed there for a few minutes to get himself under control and also to give them a moment together.

The animosity he'd felt toward Merle had quickly dissipated over the summer. The other man was wicked smart and very good at darts…*as if those are the only things that matter*, he said to himself. But they meant something. Somehow, he'd started to bond with Poppy's little band of friends. A part of him almost believed they were his friends as well. But their loyalty would always be to Poppy…rightly so.

Which ratcheted up the pressure he felt not to fuck things

up. Poppy was a big part of why he'd started to feel like this place was home. This family that was nothing like any other family he'd ever experienced.

"Hey, Ali. Poppy said I should come and try the kombucha," Merle said from the doorway of the shed. "I'm more a Powerade and Pop-Tart kind of guy."

"That stuff is horrible for you," he said. "Your parents must hate that. They pretty much exude healthy vibes."

"They do. I think that's why I love it," he said, taking the bottle that Ali offered him.

"Where's Poppy?"

"Liberty's nan's birthday is tomorrow. When we were over there, we saw she was out of the tea Poppy made for her. It really helps her keep calm, and she loves it," Merle said. "Poppy went to grab some."

Ali had learned that Liberty's nan had Alzheimer's and that Poppy's tea was one of the things that seemed to help keep her head clear. Nothing could cure Nan, but the tea Poppy brewed made her feel better. The WiCKed Sisters imbued everything they did with magic.

He hadn't realized that there was real-world magic. He'd always just pictured witches from Roald Dahl's book, the kind that turned kids into mice.

But Poppy and her friends worked together to weave a spell around the people they met. One that improved their lives. With caring and love and attention. Just being seen was the most powerful magic he'd encountered…well, that and Poppy's affection. Which was probably why he'd been hesitating to tell her he loved her.

"Also, can I get a pony keg of your summer solstice brew?

I'm running D&D tomorrow night," Merle asked as he and Ali walked back up to Poppy's house.

"Yeah, I should be able to swing that," he said. Talking to Merle about beer alleviated his fears. He was getting too in his head, which had never been a good place for him to be.

Poppy met them at the back door with a smile and a small jar of loose blended tea that she gave to Merle. "I made a double batch."

"Thanks," he said, then left.

"Where were we?" Poppy said, grabbing Ali's hand and pulling him into the living room.

The seasonal blue moon in August was the third full moon of the astrological season, so this one felt special. Liberty had led them all in filling a small, stoppered bottle with moon water, small blue crystals and deep blue dye. Sera had supplied some of the old paper she used in her journals, and they all were sitting together at the top of Hanging Hill, drinking rosé as they wrote their intentions.

They were all using blue India ink and dip pens, which Poppy freely admitted was her least favorite way of writing. Dip pens were tricky, and more times than not, she ended up with ink on everything.

But tonight, that didn't matter; the rosé was flowing, and they were listening to Train's "Hey, Soul Sister," which they all agreed they'd loved when they were ten. Sera's handwriting looked the best, but Poppy didn't read her intention. It was personal, between Sera and the universe.

For herself, she wasn't sure what to put down. Alistair had been dominating every moon ritual since he'd first reached out to ask her to be fake married. But that had changed. And she had to come up with an intention, not a question.

What did she intend to do?

I intend to be happy and content with my relationship with Ali and to continue to grow and thrive in the shop and as a tea-blending goddess.

That worked. The tiny chains that remained wrapped around her heart loosened, and Poppy put her hands behind her, tipping her head up to the sky, imagining them falling away.

It was time.

She'd been holding on to the past no matter how many times she reassured herself she was done with it. She wasn't. It was still there keeping her safe, because as long as fear dominated her emotions, she wouldn't be hurt again.

The past few weeks with Ali had made her realize she couldn't be happy either. That fear was tempering everything else, making it harder and harder to just be present.

"Done?" Liberty asked.

"Yes," Poppy and Sera said at the same time.

"Now we are going to bathe in the light of the blue moon. Let it wash over you and know that extraordinary things are coming your way," Liberty said. She followed that with some words that Poppy knew came from a book she sold in her part of the shop.

They turned off Train and joined hands. Chanting about no longer being alone, welcoming the unusual events that would soon be upon them. They opened the dreams kept deep in their hearts. Miracles and wonder, those were what this blue moon offered her.

It was time to shed the last of that girl who kept punishing herself for her lack of maturity and falling for a bad boy who wasn't a good man. With the wisdom of the past and really hard long years, Poppy now understood that girl had done the best she could.

This second chance with Alistair felt like a miracle. The one thing that she would have predicted would never happen. He'd changed, he was honest with her, and as much as she was afraid to trust that he'd stay, she also hadn't asked him to.

She had to take a risk. *Ugh*. But the truth was there. That life she wanted to manifest was right there at the edge of her current one. She had to jump toward him, let him catch her.

Or fall, her subconscious pointed out.

Or fall...but that would be better than living with the doubt.

Liberty was crying when she was done, and Sera had a huge smile on her face. Her friends were all in the same zone she was. Poppy and Sera swarmed around Liberty, hugging her until she hugged them back.

"Okay?"

"Yes. Just making peace with Nan's situation. And thanking the goddess for Merle." Liberty turned to Poppy. "You?"

"Letting go of eighteen-year-old me and finally admitting I'm ready to love again," she said.

Sera hugged her tight. "I'm glad."

"Me too," Poppy admitted. "You?"

"Just envisioned my life with Wes."

"Happily ever after?" Liberty asked.

Sera nodded.

"It's about time. You two are a perfectly imperfect match," Poppy said.

"Aren't we all?"

"Yes. I think trying to be perfect or meet an expectation was the downfall of Mrs. Alistair Miller. This time, I'm just letting him see me, hairy legs and all."

"Good for you. Merle already knew about my rough edges. I'm not like you two. I don't know how to be proper."

"We know," Poppy and Sera said at the same time, and they all laughed.

They finished their bottle of rosé, then lay on their backs, looking up at the moon. The power that had started to stir in Poppy at the Tor on the eve of the summer solstice was back. It had wrapped all around her, leading her to the power that hadn't been given to her on that night but had always been there deep inside of her.

The power she'd been afraid to admit she had. But life had forced her to use it. She'd survived and found her own way because of that strength.

It didn't come from the bonds she formed, though they certainly helped her. The bonds were there because of that inner strength. Surrounding herself with people who resonated with her and brought out the best of her.

"I love you two," Poppy said.

"Same," her friends said in unison.

Now she needed to take her new knowledge and that energy from the night and use it to tell Alistair how she really felt. She had to see if this time, they could make a real go of being a couple.

It wouldn't be easy.

But it could be perfectly imperfect. She wanted that for them, the figuring out where to live and how to blend their lives together. She knew they could do it. The couple they'd been when they married wouldn't have survived, but this time…

★ ★ ★

Waiting for Poppy at the bottom of Hanging Hill might not be his smartest idea, but he'd decided to stop hiding. And once a decision was made, he had to act on it. He still had shitty impulse control. Something that his therapist would no doubt want him to keep working on.

Not now. Not until he told Poppy how he felt.

The first time he told her he loved her, they'd been words. Just words. There hadn't been anything more than the most casual of feelings tied to them. At that time, he didn't believe that love was real or that he was even able to love the way she did.

He hadn't thought anything about them at the time. They were the words that were required to get her to marry him. He'd known from the beginning that Poppy would never marry a man who wasn't in love with her.

That man hadn't been capable of this sunny, warm feeling that was inside of him now. That feeling that was down totally to Poppy.

She and her friends made their way down the path singing "IDGAF" by Dua Lipa. His confidence, which had never been a problem for him, wavered for a second. That song was about keeping an ex out of her life. Was that where—

Fuck it.

He wasn't going down that road. He was here for himself as much as Poppy, and it was time to stop playing it safe. Actually, it was too late; he was already in his feels where she was concerned.

There was no easy way out of this.

"Ali?"

"Yeah," he said, rubbing the back of his neck. "Hoped you'd want to take a ride with me."

A car pulled in, and he noticed Merle behind the wheel. Of course nerd boy drove a sensible sedan that everyone could easily fit into.

The anger he felt toward Merle wasn't exactly the mood he wanted to be channeling at this moment. He also recognized that it wasn't anger at Merle per se, but just anger at himself because he wanted Poppy to come with him.

"I'll go with you. It was Merle's turn to retrieve us, so that's why he's here," Poppy said, waving bye to her friends.

"Retrieve you?" he asked as she took the spare helmet he'd brought for her.

"Yeah, we like to drink and get all into our ritual. I'm buzzing from the moon and the night. It's better not to drive in this state," she said. "Why are you here?"

He leaned back against the Ducati, crossing his legs at the ankle. *Be cool.* Except his heart was racing, and he realized he'd been holding his breath when he let it out in a huff. *Yeah, so cool.*

Was there ever a time when he'd stood by this woman and not lost all of his chill?

"I missed you." The truth sort of spilled out.

Her face softened, and she played with one of her curls. "Me too. So where are we going?"

"Thought you might like a moonlit ride," he said. The moon seemed important to Poppy, and she shone on nights like this in a way that he found irresistible.

There was no pretending he didn't want to have her up against the bike. Just reach up under the full skirt of the dress she was wearing and take off her panties…then put her on the bike. He moved before he fully realized what he was doing. Reaching under her skirt, he cupped her butt and lifted her onto the bike.

Her arms wrapped around his shoulders, her fingers playing with the hair at the back of his neck. "I'm sensing you want more than a ride."

"I want it all," he said against her neck.

One of her hands slipped down to stroke his erection through his jeans. He took her mouth in a long, deep kiss, his body vibrating with the love he felt for her. The words were trapped inside of the lonely boy he'd been, but the man he was now knew how to show her what she meant to him. How much he needed her in his arms and in his life.

Lifting her up, he tore her underwear off, shoving them in the front pocket of his jeans. Her hands were on the front of his jeans, lowering the zipper until she had him free.

"Back pocket," he said, not wanting to take his hands off of her to get the condom. Her skin was so soft and cool. She smelled of summer and night, and it was intoxicating.

She took the packet out and handed it to him. "Hurry."

He put it on and was back between her legs. Her hands were on his butt, pulling him closer. He drove himself up into her, burying his face in the side of her neck, sucking at the skin there.

He drove himself into her as the words kept echoing around in his head. Words that he was determined to say to her. Not while they were fucking. He wanted it to be romantic, without any doubt of his intentions.

Her hand under his jaw forced his head up, and their eyes met. The love he felt for her surged through him. There was no way she couldn't realize how much she meant to him.

He felt…oh God, he almost felt like she might welcome his feelings.

He started to talk, but her mouth was on his, sucking his tongue, exploring. Her fingers were between them as he drove into her, rubbing her clit until she tore her mouth from his, crying out his name as he felt her pussy tightening around his shaft.

He drove into her again and again until he came in a long rush, emptying himself completely. He braced his hand on the Ducati seat next to her as his other arm wrapped around her, holding her to him. Her head rested over his beating heart, her fingers still teasing the hair at the back of his neck.

"Alistair," she said.

"Moon fairy. I'm not sure I can live without you."

Her eyes went wide. *Fuck.* This wasn't the way he planned it.

Twenty-Two

Couldn't live without her. The words echoed through her joy-soaked mind as she was plastered to his back on the Ducati. The blue moon was large and full, casting the two of them in her glow. Every nerve in her body buzzed from the quickie on his bike and the energy she'd gotten from being with Liberty and Sera.

Right at the edge of her subconscious was just the tiniest—like barely present—strand of fear. He'd uttered the words and then let them fall, hustling her into the helmet and onto the bike. He'd been quiet on the ride.

The light of the moon showed signs that fall was around the corner. The fields had been harvested and no longer overflowed with berries and other summer crops. Some of the branches of the trees they flew past on his bike weren't as full as they had been just a week ago.

Fall beckoned. It was time for Ali to go back to the UK. He didn't have a permanent visa. He couldn't just decide to stay.

Did he think she'd go back to England?

Would she if he asked?

The scary part was that there was a version of herself that would be tempted to, no matter that she'd built the woman she was today in Birch Lake. That her life, her business, the family she chose, were all here.

But he wasn't. He was temporary. Except that comment... did that mean he wanted more?

It felt like the questions were going to burst out of her if she tried to stymy them for much longer. Being hesitant wasn't unlike Ali when he was trying to figure something out.

But her silence was another matter.

Be present. Make your own choices. Don't assume.

Those were things she kept writing in her journal, but somehow that little ribbon of fear had kept her quiet for far too long.

Until she couldn't take it anymore.

"What did you mean?" she asked at last.

The words felt like they were ripped from the very deepest part of her psyche, but they came out all cool, as if she hadn't spent the past ten minutes trying to figure out the best way to ask them.

"How many ways could you take that?" he asked back, his voice a low rumble in her ears.

"Alistair. We have history, and I want to know what you meant."

"I was in the moment," he said.

"So it was just a really good orgasm for you? That's why you can't live without me?"

"Fuck. Can this wait until we aren't on the back of my bike?" he asked.

"No. I mean, you could refuse to talk to me, but right now, it's all I can think about. What did Ali mean? Is he saying he wants to be back with me? Is he still leaving at the end of September?"

The bike accelerated down a straightaway, and she held him close, excited and also a tiny bit scared by the speed. When she squeezed him tighter, he slowly pulled to a stop. "I'm sorry."

He put down the kickstand, and she hopped off the bike, not as gracefully as she'd hoped. She took off her helmet and handed it to him. "What was that?"

He shook his head as he leaned against his bike. Closing her eyes, she told herself this was a conversation that was too important for her to be distracted by the hard-to-read emotions on his face. "Me trying to outrun both of us and this conversation. I didn't mean to scare you."

"Well, you did. Does that happen a lot?" she asked, suddenly worrying that he was reckless when she wasn't around. She wasn't entirely sure he'd have stopped if she hadn't been on the bike.

"Not recently."

"Ali…"

He shoved his hands in his hair and leaned forward, over his legs. *This man.* Walking to him, she touched the back of his neck, and his arms snaked around her torso, pulling her into a hug and burying his head against her shoulder.

"I don't know. That's the answer to all those questions," he muttered against her shoulder. "I just want to be with you for the rest of our lives. Do I have a plan? Nope."

As he held her so tightly, those words settled into her heart and soul, making the joy she'd felt earlier bloom again. Warmth from the late summer evening wrapped around her, and inside, that small, cold part of her soul that had always felt alone wasn't alone anymore.

"Promise?" she whispered.

He lifted his head, their eyes met. "On my very soul. I'm not kidding myself that this will be easy. I live in another country, and who knows how long it will take me to figure out how to move to this one. But I want that if you do."

He'd move here. That was big. It was the kind of gesture she hadn't believed him capable of making. "You won't be Alistair Miller here. I'm mean, the one you are in England, where everyone knows who your family is and your money makes them want to be around you."

"No great loss. That's not me, moon fairy. So do you want to try to figure this out?"

As nice as this was making her feel, this was Ali. The only man she'd ever allowed herself to love. The one man that had taken every ounce she'd had to give and thrown it back in her face. The single man that had humbled himself, coming to her and asking for her help by offering her things that she hadn't known she'd needed in return.

It was there right on the edges of her being, that love she'd never really lost. But this time, it was new. It felt solid and real and like it could last.

"Or we pretend I didn't say anything and keep doing what we have been until I leave," he said.

"I want to be with you too," she said. "I'm not sure how it's going to work. Can we take it slow?"

"I'll take you anyway I can get you," he said.

With that, her heart squeezed in agreement, and she looked up at the moon, silently thanking her.

Waking up alone in Poppy's bed was becoming his best habit. It had been two weeks since the night he told her he wanted to spend the rest of his life with her. Still, the words *I love you* were unspoken. He glanced at his phone and saw she'd left him a cute little video.

"Hey, sleepyhead. I have to get to work. Pickle's been fed, so don't let her con you into feeding her again." She smiled at him on-screen. "I'm so tempted to crawl back into bed with you, but I'm already late, and Liberty and Sera will probably show up here to get me. See you tonight."

Her video ended, and he rewatched it. He had the day off at the tavern so he'd offered to bottle their kombucha and send it to the other members of the Tea Society for tasting. So far, two other bottles from other members had arrived at Poppy's house. His were being held at the tavern for him. Owen had declined to join the society, telling Alistair he wasn't big into groups, which made sense. The man was on the quiet side. Even so, Ali was glad he'd invited him.

His phone rang and he glanced down to see that it was the tavern.

"Miller here."

"Owen. A pipe burst in the basement, and dude, if you're not doing anything, we could use some help moving everything up."

"On my way."

The basement was in bad shape, and Ali got right to work moving things up the stairs. There was a small area that they had been using as a beer garden for the summer, but now it would serve as storage for all the items from the basement. Everyone who worked for the Bootless Soldier had come in to help, and they were making quick work of the task.

As Ali worked side by side with everyone, he realized that this would never have happened at Lancaster-Spencer. He might have worked in each department at some point, but he never would have pitched in with the workers to do anything. There were days, or rather nights, like the one when a burst of anger had him speeding down the country roads in the UK to the point of a near collision, when he doubted that he'd really moved forward at all.

But the fact that he'd woken in Poppy's bed that morning… Those were things the old Alistair wouldn't have. He never could have conceived of the importance of moments like this. Being part of something bigger than himself.

The day was mercifully cool. Clouds covered the sky, and Lars and Owen were both praying it wouldn't rain. Alistair realized his friends needed someone to manage this operation, and organizing was something he was damned good at.

He called Poppy to get the name of where they stored their excess stock.

"We use Hadley's. Why?"

"Flooded basement at the tavern."

"I'll text you the number. It looks like rain," she pointed out.

"Duh," he teased, making her laugh.

"Merle isn't working for me today. I'll text him to come help. I have some space in my backroom. Tell Lars and Owen they are welcome to bring stuff down here," she said.

"Oh that'd be great, thanks. I will."

"No problem. Neighbors help each other," she said. After she hung up, she texted him the number for Hadley's.

About ten minutes later, Merle showed up. He wore a pair of basketball shorts and a gaming T-shirt with a cat on it.

The bed of Lars's truck was already full of supplies, and Merle rode with Ali to Poppy's to help unload. It made the most sense given he worked at Poppy's shop and knew the layout. It was only later that Alistair recognized that he wasn't jealous or angry about Merle's presence. He just did what needed to be done.

They rented a space at Hadley's and got them to send their driver with a moving van to collect the rest of the stuff from the basement. They were almost done when it started raining, but most of the fragile stuff, such as bar mats, napkins and paper straws, had already been moved to Poppy's.

It was another two hours before they were all back at the tavern. The plumber had been called, and Lars was tending bar—bottles only, since the taps were serviced from the basement.

"What a fucking wild day," Owen said. "Thanks for helping out."

"No problem," Ali said. "That's what neighbors do."

"Are you a neighbor now?" Owen asked.

"I'm thinking about being one. If the offer is still open for the Oktoberfest," Ali said. His honesty and slip of the tongue with Poppy had made everything in his life so much clearer than it had been before. He wanted to be here.

He wanted to live in this small town, brewing his craft beer and working in the tavern up the street from Poppy's WiCKed Sisters. It wasn't the tabloid-worthy, society-soaked life he'd always had, but this felt right.

"It's open. Lars and I have been talking about taking on a third partner...if you're interested. Didn't mean to spring that on you," Owen said.

"I'm open to it. I think it might take some time to get a visa to live and work here, but I like the idea of working with the two of you."

"We like it too," Lars said. "The hope from my perspective is that Owen will take some real time off and maybe start having a life."

Owen shot his brother the finger. "I have a life I like."

Not that long ago, he wouldn't have understood how Owen could be content, but now Ali sort of got it. There was a lot to be said for owning his own tavern, brewing his own beer and being his own boss.

It was so different from being a Miller at Lancaster-Spencer, where the board made all the decisions and tradition and legacy were the only masters they served. There was no place for growth or innovation. Two things he hadn't realized were important until this summer.

These long summer days since the beginning of June, when he'd come here to find Poppy, had woven some magic around him. Truth was, Poppy was probably way more responsible for where he was in his life now.

Everything had changed when he signed those divorce papers.

The rain had slowed traffic in the store, and Sera and Liberty were sitting at one of the tables toward the front of the tea shop on either side of her. Poppy had used the last of her summer leaves and essences, adding vanilla, to make the blend that they were now sipping. "This reminds me of when Amber Rapp came in."

"Me too," Liberty admitted. "I was just thinking about that. How we were just being chill, living our lives. We were getting ready for Thanksgiving at Mom's…"

"Little did we know our worlds were about to change," Sera said.

"And kept changing," Poppy said. Nothing had been the same since that day. Not that things would have stayed the same if Amber hadn't come into the shop and found what she'd been searching for. Like Sera said, the magic had been in Amber before she entered. Just like the solid bond of friendship between the three of them would still be there without the success.

The door to the shop opened, and a couple walked in. Poppy blinked a few of times before realizing it was George—Alistair's brother—and his wife.

"Hello, Poppy," Bronte said, coming over to them. "I finally talked George into coming here."

"I wasn't reluctant to visit. Just had business to take care of," George reminded her.

Poppy stood up and introduced everyone.

Bronte immediately asked Liberty to read her cards, which Liberty agreed to. They left, and Sera had a customer come in to collect some books they'd ordered. Leaving Poppy and George.

"Tea?" she asked.

"Thanks. I'll have the Amber Rapp blend," he said, following her to the counter.

It had been a few weeks since she'd signed the deal with

Lancaster-Spencer, and she hadn't heard anything from their side since. "Is there a problem with our deal?"

"Not at all. In fact, I brought the fully executed copy with me. Bronte has been wanting to come visit, and as she mentioned, I did promise. Thought it would be nice to give you this in person. I'm so glad you accepted our offer."

"It felt right," she admitted.

"I'm glad. Alistair told me how silenced you felt when you worked for Lancaster-Spencer. I'm sorry I didn't pay better attention to how Dad was running things," George said.

"Thanks. That wasn't really your job," she pointed out.

"No, it wasn't. But it will be now. I'm going to be the CEO starting October 1."

"Congratulations," she said. She was hopeful that George would continue to make the changes he'd already started. Lancaster-Spencer had centuries of heritage behind it, and bringing the company into the twenty-first century would ensure that continued.

"Thanks," he said.

A customer came in while George finished his tea, and when the customer left, he asked Poppy if she knew where Alistair was.

She directed him to the Bootless Soldier and assured him she'd make sure Bronte knew where he'd gone.

Bronte had Sera emboss her intention into the cover of the journal she'd purchased in Glastonbury from Solange's shop. Then she settled next to Poppy to have a cup of tea.

"I hope I haven't been too fan-girly today, but this is a dream come true," she said.

"You've been fine. It's good to see you again," Poppy said.

"Same. I've been buzzing since George told me you signed

with Lancaster-Spencer, but given that even the Earl of Win-field knew that it would be foolish not to do everything to get you to sign, I sort of figured it was a done deal."

"Everything? I mean, the terms were pretty standard, and they had the offer from Willingham that they wanted to beat," Poppy said.

"Of course, but it wasn't just your contract they were after," she said. "You know, Alistair's been on a leave of absence, and nothing that George or Howard has offered has made him leave his little beer barn."

Ali liked being in his beer barn. Also, there was some-thing passive-aggressive about the way Bronte had put that. His beer was bigger than that and meant a lot to Ali. "I don't think my contract is going to change that," Poppy said at last.

Bronte sort of went pale and pursed her lips together. Then she looked down into her teacup, avoiding eye contact.

"Right?"

"Uh, sorry. I thought you knew. George said Alistair is staying at your place now," Bronte said.

"Knew what?"

"I don't know all of the details, but George mentioned be-fore we left London that everything was in place. Howard's retirement and your fair deal were the last things keeping Alistair from accepting the chief operations officer position. George has been monitoring him since the leave of absence."

There was too much to process. Poppy's ears were buzz-ing. "What do you mean?"

"Oh, after his break, everyone wasn't sure he'd be able to come back. But the therapy and the extended time away from the office has finally been enough for HR to sign off on his return."

"Bronte, you shouldn't be talking to me about this," Poppy said. This was all secondhand news. Nothing substantial. She found it hard to believe that Alistair wouldn't have told her if he'd decided to go back to England. They'd made future plans.

"You're right. I'm just so jazzed that we are going to be like real sisters when you both move back. Now that you're not separated anymore."

"We were never separated," she said, stopping before telling the other woman they were actually divorced.

Bronte didn't seem to realize that Poppy was upset, and there was a part of Poppy that wanted to tell Bronte they'd never be sisters. A sister would have noticed that Poppy was crumbling. Like Sera and Liberty, who'd moved closer to their table, both of them coming to support her without her asking.

Bronte keep drinking her tea as Poppy waved her friends away. There was nothing to discuss with Liberty and Sera until she had a talk with Ali, which would have to wait until the shop closed.

Twenty-Three

George seemed to have lost his head. Somewhere between the conversation they'd had over the summer and the last day of August, his brother had taken full leave of his senses. The Tavern wasn't too busy, but locals had started to trickle in once they'd learned online that the Bootless Soldier had reopened. Owen and Lars were both behind the bar, the brothers laughing and joking with customers.

They were nothing like Ali and George, and not for the first time, he saw how much his privileged upbringing hadn't given him. The bond between the Krog brothers was strong. Sure, they fought at times, and each of them got exasperated with the other, but Owen and Lars understood each other. Owen got that Lars was never going to brew his own beer. Lars got that Owen was happiest behind the bar.

George got nothing about Ali. Even after all those long weeks when a hang in there text had saved him, he realized he'd never had a conversation with his brother that mat-

266   Katherine Garbera

tered. They talked about Lancaster-Spencer and about their parents, but never about themselves.

"No. Definitely not."

"Dad's retiring. Mum sprung that on me. I already got full agreement from the board. You've changed. Even Stephen agreed that you've changed a lot. Everyone saw what you did with Ali's Brew, and they are impressed. We need that knowledge and innovation at Lancaster-Spencer."

"You totally do, but I'm not the guy for the job." The words were out of Ali's mouth, but there was a part of him that was more than flattered by his brother's words. The job that had never been meant for him now handed over on a silver platter. All it had taken was, what? A total breakdown and shedding every inch of the man he'd been.

But the man he was today wouldn't be happy at Lancaster-Spencer. He was making plans for his life here with Poppy. He'd already started planning ales for the Oktoberfest.

"George, if I went back, it would kill me," he said.

"What? No, the therapy would continue. We are more aware of work-life balance—"

"That's not what I'm talking about." Ali shoved his hand through his hair. How to make George understand? "Remember when I arrived at school?"

"Yeah. You were so nervous. I told you to stick to your schedule and the right families to make friends with," George said.

"You did," Ali said. George had been the best brother he knew how to be.

"Was that not helpful?"

"For you. Everyone already knew who I was, and they were all trying to cultivate me."

"Ego much?"

"You say that, but the reality was you were already earning a reputation of having Dad's drive and Mum's charm. Everyone knew you were going places and assumed I was another version of you."

"But you're not. You never have been," George said.

"Yeah."

"So...it's a definite no to the job," George said almost musingly.

"Yeah."

"What will you do?"

Before he could answer, Bronte and Poppy entered the tavern and came over to the table where he and George were seated. One look at Poppy's face told him she'd already heard about his job offer at Lancaster-Spencer. He took her hand, but she pulled it back.

He wasn't sure what was going on. When George went to the bar to get drinks for the table and Bronte went to the bathroom, he turned to her. "What's up?"

"Bronte told me you're the COO of Lancaster-Spencer, for starts."

"I'm not," he said. "The position wouldn't open until October."

"So you're considering it?" she asked. "Which you're totally free to do. I mean, this is the offer of a lifetime."

"Do you think so?" he asked. Did she want him to take it? She had married him when he was on a path to leadership at Lancaster-Spencer, after all.

"You tell me. I don't know what you want."

"I've told you," he said, feeling that familiar tension start to build inside of him. What was Poppy doing? Had she not heard a single thing he'd said to her since he'd been in Maine?

"That was before you were handed something that I know you craved for a long time. You told me yourself before I left England that all you wanted was for the world to see that you earned your way to the top of Lancaster-Spencer. That it wasn't just handed to you because of who your parents were," she pointed out.

"I said that almost ten years ago. You said that you needed to be alone and not answer to anyone," he said, remembering that long-ago fight. "You work with two other women and have a loyal customer base. Not the loner dream you said you wanted."

She rocked back in her chair, wrapping her arms around her waist. "Yeah, so?"

"I've changed too. I'm not twenty-four anymore," he pointed out.

Her mouth opened, but she closed it without uttering a word as George returned with the drinks. "We can talk later. Come by my place."

"This morning I had the feeling that it was becoming our place."

"A lot has changed today. You might be chief operations officer of Lancaster-Spencer."

He shook his head and then put his hands down on the table hard enough to rock it, making beer spill from the pints. "There is no offer. I'm out. I sold my shares to George and Mum as soon as your deal was signed."

George started to speak, but Alistair didn't need his brother to come to his defense. Poppy should have known him better. Turning on his heel, he stalked out of the tavern. Everyone sort of cleared a path for him, which was good because he was about to explode.

No one saw him. Not even Poppy, who he had started to believe truly got him.

He saw the Ducati waiting. The open road that would take him far away from his brother, who was never going to understand that there was any job worth pursuing beyond Lancaster-Spencer. And Poppy. Damn, his moon fairy should have believed him when he'd said he wanted a life with her.

They hadn't hashed out the details, because he'd been too content. Too willing to believe that she would stay because, this time, she'd seen the changes. She knew he was a different man.

"Alistair."

Poppy watched Alistair leave through the back of the tavern as Liberty and Sera walked in the front door. Her friends saw him leaving and, she guessed, took one look at her face and figured something wasn't right.

She felt hollow inside. *Fucking hell*. She hadn't meant to do it. But she'd cut him deeply, treating him like the man he'd been at the end of their marriage.

Bronte came back to the table, but Poppy couldn't deal with her or George, who was trying to explain things to her. His voice was a drone of words she couldn't comprehend. She walked to her friends, both of them wrapping their arms around her. They stood in a huddle, with Poppy breathing deeply and trying not to cry.

"What happened?" Sera's voice was right next to her ear.

"I hurt him."

"How?" It was Liberty this time, her hand on Poppy's back, stroking her shoulder.

"By not seeing him. All this time, I was worried he'd do something to fuck this whole thing up, but it was me. I wanted him so much to still be that bad boy, that man who cared about no one else, that I treated him… I have to go and find him."

"Okay. We'll be here," Sera said.

Poppy nodded, wiping her hands on her cheeks to swipe away the tears. She walked toward the bar and the side exit. She had no idea what she was going to say to Alistair, but she had to find him.

The words didn't matter. Being with him. Talking about this the way they had on that first night in England. Those were the things that mattered. Could she get back there?

But there was no going back to the woman she'd been on that night; there was only trying to find a path forward.

His words were a mantra in her ears. *I've changed too.* Neither of them were the same people they'd been.

Remembering that was harder than she wanted to admit. Because if she let that last piece of her guard down, the lingering fear that still circled around her heart when she started to feel truly happy with him would disappear. She'd have no protection against being hurt again. Sort of like how she imagined Ali felt now.

Then she found him. He stood leaning against the outside wall of the tavern, his hands on his knees and his head forward.

"Alistair."

There was so much more she wanted to say to him. But she didn't want to screw this up.

His head turned, and he straightened up. "Poppy."

"I'm...I shouldn't have jumped to conclusions," she admitted.

"You're right. But I get why you did."

She shook her head. "Well, you shouldn't. I kept hammering home how I'm not the same woman now, but as soon as I heard you had a deal with Lancaster-Spencer, I was nineteen again, realizing that my dream marriage was a business deal. Only this time, it hurt so much more because I really love you. Not the idea of you, but the man you are."

"The flawed man. That's why you did it, Poppy, don't blame yourself for reaping the seeds that I sowed."

"I like your flaws. The rough edges are a big part of what I love about you. You were too smooth and perfect before," she pointed out. There she'd said it. Told him she loved him.

"And perfect is..."

"Overrated," she said. Hope that they could work through this, really work through it, bloomed in her heart. That fizzy feeling was back in her stomach, wrapping her in joy.

Ali strode toward her; his hair was a mess from how much he'd run his hands through it. His face was a mix of hope and something that on any other person she'd describe as trepidation. Then she chastised herself. Of course he was leery. He didn't know what reception he was going to get from her.

She'd spent so much time protecting her own heart while basking in the warmth of the affection that he showered on her. Had she shown him how much he meant to her? Had she done enough?

This was the real pain of a broken relationship. It was so hard to leave the past where it belonged and not allow everything to merge together. There were always going to be flashbacks to the time when they weren't the best versions of themselves. Always going to be a chance that this wouldn't work out. Always going to be this moment when she had to really let go of and realize that maybe their marriage had just been a prelude to the people they'd become.

Became.

They were those better versions of themselves.

"I'm sorry," she said.

"Please, don't say that."

Oh, no. It's too late. What if this was who they were now? Two people who couldn't live without the other but never quite got it right when they were together. Like some sort of demented hamster wheel where they both kept hopping in and out of each other's lives.

He was within his rights to ask for space. But she didn't know if she could give it to him. This time, there was no pretending she didn't love him. No telling herself that he'd fooled her. He hadn't. He'd been honest with her about everything.

He'd bared it all. Even the stuff that he hadn't wanted to share. Not to get her to sign a contract or to get a family tea recipe. He'd done it for her.

Oh, fuck, damn, shit.

When he needed her to see the growth he'd made, she'd given him the finger and told him they could talk later.

Why would he be open to doing anything she wanted? Why should she expect him to let her continue to dictate the terms of their relationship? She hadn't shown him any of the respect that he'd more than earned. That he deserved.

The respect they both deserved because they were flawed adults. Not two people pretending to be some idolized couple.

Listening to Poppy take any of this on herself was unbearable. She was the woman he'd shaped her into when he'd used her that first time. The fact that she loved him—he'd heard her say it—was a miracle. One he wasn't about to take for granted.

They needed to clear everything up. Now. "You don't owe me any more apologies."

"I should have—"

He put his finger over her lips. Her mouth was soft and supple under his touch. "George came to me with the offer while I guess Bronte was telling you. I was never going back to Lancaster-Spencer. I will have to return to England to close the beer barn, to honor my commitments there, but my life is going to be here with you. But only when we are both ready for it."

"Bronte made it seem like a done deal," Poppy said, her voice thready. "She said that you getting me to sign… I should have asked you instead of jumping to conclusions."

"You should have. But the divorce PTSD probably had you reeling," he said.

"It did. Except there was a part of me that didn't accept her version of you. The man I've come to know… Honestly, you'd hate it in the corporate world," she said.

"I hated it the last time too. Just took me a while to figure out there was more to life than pleasing my family," he said.

"Like what?" she asked.

"Loving you," he replied, pulling her into his arms. He held her tight, resting his forehead on hers. "I heard you say you love me."

"I do. I have for a while but was afraid…"

"Then it seemed like your fears were coming true."

"Yeah, I manifested the worst outcome for us," she said. "I hadn't realized it until this moment. But I kept waiting for you to do…"

"Do something dicky. I'm not saying I don't. I mean, I did rock that table in the tavern just now and spilled everyone's drinks. But to be honest, I didn't know it was unstable. I'll have to get Lars to fix it—"

She kissed him, stopping the flow of words. Her mouth moved under his, her hands in his hair, and her body fitted into the curve of his chest. Nothing else mattered except this woman, this moment.

"So…"

"I'm not leaving you again," he began. It was too important to not make it perfectly clear what he wanted for the two of them. "I want a life with you. However it works out. I'm going to get a visa and come to Maine and work with Owen and Lars in the tavern, brewing beer for the different seasons.

"I'd like to live with the woman I love and explore new flavors and try new brewing methods with her. I'd like to finally just be the man I've been afraid to let the world see. I don't want to end up like my parents, who are just partners in an institution they were both forced into.

"I love you, moon fairy, and my life will be dull and boring without you by my side. I'm no longer the legacy second son to the Lancaster-Spencer dynasty. I'm not a tabloid favorite or able to jet you off to places you've never been.

"What I am is a man who will keep trying to not let you down, a man who's going to fuck up sometimes and apologize as soon as it happens."

That was all he could offer. Therapy had taught him to learn to accept that he was flawed. He had tools to help him manage his anger and his emotions, such as his running, but the truth was, around Poppy, he didn't need to run as much or as far.

"I love you, too," she said. "I'm going to make mistakes too. But there isn't anything I want more than a life together. One that we make for ourselves. Not bound by a centuries-old tea recipe but new blends that we create together. I was serious about not marrying again, just so you know. I'll live with you and love you, but being man and wife...that doesn't work for me. You okay with that?"

"I pretty much just said I'm okay with anything as long as I'm next to you," he said.

"Perfect."

He shook his head. "Perfectly imperfect."

Poppy laughed, and he lifted her into his arms, spinning them in a circle. His heart was beating nice and steady, and the feelings that were flooding through him were more intense than his anger ever had been. They were happy and joyful, making him realize how long he'd been waiting to be back in her arms.

Really back.

He'd been edging his way back to her since the moment they signed the divorce papers. The moment she forced him into when she refused to let him drag out their connection any longer. The moment he realized that losing her was the worst thing that ever happened to him.

Nothing had mattered after that except getting her back. He'd been prepared to work the rest of his life to do it. But was glad he wouldn't have to.

Tears stung his eyes, and he buried his face in her hair. "I really do love you."

"Took you long enough."

Someone cleared their throat behind them. His family was waiting for him in the tavern. But when he turned, he saw that it wasn't just George, but Liberty and Sera and Owen had also popped around the doorframe.

"You two good?" George asked. "I'd hate for Lancaster-Spencer to be responsible for ruining things a second time."

Poppy ducked under Ali's arm, keeping hold of his hand. "We're very good."

They went back in the tavern with their family. They pushed tables together, and Wes and Merle came to join them, both of them treating Ali like a brother-in-law.

The family he'd always secretly craved was his. Thanks to his moon fairy and the magic she'd woven around them.

Epilogue

Alistair stood in the archway between the tea shop and the bookstore, leaning against the wall, looking badass in the navy suit he'd brought with him from England. They'd spent the Christmas season together in Poppy's house. Her parents, George and Bronte had flown over as well. They'd had a big celebration combining the winter solstice and Christmas at Liberty and Merle's new house.

Today was Sera's wedding to Wes. It was a small ceremony to be held in WiCKed Sisters. Wes, his dad and brother were all waiting at the end of an aisle that had been formed by moving the book tables around. Liberty had made an arch out of branches and seasonal flowers for them to be married under. Greer and their partner were off to one side talking to Merle and his entire family.

"I can't believe they all came," Liberty said.

"I invited them," Sera said. "His brothers are sweet, and your aunt Regina has definitely warmed up lately."

"She has," Poppy agreed. "She asked me about the journals you make, Sera. I think she might buy one."

"She also had me do a reading for her," Liberty admitted. "But I'm not allowed to ever mention it in front of Coach."

"Ha. That sounds like her. She has loosened up a lot since you and Merle got together."

"I still can't believe I'm getting married today," Sera said. "You guys have changed my life so much. I don't think I ever would have been able to trust any man without your friendship. You two have helped me to be the main character in my own life instead of just the best friend."

"You were always the main character, you simply didn't see it," Liberty said.

"Agreed. From the moment I met you, I saw it." Poppy adjusted the flower wreath she'd made for Sera on her head. Her friend's brown curls were perfect today. Her wedding dress featured a fitted corset-type bodice with a skirt of tulle and layers of beaded lace.

"While we're doing the thanks thing…I wouldn't have even met Merle if not for you, Poppy. I totally wouldn't have made it through Nan's Alzheimer's without you both by my side," Liberty said.

Poppy just hugged her tight. Nan and Lourdes, Liberty's mom, were both out in the shop as well, talking quietly to Hamish, who had been Sera's mentor Ford's best friend.

"Writing in the journals you made for us gave us this," Poppy said. "I never would have dreamed this big on my own."

"You always dreamed big," Liberty said. "When we first

met, you told me that one day Lancaster-Spencer would come crawling to you."

"That's right," Poppy said with a laugh. "I didn't really believe it."

"I didn't believe that we'd be able to make this place a success. Mom tried to have a shop here when I was ten. She was only able to keep it open for a few months," Liberty added. "But we did it."

"Together," Sera said. "We were all strong on our own, but together, we're...unstoppable."

Sera and Wes's ceremony was simple but sweet, making Poppy tear up seeing the love they shared. Alistair handed her a monogramed handkerchief, which she used before tucking it back into his pocket.

"Thanks for asking me to be your fake husband for the day," he whispered in her ear as they swayed to "Dancing in the Moonlight" at the reception in the tea shop.

"I figured you owed me," she said.

"I owe you my life, moon fairy."

She owed him hers. By forcing her to realize that the life she'd thought she wanted was an illusion, he'd given her a gift. His business marriage had forced her to find these women and this place.

The magic of Birch Lake and WiCKed Sisters had enriched all of their lives. Glancing around, she saw Merle and Liberty holding each other tight; Wes and Sera hadn't taken their hands off each other since they'd exchanged I dos. But more than that was the larger community they'd created.

Owen had a date with the woman he'd been seeing in Bangor, and Lily and Lars were still here. Wes's dad and brother were both dancing with their dates, and Lourdes had returned from dropping Nan back at the care home.

"*Our* life. You owe me our life," Poppy said with a smile.

★ ★ ★ ★ ★

For more spicy romance with a touch of magic, check out
USA TODAY *Bestseller Katherine Garbera's*
Ghost of a Chance, *coming this fall.*

Acknowledgments

I can't believe this is the last WiCKed Sisters book. From the moment Serafina popped onto the page, I knew her world would be fun and interesting to delve into. As an author, I wanted her to have good friends, but even I wasn't ready for Liberty and Poppy. The bond these three women share is the backbone of the stories, and I've loved every minute of exploring their relationships with each other, their families and the men who come into their lives.

The people in my life who make writing possible mean the very world to me, and that starts with you, dear reader. Thank you for picking up these books and getting as swept up in their lives as I did.

Thank you to my wonderful agent, Sandy, who is smart and savvy and a very good cheerleader when I need one. Thanks to my editor, John, who is always there for my ideas and knows just the right things to say to make them sing.

Thank you to my sprinting partners Joss and Tina, who

are there every day when I show up to the page and keep me honest and on track.

My family gets the biggest thanks, and I can't ever thank them enough. My husband, who listens to me ramble about stories and ideas that never become books; my kids, who are writers and love to talk story with me; my parents, who might not have thought I could make a living as a writer but never did anything but encourage me to try.

Until next time, happy reading!